PATTERN OF
BEHAVIOR

PATTERN OF BEHAVIOR

A Short Story Collection

Paul Bishop

Five Star
Unity, Maine

Five Star First Edition Mystery Series.
Published in 2000 in conjunction with Tekno Books and
Ed Gorman.

Additional copyright information on Page 285.

Cover concept and artwork by Paul Bishop.

The text of this edition is unabridged.

Set in 11 pt. Plantin.

Printed in the United States on permanent paper.

Library of Congress Cataloging-in-Publication Data

Bishop, Paul.
    Pattern of behavior : a short story collection / by Paul Bishop.
      p. cm. — (Five Star standard print mystery series)
    ISBN 0-7862-2670-6 (hc : alk. paper)
    1. Detective and mystery stories, American. I. Title. II. Series.
PS3552.I7723 P38   2000
  813'.54—dc21   00-030841

DEDICATION

To those who said the first yes
to the various stages of my
writing career.
Stephen Smoke (non-fiction)
Charles Fritch (short stories)
Raymond Obsfeldt (work-for-hire)
Michael Seidman (novels)
Lee Goldberg (teleplays)
Thanks

TABLE OF CONTENTS

INTRODUCTION

I am a very lucky guy.

For over twenty years, I've been able to pursue two careers that continue to excite me and reward me—putting villains in jail, and putting words on paper. As a detective with the Los Angeles Police Department specializing in sex crimes, I continue to chase bad guys and solve crimes. Under the cover of darkness, however, I slip into my writer's cloak and find cathartic release by telling stories in the form of novels, screenplays, and short stories for a (hopefully) growing audience.

Such a deal.

There is no doubt each profession feeds the other, occasionally colliding in a mix of coincidence no fiction reader would ever accept. The first time it happened, I was the investigating officer during the trial of a child molester. In court, potential jurors were being asked if they knew anybody connected with the case. A frail, older lady in the back of the jury box answered by stating, "Does it matter if I'm reading Detective Bishop's book?" With that, she reached into the stereotypical knitting bag at her feet, removed a copy of *Citadel Run*, and waved it over her head with a flourish. The defense attorney immediately removed her from the jury. Order was eventually restored and the trial proceeded. After the lunch recess, however, five other jurors and the judge returned to the courtroom with copies of the book and asked for signatures. The defendant didn't stand a chance.

On another occasion, my partner and I responded to a suspect's residence to arrest him for rape. It was early by *dirtbag* standards and we were forced to rouse the suspect from his slumbers. Wearing only a tattered robe over his birthday suit, the suspect failed to follow the rules (admit nothing, deny everything, demand proof) by helpfully acknowledging his guilt and effectively *talking his way to jail.*

Since he was cooperating, the suspect was given the chance to get dressed before being unceremoniously dragged off to his reservation at the *Gray Bar Motel.* This involved having the handcuffed suspect stand in the doorway to his bedroom while directing my partner to what clothing he wanted to wear. Attempting to retrieve a pair of grubby undershorts from the far side of the bed, my partner (a trained observer) noticed a paperback copy of my novel *Kill Me Again* splayed open on the nightstand. He held it up and showed it to me with an amused look on his face. We both knew it would be at least twelve years before the suspect had a chance to finish the final chapter.

How strange to be reading a book by an author at night, only to have him turn up to arrest you the following morning. How much stranger for the detective/author to attempt to get additional charges filed for cracking the book's spine. Some things deserve severe punishment.

As a detective, I often get calls from other writers looking to enhance their knowledge of police procedures. I experienced a twist on this scenario after reading *The Devil's Waltz* by bestselling author and child psychologist Jonathan Kellerman.

The morning after finishing the book, I began an investigation of a bizarre child abuse case. Fresh in my mind was Kellerman's detailed description of a rare disorder known as *Munchausen by proxy* (a parent who purposely and repeatedly injures or makes a child sick in order to get sympathy for themselves). In short order, I realized what I was up against and called Jonathan for an expert's confirmation. The collaboration led to the arrest and conviction of the suspect, and a new life for the victim. Satisfaction doesn't get much better.

In November of 1993, I sold the second book in my Fey Croaker series, *Twice Dead*, based on a twenty-page outline. The storyline, which was set in the LAPD's West Los Angeles Division where I work, involved a series of murders possibly committed by a black ex-football player turned actor. I was halfway through writing the book when, on July 12, 1994, the OJ Simpson case exploded. Not only were the inner workings of the virtually unknown West Los Angeles Division suddenly thrust into the national consciousness, but the parallels between the two stories would make the book look like nothing more than a headline rip-off by the time it was published.

I scrambled to restructure the novel. The black ex-football player turned actor became an NBA star rookie, the victims male instead of female. As this was the second book in an ongoing series about a female homicide supervisor assigned to West Los Angeles Division, the background of the character had to stand.

Near the end of the book, a subplot involving audio tapes of my main character's psychiatric sessions being made public has a bearing on the outcome of the story. The day I turned the book into the editor, the controversy over the Mark Fuhrman tapes broke in the OJ Simpson case. As usual, fiction couldn't stay ahead of real life.

Inspiration also strikes at inconvenient times. During the LA riots in 1994, all detectives were back in uniform, working twelve-hour shifts, three to a patrol car. We spent our time confronting looters, facing down angry mobs, and racing up ladders behind firemen to protect them from snipers (as we had body armor and they didn't—a situation since rectified). I was in more physical confrontations in those five days of civilian rage than any other intense period during my career.

Four days into the debacle, I found myself in the passenger seat of the patrol car scribbling madly into my two-inch by three-inch officers' notebook. When my partners demanded to know what I was doing, I tried to explain I had to do a brain dump—get the images and impressions of the prior days onto paper—so I could continue to focus without fear of losing my writer's edge. They thought I was nuts, but by that time in my twin careers, writing had become a habit. Four days away from the word processor and I was going through withdrawals.

Even minor career crossovers can cause problems. In 1988, while assigned to a nationwide terrorist task force, I was interrogating a suspect with the assistance of a southern FBI agent. After the suspect had told a particularly bald lie (we knew he was lying because his lips were moving), the southern FBI agent moved in close and drawled, "Son, that hound just won't hunt. And if you don't tell me the truth you're gonna find yourself taking a dirt nap." What did he say? What a great couple of lines!

I knew I'd forget the verisimilitude of those statements if I waited any length of time before writing them down, but I had an obligation to concentrate on the interrogation—not on the perfect place to put the words. Thinking fast, I unobtrusively excused myself from the interview room and scribbled down the lines of dialogue on the back of a candy wrapper. I then returned to the continuing interrogation safe in the knowledge my two masters were being served.

And so we come to the stories in this collection. A couple are from the early days of my fiction career, when I struggled under the misconception that writing short stories was a good way to learn how to write a novel (in actuality the reverse is true). Most are from other points along the way, with the title novella written especially for this collection. Many, however, were conceived from an idea or a *what if?* generated by a scenario from my day job—career crossover of the best kind.

As you read, remember truth is always stranger than fiction, and the realities learned *on-the-job* are the strangest truths of all. Enjoy.

"Cheers!"
Paul Bishop
North of LA
2000
http://www.BookRadio.com/Bishop

THE COP STUFF

Pattern of Behavior started life as a "spec" script for a popular television series. You can probably tell which one by the structure of the story. While the script was never produced by the show for which it was designed, it did act as a strong writing example that enabled me to get work on other shows. However, not wanting a good tale to go unpublished, I adapted the script to make it an original novella for this collection. It now features my current novel series character, Fey Croaker, and is chronologically set after the fourth book in the series, **Chalk Whispers**.
The storyline itself is drawn from a rape case I investigated in 1998. It was filled with enough bizarre twists, turns, and coincidences to make it one of the most interesting cases with which I've ever been involved. While the prosecution won a conviction in the end, I was never sure if the truth was served or only justice.

PATTERN OF BEHAVIOR
A Fey Croaker LAPD Crime Story
PROLOGUE

In the center of the darkened banquet room, Anna Havilland was curled into a fetal position. Her long blond hair was scattered across her twenty-something face, obscuring her features. Her short, black skirt was rucked up around her thighs, exposing her lack of underwear or pantyhose. A rope was bound around her ankles, and a colorful man's tie secured her wrists behind her back. Across her mouth was a single slash of duct tape. A large, ornate restaurant sign proclaiming *Tony V's* leant drunkenly against the wall behind her.

Whimpering, she struggled to pull her hands under her buttocks. Painfully she threaded her legs through until her hands were in front of her. She paused to rest for a few seconds—time was meaningless—before reaching up to pull the duct tape from her mouth with a swift tear. She burst into tears from the pain.

Eventually gaining control of her emotions, Anna crawled slowly toward her abandoned purse. With shaking fingers she reached into the purse and removed her cell phone. Massive effort was required to pick out and push the proper numbers—911.

When the connection was made, a recording came on the line asking her to wait. Anna lay her head on the floor, the phone under her ear, and the recording repeated twice more. Finally, a live voice came on the line. "Operator fifteen-eighteen. What is your emergency?"

Anna sucked in a breath. "Please help me. I've been raped."

Fey Croaker sat at her desk in the Robbery-Homicide squad room and pushed keys on her computer with desultory interest.

"Do you have a minute, Fey?" The question came from Whip Whitman who was leaning out of his Captain's office at the far end of the squad bay.

Happy for any interruption, Fey stood up and grabbed her coffee cup as she left her desk. Inside Whitman's office, Whip sat in a high-backed chair behind his desk. Next to the desk stood a dark-haired man with sun-blackened skin. He was only slightly over five-six and wiry thin, but there was an inner stillness about him that was slightly spooky.

"How's your team," Whitman asked Fey without introducing his other guest.

"What team?" Fey replied. "We still haven't replaced Hammer and Nails. Brindle and Alphabet are on vacation. And Monk is down with this damn flu."

"Situation normal then? All screwed up?"

Whitman noticed Fey looking pointedly at the other visitor. "This is Mickey Crow," Whitman said finally. "I need you both to respond to a stranger rape on your old turf in West Los Angeles Division."

"A rape case?" Fey cut her eyes back to Whitman in surprise.

"You know that since the start of the year RHD Rape Special has taken over city wide jurisdiction of all stranger rapes."

"Sure, but I run a homicide team."

"There's nobody available from Rape Special to handle the case. Like everyone else they've been decimated by the flu. You don't have a team, and Mickey just transferred in. The case is down to you. Get on it."

Fey and Mickey Crow approached Officer Tina Delgado outside of Tony V's restaurant. Tina's uniform shirt was pulled tight across her impressive chest, but Mickey Crow didn't appear to pay any attention. He'd talked little to Fey on the trip out from downtown. Fey had only learned he recently surfaced from a deep cover assignment with Organized Crime and Vice Division. He had nine years on the job, and appeared apathetic toward his new assignment to RHD.

"How's the victim?" Fey asked Tina.

"As good as can be expected."

17

"She give you anything on the suspect?" Crow asked.

Tina consulted a small officers' notebook. "Male, Caucasian, six-foot-one, two hundred pounds. Black hair, razor cut and slicked back. Paul Newman eyes—her description not mine."

"Anything else?" Fey asked.

Tina looked back at her notebook. "The victim was coming out of a play at the Shubert last night with a female friend, when the suspect approached them. He said he was a movie producer—wanted to make the victim a star."

"And she believed him?" Fey's question was rhetorical. She'd become cynically endured to the average citizen's gullibility.

"Everyone wants to be a star in this town," Delgado said. "Suspect told the victim to meet him this morning in the lobby of the Century Towers."

"How'd they get here from there?"

"Suspect told her he wanted to take some publicity stills in his studio. The victim followed him over in her own car, but once the suspect got her inside—bada-bing, bada-boom."

Fey shook her head. She looked at Crow. "You know what this country needs?"

"What's that?" Crow asked, surprisingly willing to play straight man.

"A good twelve-step program for stupidity."

PART ONE

Fey and Crow made their way around the building to find criminalist June Sweetwater fingerprinting the door of Tony V's back entrance. The closed restaurant occupied the lower left corner of a two-story office building. June looked up as the two detectives approached.

"Is this the POE?" Fey asked.

"Looks that way," June said with a smile for Fey. "I lifted a couple of prints from the door knob. There's also a couple of tool marks on the jamb. Find the tool, I'll give you a match."

Crow moved forward to examine the pry marks. "You find anything inside?"

"Not much—rope from the victim's ankles, the tie used to bind her hands. The victim said the suspect used a condom, but he must have taken it with him."

"Done this before, then?" Fey said.

June shrugged. "Probably."

Crow stood back to look at the building. "How long has the restaurant been out of business?"

June shrugged again. "A couple of months. Lousy food, lousy service."

"Go figure," Fey said. "You would have thought the LA's nouveau riche would embrace it."

Anna Havilland sat on a small couch in the *soft room* provided by Santa Monica Hospital's Rape Treatment Center. Vicky Torrance, the comfortable looking rape counselor sat next to Anna on the couch holding her hand. Fey and Crow were forced to stand as there were no other chairs in the small room.

"I know it sounds stupid," Anna told Fey and Crow. "But he was so convincing."

"Who was the friend you were with at the theatre?" Fey asked.

"Tiffany Bannister."

"Do you have her address?"

"In my purse," Anna said. She rummaged in the black leather bag on her lap and produced an address book. Crow took it and began leafing through the pages.

"Had either of you seen this guy before?" Fey asked.

"Never. He just came up to me in the parking lot and asked if I was an actress."

"Are you?"

"I've done a couple of soap opera walk-ons, but nothing major."

"This guy told you he was a producer?"

"He said I was perfect for a part in the next Mel Gibson film he was casting."

"You didn't question him," Crow cut in coldly.

Anna was close to tears. "He seemed legit—nice suit, clean cut, good jewelry."

"Did he tell you his name?" Crow asked.

"John Clark."

"He have any identification?"

"She's not a cop," Vicky Torrance interrupted, her anger showing. "Normal people don't meet somebody and ask to see their driver's license."

Fey stepped in to smooth things over. "When you met Clark in the hotel today, did you feel he was staying there?"

"I guess," Anna said. "I gave him my portfolio. He was sitting in the lobby sorting through a bunch of papers."

"Props," said Crow.

Fey shut him up with a look. "After you left the hotel, you drove to the restaurant?"

"Actually, the front of the office building," Anna said. "He told me it was his production company. I could see movie posters on the walls through the glass doors, and the name—Lionheart Pictures."

"Why did you take your own car?"

"I'm not naïve enough to come to the city without my own ride."

Fey and Crow exchanged a glance.

"How did you get into the restaurant?"

"He wanted to start taking photos in his studio around the side of the building."

"How did he open the door?"

"It was already partially open. He stood back to let me enter, but I saw it was dark. I turned back, but he shoved me inside, and then—" Anna suddenly burst into tears and buried her face into Vicky Torrance's shoulder.

Back in the Robbery-Homicide offices, Whip Whitman stood next to Fey as Crow fiddled with the remote control of an industrial VCR.

"You picked the security tape up from the hotel?" Whip asked.

"After we had an artist do a composite with the victim," Fey confirmed.

Crow finally found the right button and the tape in the machine began to play.

"There are ten security cameras in the hotel," Crow said. "They rotate every two seconds." He suddenly froze the image on the screen. "That's the suspect—the back of him anyway."

"And he never turns around?" Whip asked.

"Never."

"What do you think?"

"It's like he knew the cameras were there," Crow said.

"You check out the restaurant?"

Fey nodded. "The property is owned by Elgin Tremayne, the same guy behind Lionheart Pictures."

"No John Clarke?"

Fey Shook her head. "Too easy."

"Then you better get over to Lionheart and do it the hard way."

★ ★ ★ ★ ★

Elgin Tremayne's office was not plush. Cast-off furniture blended in functional mismatch under the framed posters of numerous B-movies. Sitting behind his desk Tremayne was a wizened man in his seventies. His lawyer, Susan Lawrence, sat next to him like a handmaiden. Greta Martin, the Lionheart office manager leaned against the door as Fey and Crow conducted their interview.

"Mr. Tremayne," Fey said. "The business license registry shows you own both these offices and the attached restaurant—Tony V's."

Tremayne's voice was thin and reedy. "My company owns the property where Tony V's was located, but the restaurant was owned by two men who we are now engaged with in major civil litigation. Can you tell us what this is all about?"

Fey nodded. "Were you aware somebody broke into the restaurant premises yesterday and committed a rape?"

"No! How horrible." The outburst came from Susan Lawrence.

"Didn't we change the locks on the restaurant two weeks ago, Greta?" Tremayne asked his office manager.

"Yes," Greta replied. "I have a set of keys, you have a set, and John has a set."

"John?" Crow jumped on the name. "Who's John?"

"John Clark," Tremayne said. "He's our maintenance man."

Crow slid a copy of the suspect's composite across the desk to Tremayne. "He look like this?"

"No way," Tremayne said, giving the composite a cursory glance. "He's about five foot tall, bald, and sixty. He wishes he looked like this." Tremayne picked up the composite and studied it closer. "Wait a minute," he turned to hand the paper to Susan Lawrence. "What do you think?" he asked her.

"You know this guy?" Crow asked.

"Maybe," Tremayne said. "It's the eyes mostly."

Greta Martin moved in to take a look at the composite in Lawrence's hand. Her face paled.

"So who is he?" Fey asked.

"His name is Rafe Vandermere," Lawrence said, putting the composite back on the table. "He's one of the men who owned Tony V's."

"The guys you're involved in the civil litigation with?"

"Yes," Tremayne confirmed. "They stole all the ovens and other fixtures when we evicted them."

"But there's more," Lawrence said. "Vandermere has a prior record for rape."

Fey was in Whip Whitman's office bringing him up-to-speed when Crow entered with a sheaf of printouts.

"Vandermere is a registered sex offender," Crow said, handing the printout to Fey.

Putting on her glasses, Fey scanned the sheets. "Two priors for rape that stuck, and a forced oral cop arrest that bounced behind a reluctant witness."

Whip was reading over Fey's shoulder. "How'd he get nailed?"

Fey turned several pages. "Leaving the scene of the second rape, he hinked up a couple of uniforms. The M.O. tied him to the first rape, and the first victim then picked him out of a line-up."

"Can we get a quick picture to do a photo line-up with our victim?" Whip asked.

Crow held up a line-up card with six photos inside. "Already put the *six-pack* together. The victim is on her way in."

Whip gave Crow an assessing look. "Any idea where

Vandermere is now?"

Crow nodded. "He and his partner, Anthony Picardi, have opened another restaurant called La Scala. Vandermere shows it as his parole address."

Whip checked his watch. "If you hurry, you can get the victim to ID and still beat the lunch crowd."

"Apache," Crow said out of the blue, as he and Fey parked down the street from the La Scala restaurant and exited their detective sedan.

"What?" Fey looked confused.

"You want to know what kind of Indian I am. Everyone does. I'm an Apache."

Fey stopped walking. "First of all, I didn't ask the question. Second, if you've got some kind of chip on your shoulder because you're an Indian, get over it if you want to work for me. And third, you aren't an Apache. Your facial structure isn't right."

Crow smiled for the first time. "How would you know?"

"All palefaces aren't stupid. I'd say you're either Creek or Iroquois."

"Iroquois with a little French thrown in," Crow said.

"Then why say you're Apache?"

"It's what everyone expects to hear."

"If I want to know something, I'll ask. And don't ever make the mistake of lumping me in with everyone."

"No," Crow said thoughtfully. "I stand corrected."

"Damn straight," Fey said. "Now, let's do this."

The two detectives crossed the street during a break in traffic.

"This guy is being served up to us like a pig on a spit," Fey worried as they approached the front of the restaurant. "It's almost too easy."

"So what? Let's put an apple in his mouth and send him back to jail. His pattern of behavior in this case is the same as the priors."

"I know," Fey said. "It all fits, but—"

"What's the problem? The victim immediately picked Vandermere out of the *six-pack*. He's a predator."

"I'm not arguing, but I've still got an itch."

Crow opened the restaurant's front door and stood back. "Maybe you should try a little baby powder in your shorts," he said in a low voice as Fey passed through.

Inside, the restaurant was empty of customers. A busboy was setting tables, and a bartender was busy with his bottles. The bartender's nametag read, *Rand*.

"Sorry, folks," Rand said. "We don't open for another half-hour."

"Tony or Rafe around?" Fey asked.

Rand gave them a look. "You friends or something?"

Crow smiled and extended his hand toward Rand. "Mickey Crow. How ya' doing?"

As Rand reflexively took the proffered hand, Crow tightened his grip and pulled Rand off balance across the bar.

"Hey!" Rand yelled.

"Actually," Crow said, maintaining his grip. "We ain't friends. We're the *or something*."

The busboy looked over, but Fey pointed a gun finger at him. "Relax. No problem here."

"Cops or leg breakers?" Rand asked.

"Glad you make the distinction," Crow said. "Now, are Tony or Rafe around?"

"Tony's in the back office."

"What about Rafe?"

"Not my turn to watch him."

Crow nodded to Fey, letting her make a start for the back

25

room before releasing Rand. "Be a good boy," Crow said and patted Rand's cheek.

With Crow behind her, Fey walked briskly to the back of the restaurant and pushed open the door to a small office. Inside, Tony Picardi sat at a tiny, cluttered desk talking on a cell phone. He was in his thirties with Italian good looks. He looked up, startled, as Fey and Crow crowded in.

"What is this? No customers are allowed back here."

"What about cops?" Fey asked displaying her badge.

"I'll call you back," Picardi said into his phone.

"Are you Anthony Picardi?" Fey asked.

"Yeah, I'm Tony. Why the roust?"

"Where's your partner—Vandermere?"

"He's at the bank. He'll be back any minute. Hey, does this have anything to do with those jerks at Lionheart?"

"Why do you think that?"

"It's the only thing we're into."

"They say you stole all their ovens and fixtures when you closed down Tony V's," Crow said.

"That's crap," Picardi said. "We didn't steal nothing. They wanted the restaurant space back, so they put us out of business. Cost us a fortune. We're suing them for breach of contract."

"Still doesn't justify grand theft," Fey said.

Suddenly, a slim, dark complexioned man opened the door to the office.

"Cops, Rafe!" Picardi yelled.

Rafe Vandermere slammed the door shut before Crow could react. Picardi stood up forcing Fey to push him backward to get room for Crow to open the door. Pulling out their guns, the two detectives ran for the front of the restaurant.

"There!" Crow yelled, pointing as Vandermere disappeared through the front door.

Fey was still running when Rand, the bartender, hip-checked a table and sent it skittering across in front of her. Colliding with the awkward object, Fey crashed to the floor. Right behind her, Crow tripped over Fey's legs and slammed down on top of her.

"Go, damn it! Go! Go!" Fey yelled as Crow scrambled back to his feet.

Dashing out the restaurant entrance, Crow pushed hair out of his eyes to look up and down the street. There was nothing but a blur of traffic and pedestrians. No Vandermere.

PART TWO

Fey and Crow stood in front of Whip Whitman's desk like children in the principal's office.

"I expected better from you, Fey. You were sloppy out there. If things had gone differently, you might have ended up with more than a few bumps and bruises."

"We screwed up," Fey said, defiantly. "So fire me."

Whitman looked about to burst.

"We did get Vandermere's car," Crow said, in a deflective action.

"Congratulations," Whip said, turning on the other detective. "You gonna charge it with rape?"

"We found a jimmy under the front seat," Crow persisted. "Forensics has matched it to the pry marks on the door to Tony V's."

"Doesn't do you much good without Vandermere in custody."

The phone rang on Whitman's desk. He scooped it up with short, pudgy fingers.

"Whitman." He listened for a few moments. "I'll send them over," he said finally before hanging up. He sighed and gave Fey and Crow a dark look. "Somebody must be watching out for you two. That was Gerald Shultz, Vandermere's lawyer. He wants to surrender his client."

Shultz was pot-bellied, balding, and aging fast. He ushered Fey and Crow into his office. A willow blond in her thirties with sharp features was sitting in a client's chair. Shultz moved forward to make introductions.

"This is Janet Kent." Shultz indicated the blond. "She is Mr. Vandermere's civil counsel."

Kent loosened off a predatory smile. "I represent Mr. Vandermere and Mr. Picardi in their action against Lionheart Pictures."

"How nice for you," Fey said. "Where is Mr. Vandermere? We were told you wanted to surrender him."

"Why do you want to talk to my client?" Kent asked.

"We want to arrest him," Fey said blandly.

"Even if he's an innocent man?"

"Innocent men don't run from the police."

"Oh, please," Kent gave a harsh half-laugh. "Don't be ridiculous."

"Rafe Vandermere has been identified as the suspect in a rape investigation," Crow said.

"When did this alleged rape occur?" Kent asked.

"Yesterday morning."

"Where?"

"At Tony V's," Crow said. "The restaurant he owned with Anthony Picardi."

Shultz stirred himself. "Are you aware of the civil litigation surrounding that location?"

"We're aware," Fey said. "But it isn't relevant."

"Of course it's relevant," Janet Kent almost shouted. "Elgin Tremayne has already ruined my client's business. Now, he's trying to ruin my client's life."

Fey kept her voice level. "It's your client who has ruined a young woman's life."

Gerald Shultz put a restraining hand on Janet Kent's shoulder. "How can you be sure?" he asked. "Wasn't it Tremayne who pointed you at Mr. Vandermere?"

"And how would you know that?" Fey asked.

"It stands to reason," Kent told her. "I'm sure Tremayne, or one of his lackeys, told you about Rafe's prior criminal record."

"Let's stop playing games," Fey said. "Where is Vandermere?"

"Do you have a warrant for his arrest?" Shultz asked.

"We don't need one," Crow said. "We have more than enough probable cause—"

"All of it fabricated by Tremayne," Kent interrupted.

"That's for a jury to decide," Fey said. "Somehow, I don't think they're going to believe the victim is a figment of Tremayne's imagination."

Back in the RHD squad room again, Whip Whitman had played the mountain to Mohammed and was standing by Fey's desk.

Whip scowled. "So they refused to produce Vandermere?"

"All they wanted was a tip-off to what we had," Fey told him.

"Any ideas on where Vandermere might be?"

Crow slid a haunch onto the corner of Fey's desk. "We got the impression Janet Kent is involved with Vandermere on more than just a professional basis."

"Are you doing anything about it?"

"We've parked surveillance on both her office and residence," Fey said.

"What about Tremayne? You think he's setting Vandermere up?"

Fey shook her head. "As a frame-up, it's far too complicated."

"The civil litigation is real enough, though," Whip said. "And the victim did tell you she's an actress."

"Are you saying you think the whole thing is a hoax?" Crow asked. There was a belligerent edge to his voice.

Whip hardened his gaze and shifted it to the new detective. "I'm saying let's make the case tight. Tomorrow, reinterview the victim, and confront Tremayne with the accusations. Let's see what shakes loose." He paused for a moment thinking. "And what about Tiffany Bannister, the friend the victim was with at the theatre. Let's see if she can pick Vandermere out of the photo line-up."

The next morning Fey and Crow arrived early at Tiffany Bannister's apartment. Answering the door to their knock, Tiffany appeared to be in her early twenties. Her hair was tousled and she wore a soft collar-brace around her neck. Fey and Crow identified themselves and were invited in.

"You'll have to excuse me," Tiffany said. "I look a wreck, but I'm still not used to this thing." She touched the collar at her throat.

"Traffic accident?" Crow asked.

"Yeah. My car was totaled. I'm very lucky I wasn't injured worse."

"Are you aware of what happened to your friend Anna Havilland?" Fey asked, getting down to business.

"Sure, but I still can't believe it. I told Anna the guy was handing her a line."

30

Crow gave Tiffany a look. "You didn't believe his producer story?"

"Come on," Tiffany said with emphasis. "Everybody in this town is a producer."

"Have you ever heard of Lionheart Pictures or Elgin Tremayne?" Fey asked.

"Who are they?"

"Doesn't matter," Fey said. "We'd like you to look at a photo line-up and see if you can pick out the man who approached you and Anna in the parking lot."

"I'll try," Tiffany said.

Crow held out the photo six-pack face down for Tiffany to take.

"Before you turn it over," Crow said, "I need to give you a legal admonition." His voice became more formal. "A picture of the suspect may or may not be in this line-up. Remember, hair styles and facial hair can be changed, and skin complexions can be lighter or darker than in these pictures. Do you understand?"

"Yes." Tiffany took the proffered line-up and turned it over. She ran her eyes quickly over the photos. "That's him," she said, pointing to Vandermere's photo in the number five position without hesitation.

"Are you sure?" Crow asked.

"Positive," Tiffany said. "It's the eyes."

Leaving Tiffany Bannister's apartment, Fey and Crow returned to Lionheart Pictures to reinterview Elgin Tremayne in the presence of his lawyer, Susan Lawrence.

Tremayne was into his Hollywood powerbroker intimidation mode. "We've shown you all of our employee records. Anna Havilland has never worked for Lionheart."

"I've check with the SAG, which is something you should

have done before coming here," Susan Lawrence said with condescension. "Havilland's acting career consists of six weeks' work on two different soap operas produced by the same company—neither of which has any connections to Lionheart."

"What about the allegations you put Tony V's out of business?" Fey asked. "Vandermere's lawyer claims you are now trying to frame Vandermere because of the civil suit."

"You can't possibly believe that crap," Susan Lawrence said. "It's crazy."

"What I believe doesn't matter," Fey said, calmly. "The question still has to be addressed."

"Rafe Vandermere and Tony Picardi sold us a bill of goods," Tremayne said. "There had been several other attempts to run a restaurant on the premises without success. We were going to convert the location into office space, but Rafe and Tony convinced us to rent it to them for another try as a restaurant."

Lawrence laid her hand on Tremayne's arm. "Elgin gave them all the backing he could," she said. "He provided advertising and other promotions, even used them to cater to our other business functions."

"None of it helped," Tremayne said. "There were health code violations, unhappy customers—the menu was a disaster."

"Picardi was the brains?" Crow asked.

"I don't know about brains," Tremayne said. "He was the head cook and busboy anyway. Vandermere was the showman, but he was all show and no do. We had no choice but to evict them when they consistently failed to meet their financial obligations."

"What do you intend to do with the property now?" Fey asked.

Tremayne shrugged. "When the civil suit is settled, we'll convert it to office space. Lionheart is out of the restaurant business."

From the Lionheart offices, Fey and Crow moved on to Anna Havilland's apartment. Both detectives had been thoughtful while driving to the location. However, walking through the entrance to the complex, Crow broke the silence.

"This whole set-up theory doesn't make sense. You saw the victim at the hospital. Do you believe she wasn't raped?"

"Maybe she's an Oscar class actress."

"You can't be serious?"

"No," Fey said. "But I learned a long time ago that trusting gut instinct was a loser's game. We check everybody's story out. We get proof."

They were now approaching the door to Anna's apartment when Fey saw it was slightly open. She tapped Crow's shoulder and pointed.

"Your gut instinct telling you something?" Crow asked assessing the situation. "Or do you need proof?"

"Shut up," Fey said, knowing he was right.

Approaching cautiously, Fey knocked on the door. It swung open slightly, but there was no response from inside. The two detectives drew their guns, holding them down by their sides.

"Ms. Havilland?" Fey called out. "Anna?"

Crow pushed the door open wide and stepped in. "Anna Havilland?" He called out loudly. "Police."

They walked through the small apartment. Fey checked the kitchen as Crow pushed open the door to the single bedroom. He looked inside and immediately withdrew his head.

"Fey," he called out softly.

Fey moved to his side and looked into the bedroom for herself. Anna Havilland's body lay naked across the bed, a man's tie wrapped tightly around her throat.

Fey let out a deep sigh. "Oh, hell."

Deputy Coroner Elsie Manning talked to Fey as they stood next to the stainless steel autopsy table bearing Anna Havilland's body.

"Cause of death was definitely asphyxiation," Elsie said. She was drying her hands on a small towel.

"Any sexual trauma?" Fey asked.

Crow entered the autopsy room and came to stand next to Fey, picking up the thread of the conversation.

"None," Elsie reported. "But she did put up a struggle. I found a fair amount of skin under the nails of her left hand. There were some black beard hairs in the skin."

"So, you're saying whoever did this is walking around with a hell of a set of scratches on their face?" Crow asked.

Elsie nodded. "Best guess would be the suspect's right cheek."

Crow turned to Fey. "Surveillance just called in. They spotted Vandermere sneaking in to Janet Kent's townhouse."

"Tell me they had a close enough look to see scratches on his face," Fey said.

"Got it in one," Crow said with a grim smile.

Fey and Crow quietly approached the front door of Janet Kent's darkened townhouse. Wearing bulletproof vests and raid jackets, they led the way for several other similarly clad RHD detectives. There were also two uniformed officers, one of them carrying a battering ram.

"Better knock and identify ourselves," Fey whispered as

she and Crow reached the front door. "Wouldn't want to break the law."

Crow tapped ever so lightly on the front door. "Police," he whispered. "We have a search warrant." He looked at Fey.

"Better break it down," Fey said, continuing to whisper, "before they can destroy any evidence."

Crow grinned and waved to the uniformed officer carrying the battering ram.

The door to the townhouse burst open with the first swing of the heavy metal ram. Fey and Crow surged in followed by the other detectives, all with their guns drawn and ready.

"Police!" Crow yelled.

He and Fey swarmed down a short hallway and kicked open a door leading to the main bedroom. Inside, Janet Kent was pulling a sheet up to cover her nakedness. Rafe Vandermere had already rolled out of the bed and was heading for a window. Fresh scratches were visible on his right cheek. Fey's gun came unwaveringly to bear on him.

"Don't even think about it," she said through gritted teeth. "Just give me an excuse."

Vandermere froze in his tracks. Crow moved past Fey, careful to stay clear of her line of fire, and cuffed Vandermere.

"What's the meaning of this?" Janet Kent demanded.

"Search warrant, counselor," Fey said. She holstered her gun before tossing a copy of the warrant fact sheet on the bed. "I'm sure you're familiar with the concept."

One of the other detectives entered the room. "Look what we found," he said, holding up a man's shirt with blood on the collar and Anna Havilland's acting portfolio.

"Let's go, Vandermere," Crow said, pushing his captive toward the bedroom door. "You're under arrest for the rape and murder of Anna Havilland."

Fey started to follow Crow. She looked back over her shoulder at a shocked Janet Kent. "See you in court, counselor."

PART THREE

Assistant Deputy District Attorney Winchell Groom sat behind his desk. The office was utilitarian, much like Groom himself. Tall and rapier thin, the black skin of his shaved skull glinted under the fluorescent lighting. Arlene Lancaster, another, younger, DA leaned against the side wall watching Groom verbally fence with Gerald Shultz and Janet Kent.

"Our client is being framed by Elgin Tremayne." Kent made the statement in a fashion demanding it be taken as fact without further question.

"That's not what the evidence shows." Groom was unruffled. "Just insisting Vandermere is being framed accomplishes nothing."

Arlene Lancaster pushed herself upright with a shove of her shoulder. "Ms. Kent, is it possible your personal involvement with your client is hindering his defense?"

Gerald Shultz immediately responded before Janet Kent could get any words out. "I'm handling the criminal defense in this case. Due to the civil overtones, Ms. Kent is assisting me."

"Then you should know you need more than supposition and innuendo to support an affirmative defense," Lancaster told him. "There is a mountain of forensic, situational, and eye-witness testimony on the people's side."

"If you'd like to make a plea," Groom offered, "the people will accept murder-one with a life sentence."

"Out of the question," Kent said rising from her chair.

Shultz placed a restraining hand on her shoulder.

"We believe accepting a plea at this juncture would be premature," he said.

Groom made a gesture with his hands. "My door is always open."

Shultz stood up to follow Kent who was leaving in a huff. He almost bumped into her, however, when she turned on her heels in the doorway.

"This is far from over," Kent said, before storming on her way.

When they were out of earshot, Lancaster turned her head toward Groom. "She's wound a little tight."

"Tight enough to manufacture evidence?"

"Maybe," Lancaster said. "Perhaps we should get Croaker to find out."

Greta Martin, the office manager for Lionheart Pictures, took her coffee from the Starbucks service counter and carried it across to a small table. Fey and Crow walked across to join her.

"Hello, Greta," Fey said. "Do you remember us?"

Greta looked up. "Sure. You're the detectives."

"That's right. The district attorney's office has filed charges against Rafe Vandermere, but we need to ask you a few more questions."

Greta took a sip from her coffee. "It's a horrible situation, but what could I possibly tell you?"

Fey sat down in the chair next to Greta. "Vandermere's lawyers want us to believe Elgin Tremayne is attempting to frame their client."

"And you believe them?"

"Frankly, no. But I need to gather all the information I can about the situation so the district attorney isn't blindsided in court."

"What do you want to know?"

Fey leaned back in her seat. This was the tricky part. "It appears to me there's more to the closing down of Tony V's than wanting to turn the space into offices."

Greta looked down at her coffee for a beat, fiddling with the cardboard holder.

"I have a good job with Lionheart," she said eventually.

"But?" Fey probed.

Greta appeared to weigh her options before continuing. Finally, she said, "Mr. Tremayne has some tax problems. He needs to sell the building. To do so, he needed to break the lease with Tony and Rafe."

"So he forced them to close down and get out?" Fey asked.

"Yes," Greta said. "But their lawyer got an injunction stopping the sale of the building until the civil suit is settled."

"So, why doesn't Tremayne settle?"

Greta took a long swig from her cooling coffee. She put the cup down on the table. "I said Mr. Tremayne had tax problems. What I meant was he has huge tax problems."

Fey stood in the office of head filing deputy Owen Overmars. Winston Groom perched himself on the rolled arm of a leather couch next to Arlene Lancaster as Fey and Crow reported on her findings.

"We talked to an IRS investigator I know named Craven," Fey told the lawyers. "He said Tremayne is about to be put under indictment for tax evasion."

"And selling the building could forestall the situation?" Overmars asked.

"The building is Tremayne's largest asset," Crow said. "He needs to sell it before it is seized."

"Okay," Overmars said. "So you've found a reason for Tremayne to want to get Vandermere and his partner, but what good does having Vandermere in jail do him?"

Fey began to pace slowly. "What if Tremayne's best-laid plans went south on him? What if Tremayne manipulated Vandermere into attempting to rape Anna Havilland—wanting to catch him in the act?"

Winston Groom made a face. "You're thinking, if it happened that way, then maybe something went wrong and Tremayne didn't get there in time?"

Arlene Lancaster nodded her head, seeing where Fey was leading. "If Tremayne had caught Vandermere in the act, he could have forced him to drop the civil suit."

"Probably," Fey said. "Then he could sell the building and deal with his tax problems."

"Or make a run for the border," Crow said from his position leaning in the doorway.

"You have a nasty mind," Overmars told him. "But even if it was a set-up gone wrong, Vandermere is still guilty of rape at the very least."

"Only if Anna Havilland wasn't a willing participant," Arlene said.

Overmars and Groom exchanged a glance as this sunk in.

"Okay," Groom said. "But how do you get from there to murder?"

Fey shrugged. "When everything went south, perhaps Anna Havilland did too. Maybe she turned on Tremayne—threatened blackmail, forcing him to kill her."

"If this was my idea," Groom said, "you'd be throwing a feminist fit."

"Maybe so," Fey said smiling. She'd worked with Groom for a long time and liked him.

"Wait a minute," Overmars interrupted. "There's something that doesn't fit. What about the scratches on Vandermere's face?"

"We haven't got that figured yet," Fey admitted. "But give us time."

"Maybe we can let Vandermere explain," Groom said. "We'll get Shultz to agree to an interview after the arraignment."

The courthouse interview room was cold and featureless. A scarred wooden table sat in the middle of the room surrounded by several rickety metal chairs. Owen Overmars had suggested letting a male interview Vandermere, so Winchell Groom was sitting across the table from the prisoner. Gerald Shultz sat next to his client. Arlene Lancaster and Janet Kent hovered off to the side.

"Chicks like her are all the same," Vandermere was saying. "They'll do anything to get into the movies."

"Movies you have nothing to do with," Groom said.

"Since when is it a crime to lie to somebody to get into their pants?" Vandermere asked.

"Since you started tying them up to do it," Groom fired back.

Gerald Shultz entered the fray. "Isn't moralizing about sexual kinks between consenting adults counterproductive at this point?"

Vandermere leaned forward. "We were having fun. I didn't rape anybody, and I didn't murder anybody." There was no modesty in the man.

"Then what did happen?"

Vandermere slumped back in his chair. "When I found out about the rape charges, I knew this had to be a scam."

"Why?" Groom asked.

"Elgin Tremayne's lawyers found out about my past record. They've been trying to use it against me ever since to get the civil suit dropped."

"How did you know where Anna Havilland lived?"

"From the portfolio she gave me at the hotel. I went to confront her, but when she opened the door and saw me, she went off the deep end—screaming and stuff."

"Let me guess," Groom said. "You grabbed her to calm her down, and she scratched your face."

"Yeah," Vandermere nodded. "And then I got the hell out. She was a psycho, but she was alive when I left."

"Your lawyers are working very hard to convince us you've been framed," Groom said. "But as far as I'm concerned it's a pretty pathetic effort."

Vandermere's eyes flashed. "I swear I didn't kill the girl."

"You've admitted to raping her. If you didn't kill her, who did?"

"Wait a minute," Shultz jumped in. "Mr. Vandermere has not admitted to rape."

"I told you," Vandermere said. "The sex was consensual. Kinky maybe, but consensual. She asked to be tied up."

"No jury is going to buy that line," Groom said.

"She thought she could get into the movies by taking care of me," Vandermere insisted.

"Where did she get the idea you ran a casting couch?"

"Beats me." Vandermere's grin was goading.

"But you didn't dissuade her?"

"Would you?"

"Yes, I would," Groom said. After a pause, he resumed. "So, what happened next?"

"I told her to meet me Sunday in the lobby of the Century Towers. When I suggested we go and take some pictures, she jumped at the idea."

"Why did you go to Tony V's?"

"I live in a room over the new restaurant. Like I'm really going to take a chick there."

41

"Okay, so what happened at Tony V's?"

"The locks had been changed, so I jimmied the door. Then I waited out front."

"How did Anna react when there weren't any cameras?"

"She didn't. She knew the score."

"What score? Sex now, movie part later?"

"Hey, she got into it. Anything I wanted. When I was done I split."

"Quite the gentleman."

Vandermere shrugged. "I didn't need no grief."

Groom pushed open the door to his office allowing Arlene to enter ahead of him.

"I don't get the point," Arlene was saying. "You could tell Vandermere was lying. His lips were moving."

"The point is, Shultz wants us to drop the murder charge and offer a plea on the rape."

"On the basis of their dreamed-up conspiracy?" Arlene was offended. "Vandermere hasn't even copped to the rape yet."

"Come on," Groom said. "You were there—that's what they were hinting around."

"You think they're that desperate?"

"Don't you? We go with what we've got and a jury will slam-dunk Vandermere. It's going to take a magician to produce an affirmative defense."

Arlene pursed her lips. "I'm not so sure. I'd like to ask Croaker to take a direct run at Elgin Tremayne."

"You're asking her to spend ten dollars on a five-dollar job. Go with what we have and move on."

"Not yet. I want to be sure Tremayne isn't a card hidden up the defense's sleeve."

While Crow did his usual supporting the wall trick, Fey sat

opposite Elgin Tremayne at one end of a low couch in Tremayne's office. Susan Lawrence was also present. Fey fleetingly wondered if Lawrence and Tremayne were sleeping together despite their thirty-plus-year age difference.

"Sure I've got tax problems," Tremayne said in response to Fey's question. "Doesn't everybody in business?"

"Not everybody is about to be indicted by the IRS," Fey said.

"We are prepared to deal with any tax evasion allegations," Lawrence said with a lawyer's glib assurance.

"I would love to sell the building," Tremayne said. "It would free up a lot of cash, but the civil injunction is not the end of the world."

"No?" Crow asked bluntly. "I hear your company is in the dumper."

"All independent film companies are in the dumper," Tremayne assured him with a chuckle. "At least until the next deal comes along. It's typical Hollywood bookkeeping."

"I take it, you have the next deal?" Fey asked.

"I have three straight-to-video teen sex-and-slasher flicks ready for release." Tremayne scattered a collection of stills onto the glass top of the coffee table in front of the couch. Fey leaned forward to examine them.

"Not exactly material for the art house circuit," she said.

"Who cares as long as they make money?" Tremayne came back.

Susan Lawrence touched the photos before adding her comments. "Overseas feature release will recoup the production costs. Domestic, Canadian, and video sales are pure profit."

"The IRS bloodsuckers know the money is coming," Tremayne said. "They're simply saber rattling to make sure they get their share."

Fey picked up one of the stills and studied it. "Is that who I think it is?" she asked Crow, handing him the photo.

Crow grunted in recognition.

"What's the matter?" Tremayne asked.

Crow handed him the photo. Susan Lawrence moved around to look over Tremayne's shoulder.

"Is that a photo of Tiffany Bannister?" Crow asked.

"Yes, that's Tiffany," Tremayne said. "Terrible actress, but big boobs. She gets impaled on a marlin spike halfway through Hatchet Harvest."

Fey and Crow returned with their bounty to Owen Overmars's office. Winchell Groom and Arlene Lancaster were summoned to join them.

"Tiffany Bannister is the girl who went to the theatre with Anna Havilland," Fey explained.

"How did you recognize her?" Overmars asked. He was looking at the publicity still Fey had brought from Tremayne's office.

"You're a guy. You're only looking at her exposed chest," Fey said. "It's her hair."

"Her hair?" Overmars asked.

"It's a girl thing," Fey said. "I've been thinking about getting my hair cut, and her hairstyle in the photo caught my eye."

Arlene Lancaster laughed. "You go, girl. I know exactly what you're saying."

Fey smiled. "When we interviewed Bannister, her hair was a mess and she wore no makeup. She wore a soft collar around her neck from a recent car accident. I wouldn't have recognized her as the actress in the publicity still, if I hadn't been sure I'd seen the hairstyle before."

"Where?" Groom asked.

Fey picked up a remote control and pointed it at a TV/VCR set-up on a shelf in the corner of the office. "Watch," she said, and pressed the play button.

The screen of the television lit up with the video of the security tape from the Century Towers Hotel.

Crow suddenly moved forward. "There," he said, pointing.

Fey froze the frame. "That's her standing off to the side. Anna and Vandermere couldn't have seen her, but the camera picked her up from the opposite angle."

"I still don't see how you recognized her," Overmars said.

"I didn't until after I saw her hairstyle in the publicity still. It's done the same way on the security video."

"Talk about magic tricks," Arlene said.

"There's more," Fey said.

"I can't wait," Overmars told her.

"We checked on Tiffany's traffic accident. There was a report at West Traffic because of the injuries. It occurred the day of the rape after the time on the hotel security video," Fey said.

"Where?" Groom asked, knowing the answer.

"Halfway between the Century Towers and Tony V's."

Fey and Crow had convinced a reluctant Tiffany Bannister to talk to them at her apartment. Tiffany sat on the couch wearing her neck brace. Fey went straight for the jugular.

"Tiffany, can you explain your presence in the lobby of the Century Towers Hotel on the day Anna Havilland was raped?"

"I wasn't—"

Crow held up the security video. "Before you answer, we should explain that you appear on the lobby video tape."

Tiffany looked shocked and took in a deep breath. Tears burst from her eyes.

"Anna wasn't supposed to get raped. I thought I could stop him."

"What do you mean?" Fey asked.

Tiffany sniffled. "When Rafe approached us in the theatre parking lot, he didn't recognize me. He only had eyes for Anna."

"You knew him?"

"We'd never been introduced, but I'd eaten at Tony V's with some of the cast from Hatchet Harvest. They all knew about his rape convictions, it was common gossip, and Rafe told me to stay away from him."

"What happened in the parking lot?" Crow asked.

"Rafe laid this crap on Anna about being a producer. I told her he was feeding her a line, but she thought I was jealous."

"Why didn't you tell her about his rape record?"

"I don't know. I thought—"

"Yes?" Crow pushed.

"I knew Mr. Tremayne was having problems with Rafe. I thought I could follow them. If Rafe tried to rape Anna, I could video it, and then stop it before it went too far."

"Why?" Fey asked.

Tiffany cried even harder, her words difficult to understand through the flow. "I thought—" she gasped for breath. "I thought, I could trade the tape to Mr. Tremayne for a big part in his next film."

Fey ran her hands through her hair as she slid into the passenger side of the detective sedan after leaving Tiffany Bannister's apartment.

"Why does everyone in this town want to be rich and famous?"

46

"Don't you?" Crow asked. He started the car and pulled away from the curb.

"No," Fey said. "And certainly not like that. Can you imagine allowing a friend to be set-up by a known rapist?"

"She was blinded by ambition," Crow said. "She thought she could stop the action before it got out of hand."

"It was already out of hand."

Crow looked over at Fey. "She certainly didn't plan on getting into an accident on the way to the rescue."

"I can't believe you're defending her."

"I'm not. I just don't see how it changes anything. Tremayne didn't put Tiffany up to the ruse. The set-up was Tiffany's own decision."

"And we've still got a rape and a murder," Fey agreed reluctantly, seeing the point.

"And Vandermere is still elected to take the fall," Crow concluded.

"For the rape anyway," Fey said.

"What?" Crow asked. "Now, you think somebody else committed the murder. For Heaven's sake, who?"

"The woman scorned," Fey said.

"Janet Kent? You must be kidding?"

PART FOUR

Arlene Lancaster and Whip Whitman stood next to Fey's desk in the squad room. Fey was flipping through files.

"I knew all along this case was too easy," Fey said. "But would anybody listen to me?"

"Do you have anything at all to tie Kent to the murder?" Arlene asked.

Fey held up a sheaf of papers in triumph. "Maybe," she

said. "This is the surveillance log from the team that was staking out Kent's residence. When they spotted Vandermere, they called us in, but it took us a while to get there and get organized."

Fey handed the log to Arlene, who began thumbing through it.

"And?" Arlene asked, not immediately seeing the significance.

"Look at the last page," Fey said. "Guess who arrived thirty minutes after Vandermere."

Arlene stared at the page. "Janet Kent."

"She could have followed Vandermere to Anna Havilland and murdered her after he left," Fey suggested. "Setting Vandermere up to take a murder rap in revenge for cheating on her."

"Pretty sick," Arlene said. "Murder the rape victim to punish the rapist."

"In her warped mind, she could have decided Havilland led Vandermere on," Whitman said. Fey never ceased to amaze him with the convolutions of the cases she became involved in.

Arlene nodded. "So, you're saying Kent blamed Havilland for luring Vandermere back into his known pattern of behavior?"

"Stranger things have happened," Fey said.

Crow suddenly entered the squad room waving a file folder.

"Bingo," he said as he approached the gathering.

"You got something?" Whitman asked.

"Latents compared Janet Kent's prints to all unidentified prints from the crime scene and they matched ten points on two prints as belonging to Kent."

"We need sixteen matching points for court," Arlene said.

"But you only need eight points to actually identify somebody. With ten points we may not be able to go to court, but we know the prints belong to Kent."

"So you've only got half a bingo," Whitman said. "No sixteen points, no court."

"Still," Fey said. "Coupled with the surveillance log, we've got enough probable cause to haul Kent in."

Arlene smiled. "Sounds as if she's going to need a good lawyer."

Outside of the courtroom the following day, Arlene Lancaster approached Gerald Shultz. She matched him stride for stride as they walked.

"Busy day?" she asked.

"I've been like a long-tailed cat in a room full of rocking chairs," Shultz said.

"Did Kent and Vandermere come to you as a package?" Arlene asked.

"She brought the case to me," Shultz said. "But she wanted to stay involved because of the civil side."

"Her personal relationship with Vandermere causing you problems?"

Shultz stopped walking. "Where is this leading?"

"Humor me," Arlene said.

Shultz shrugged. "Okay, Kent's in love with the guy. Actually, obsessed would be a better word. I don't see it myself, but I guess the guy's got something."

"Is she advising Vandermere to fight the murder charge, even with all the evidence stacked against him?"

"Despite his record," Shultz said, "she refuses to even consider Vandermere might be guilty."

"What does he say?"

"He's not admitting to the murder, if that's what you mean."

"What about you?" Arlene asked.

Shultz looked at her evenly. "Don't get me wrong, counselor. I do my best for my clients. But if it were up to me, I'd plead the bastard out and move on."

"What if I told you he didn't murder Havilland?"

"If not him, who?"

"Kent."

Shultz's eyes widened in surprise.

Arlene sat in Owen Overmars's office discussing the case with Overmars and Groom.

"Shultz doesn't like the courtroom. He's a deal maker. He'll get Vandermere to testify against Kent in return for an offer on the rape charge."

"Did Vandermere know or suspect Kent killed Havilland?" Overmars asked.

"No," Arlene said. "But with hindsight, he's able to fill in a lot of the blanks."

"What does Shultz want on the rape?" Groom asked.

"Felony sexual battery—three to five, no strike."

"He's kidding, right?" Overmars was scornful. "Vandermere is a twice convicted rapist."

"The question was what does Shultz want, not what will he settle for."

"Okay," Overmars said. "So, what will he settle for?"

Arlene tilted her head slightly in thought. "One count of rape. Vandermere serves eighty-five percent of a twelve-year sentence."

"What about the third strike problem?" Groom asked.

"Retrospective record amendment," Arlene said. "Change the first rape conviction to sexual battery."

Overmars fiddled with a cold pipe. "That makes this case only a second strike. It's a good deal for him."

"It's only worth it if Vandermere can make our case," Groom said.

"I'm holding the third strike over his head," Arlene said. "We don't get Kent—Vandermere doesn't get his record amended. He strikes out and gets life."

Overmars set his pipe down on his desk. "Make sure you don't open the door for Kent's defense to bring in Vandermere's record. You're also going to have trouble with the fingerprint evidence."

"Court wouldn't be fun without a challenge," Arlene said.

"Kent say anything to Croaker when she was arrested?"

"Nothing you could repeat in church. She lawyered up immediately."

"Who?" Groom asked.

"Bernie Easterbrook."

"He's a heavy hitter. He'll fight you right from the preliminary hearing."

"That's why I want to avoid it. I want to take the case to the grand jury, get an indictment, and go straight to trial."

Arlene Lancaster had checked her new suit several times before going into court. The skirt was long enough not to offend the women on the jury, but short enough to give the men a glance at her nicely shaped legs. The white blouse under the well-cut jacket, was tight across the bust, but revealed no cleavage. Some days it pissed her off that she had to be more worried about how she looked than how strong of a case she could present, but juries were notorious for turning against the evidence based on their like or dislike of either attorney.

Fey had also dressed carefully as she was to sit next to Lancaster as the investigating officer in the case. Her role was more supportive at this point. The investigation was over.

The courtroom was Lancaster's playground.

Officer Jim Breland was on the stand being questioned by Arlene. He was young and wore a hip suit, which would have looked better at a nightclub. On the bench, Judge Julia Faversham presided over the proceedings from behind heavily hooded eyes.

"Officer Breland, what is your occupation and assignment?"

"I'm a police officer assigned to LAPD's Special Intelligence Services' surveillance unit."

"On the day Anna Havilland was murdered, were you surveilling the defendant's residence?"

"Yes."

"Previous testimony by the coroner has established the time of Anna Havilland's death as approximately four p.m. Please tell us what your log shows happening at five-thirty."

Breland briefly checked the notes on the counter in front of him.

"The subject identified as Rafe Vandermere approached the door of the residence on foot and entered through the rear door."

"Was there anything strange about his appearance?" Arlene asked.

"Several prominent scratches on his right cheek were noted."

"Now, please tell us what your log notes reflect for six p.m."

"The defendant, Janet Kent, parked her car in front of the residence and entered through the front door using a key."

"Anything unusual about her appearance?"

"She appeared upset and disheveled."

"Objection!" Bernie Easterbrook had risen to his feet to earn his fee. He was solid and senatorial. His mass of silver hair set off with piercing green eyes drew many a younger woman to him. "Calls for speculation."

"Sustained." Judge Faversham waved a hand slightly from her position on the bench.

"Prior to six p.m.," Arlene continued, "did you see the defendant at the residence?"

"We saw her leave shortly before noon. We didn't see her again until she returned at six."

"No further questions," Arlene said. She walked around the edge of the prosecution desk holding the original SIS surveillance log. "We would ask that the surveillance log be marked as people's seven."

"So marked," Faversham said, as Arlene handed the log to the court clerk.

Arlene sat down and whispered to Fey, "I miss anything?"

"Not so far," Fey told her. She then sat back as Bernie Easterbrook rose for cross-examination.

"Officer Breland, is there anything unusual in somebody leaving their house at noon and not returning until six?" Bernie's voice was full and measured.

"I guess not," Breland said.

"Did you ever see Ms. Kent anywhere else? At the market? The mall?"

"No."

"Have you ever seen Ms. Kent anywhere even remotely close to Anna Havilland's residence?"

"No."

Bernie smiled. "No further questions."

Arlene called latent print technician June Sweetwater as her next witness. After establishing Sweetwater's credentials and expertise, Arlene got quickly to the point.

"How many latent prints did you recover from the scene of the murder?"

"Twenty-seven," Sweetwater reported.

"How many of those were positively identified?"

"Fifteen."

"At some point did you compare the remaining unidentified prints to the defendant's fingerprints?"

"Objection!" Easterbrook was on his feet again. "The prosecution is attempting to force in evidence that may be unfairly prejudicial to my client by its nature."

Judge Faversham's heavy eyelids moved a fraction upward. "Ms. Lancaster?"

"I'm simply trying to establish possibilities, your honor."

"We'll take a fifteen-minute recess," Faversham said, with a bang of her gavel. "Counselors, my office."

Inside Faversham's chambers, Arlene Lancaster and Bernie Easterbrook sat in uncomfortable, straight-back chairs.

Easterbrook was elucidating his objection. "To serve as identifying evidence in a criminal matter, a fingerprint must have sixteen points of identification."

"Do you have sixteen points, Ms. Lancaster?" the judge asked.

"No," Arlene said. "Only ten, which is two more than needed in a civil case."

"It's still six points short for criminal proceedings," Faversham pointed out.

"Two of the recovered prints each matched ten points with those of the defendant," Arlene explained. "The matching points of the two prints, however, are different. Combined, the two prints match seventeen points with the defendant."

Easterbrook snorted. "Seventeen points from two prints does not equal sixteen matching points from one print."

"He's right," Faversham said. "You don't have criminal ID from either singular print."

"I'm not trying to get positive ID," Arlene said. "I simply want to show the possibility that the prints could belong to the defendant."

Easterbrook disagreed. "They could also come from somebody else. It's prejudicial to allow the comparison testimony."

"There are precedents for allowing the admission of partial prints in both Hays-versus-California, and Denniston-versus-Ohio," Arlene pointed out.

"Denniston was overturned on appeal," Easterbrook said.

"Yes," Arlene agreed, "but not on the print evidence."

"Both of you settle down," Faversham said. "I understand your feelings, Mr. Easterbrook, but I'm familiar with Ms. Lancaster's cites. As long as she doesn't claim positive ID, you can argue the significance of the ten points with the jury."

Back in the courtroom, Arlene started in again with June Sweetwater.

"Did you compare the defendant's fingerprints to the twelve unidentified latents from the crime scene?"

"Yes."

"And what did you determine?"

"Two of the twelve unidentified prints had ten matching points of identification with the defendant's prints."

"Not enough for a criminal ID?" Arlene asked, trying to steal Easterbrook's thunder.

"No," Sweetwater agreed.

"But enough for a civil identification?"

"Objection!" Easterbrook was on his feet again.

"Sustained," Judge Faversham said. "You're dangerously close to the edge, Ms. Lancaster."

55

"No further questions," Arlene said. She sat down quickly and gave Fey a smile.

Easterbrook had remained standing. He began his cross-examination.

"Isn't it true you need sixteen matching points to positively identify a print in a criminal case?"

"Yes," Sweetwater replied, unruffled. She had testified in hundreds of other cases.

"So," Easterbrook said. "Ten points doesn't cut it?"

"The odds—" Sweetwater began.

Easterbrook interrupted quickly. "Your honor, the question calls for a yes or no response."

"Answer yes or no," Faversham directed the witness.

"No," Sweetwater said sourly.

Easterbrook smiled. "Therefore, the two prints with the ten matching points of identification are worthless for identification in this courtroom, aren't they?"

"Correct." Sweetwater sighed. She'd seen this coming.

"You can't prove they belong to my client, can you?"

"No."

"As far as this court is concerned, they could belong to anyone?"

"Yes."

"No further questions," Easterbrook said, and sat down.

"Any recross?" Faversham asked.

"No, your honor," Arlene said.

"Then call your next witness."

Arlene put Rafe Vandermere on the stand. This was make-it or break-it time. From her seat at the prosecution counsel, Fey turned to look at Janet Kent. She was pleased to see her previously calm exterior beginning to wear around the edges. Kent was looking anywhere except at Vandermere.

She was uncomfortable and agitated. Maybe we're getting somewhere, Fey thought.

"During the time you lived with Janet Kent were you ever unfaithful to her?" Arlene asked Vandermere.

"Sure," he replied in his cocky manner.

"And was she aware of these wanderings?"

"Objection!" Easterbrook broke in. "Calls for speculation."

"Sustained," the judge agreed.

"Did the defendant ever accuse you of being unfaithful?" Arlene restated her question.

"She accused me of screwing anything that would hold still long enough, and we'd fight about it. She'd threaten to kill me and whoever I was screwing."

Fey saw Janet Kent start to stand. She was immediately restrained by Easterbrook and subsided back into her chair.

"What else did the defendant do as a result of her accusations?" Arlene continued.

"She started to follow me," Vandermere said. "I'd lose her if I had something going on the side, but it just caused more arguments."

"What happened when Anna Havilland made accusations against you?"

"I went to confront her."

"Did you see the defendant following you?"

"Yeah, but I didn't care. I wasn't going over there to fool around. I wanted to get the Havilland bitch off my back."

"Was Anna Havilland alive when you left her?"

"Absolutely."

"And did you see the defendant when you left the victim's residence?"

Vandermere nodded. "She was sitting in her car, which was parked across the street."

"Why did you live with the defendant if you felt the need for other women?"

"She was paying the bills."

Vandermere smirked at Janet Kent, making the woman squirm in her seat. Fey could see Kent was on the boil.

"That's not very honorable," Arlene said to Vandermere.

"She knew I was a scorpion when she met me," Vandermere said.

"What does that mean?"

"You know. The story about the scorpion who convinces the frog to give him a ride across the pond?"

"Enlighten us."

"The frog refuses, saying the scorpion will sting him. The scorpion promises he won't. Finally, the frog agrees, but halfway across the pond, the scorpion stings the frog. As they're both dying, the frog asks the scorpion why. The scorpion says, 'You knew I was a scorpion when you gave me the ride—you knew I would sting you.' It was the frog's fault not the scorpion's," Vandermere concluded.

Janet Kent jumped up from her chair—out of control.

"I loved you, you bastard!" she screamed. "But you couldn't keep it in your pants!"

Judge Faversham began banging her gavel in earnest as the courtroom erupted.

Bernie Easterbrook was sitting in Owen Overmars's office with Fey, Arlene Lancaster, Overmars, and Winchell Groom.

"You don't play fair, Ms. Lancaster," Bernie said. "You worked my client over deliberately."

"My heart bleeds," Arlene said.

"It doesn't matter what her provocation," Owen Overmars stepped in. "Janet Kent is guilty of murder."

"We'll plead to man-two."

"No way," Overmars said. "Murder-one. No special circs."

Easterbrook shook his head. "You don't want this to go to a jury. Premeditation isn't even in the ballpark. Manslaughter-one. Eight years."

"Murder-two," Overmars shot back. "Twelve to fifteen."

"I can sell ten to twelve," Easterbrook said.

Overmars glanced up at Fey and Arlene. They both nodded agreement.

"Deal," Overmars said.

After Easterbrook left, Arlene and Fey walked out together toward the elevator.

"We got away with one," Fey said.

"Sometimes, you have to take your chances," Arlene agreed.

"I wonder if we don't push our luck too often," Fey said.

Arlene smiled. "Hey, they knew we were scorpions when they hired us."

Chuckling, Fey followed Arlene into the elevator.

*In December of 1998, Audrey Moore, owner of
the independent bookstore, Mysteries To Die For,
asked me to write a short story she could give to her
customers as a Christmas gift. The result was a tongue-in-cheek
case for my novel series detective,
Fey Croaker, involving a rash of Christmas tree thefts. The
Christmas season is hardly the time for one of Fey's
more typical dark-edged investigations, so
The Thief of Christmas takes a lighter than normal
look at crime and the meddling of old St. Nick.*

THE THIEF OF CHRISTMAS
A Fey Croaker LAPD Crime Story

Fey Croaker sat at the bar of The Blue Cat sipping morosely
from a large mug of brandy-laced coffee. The stylized Christmas decorations that adorned the small jazz club only added
to her personal depression, as did the clever jazz arrangements of Christmas favorites being enthusiastically performed by the trio of musicians on the club's small stage. The
usual crowd was really digging the scene, leaving Fey feeling
as if she were a visitor from another planet.

"You all right, Frog Lady?" Booker Nelson, the club's
owner and bartender, asked her from his position behind the
bar. "Tough day crushing crime at the cop shop?" The use of
Fey's nickname by anyone else would have sent her ballistic,
but Booker's wrinkled features expressed only concern, not
mockery.

"I'm fine," Fey said, giving up a small smile. As the supervisor of LAPD's West Los Angeles Area Homicide Unit, Fey's day had been rough, but that wasn't what was bothering her.

"Don't be lying to ol' Booker, now," the bartender said. "Christmas ain't the happiest time of the year for a lot of us."

Fey pushed her mug back across the bar. "Your job is to keep pouring coffee with double shots, Booker," Fey told him. "I pay my shrink a hundred-and-fifty dead presidents an hour to mess with my head. I don't need you doing it for free."

"You know, you're supposed to mellow with age," Booker said without taking offense. He turned to grab a coffeepot from a hot plate on a shelf behind him. "You keep the Scrooge act up and Santa's gonna leave nothing but a lump of coal in your stocking." Booker set the refilled mug in front of Fey and then splashed in a liberal quantity of brandy.

"I hate the holidays," Fey said after a pause. "Crime and suicides are up. Panties at office parties are down. Everyone rushes around acting like happy jackasses, spending money they don't have on people they don't like, saying 'Merry Christmas'—as if the problems of the world can be made to disappear behind that sentiment—and you get to sit around eating dried-out turkey with inbred relatives you wouldn't be caught dead with at any other time of the year. Big whoopee." She took a swallow of the fresh coffee and made a face as the hot liquid burned her mouth.

Booker reached across the bar and put his hand on Fey's arm. "I miss him too, you know," he said, sensing Fey's true feelings.

"Ah, hell, Booker." Fey turned away to hide the tear that spilled out of the corner of one eye. She had to force down a couple of deep breaths before regaining control.

61

Fey had been introduced to Booker and The Blue Cat through a friend who they had both loved—albeit in very different ways—and who had been tragically lost to them a few months earlier. Fey had become a regular at The Blue Cat as a way of staying close to a memory, and as a result, her relationship with Booker had grown. For the lack of a decent one in her own life, Booker had become a father figure of sorts.

"Let's change the subject, okay?" Fey asked as she turned back to the bar.

Booker nodded sagely and moved away to fill an order for one of the waitresses.

Fey took another sip of her coffee before she felt the pager attached to her belt begin to vibrate. She unclipped the plastic square of modern technology and checked the display. Sighing in resignation, she took a cell phone out of her purse and punched in a number she knew by heart.

A gruff, harried, female voice answered. "Watch Commander's Office, Lieutenant Kopitzki."

"It's Fey. What's up, Ruth?"

"Hey, I'm sorry to call you when you're off duty, but we've got another one."

"Oh, hell," Fey said.

Ruth Kopitzki laughed. "Look at it this way, Fey. Normally when I call you to tell you we have another one, I'm talking about dead bodies. At least this time around it's only another stolen Christmas tree."

"At this point, I think I'd be better off with a dead body," Fey said. "Give me twenty minutes," she added, giving Kopitzki her ETA, and hung up.

Fey stuffed the cell phone back in her purse and took another quick swallow of coffee. When she stood up, Booker looked across the bar at her askance.

"I told you," she said, answering the question on his

face, "I hate the holidays."

The first tree had been stolen five days before Christmas. The responding uniformed officer thought he was being cute when he mentioned that it was a seasonal coincidence that the victim's last name was Partridge and his family lived on Pear Tree Avenue.

Apparently, the Partridges had heard this joke a million or so times before, because they didn't laugh. All they were interested in was who stole the damn Christmas tree they had just finished decorating. It was quickly evident that when a Christmas tree is stolen, the thief also gets away with the victim's sense of humor as an unintentional extra.

It didn't help matters that William Partridge was president of the Brentwood Homeowners Association. As such, he expected immediate action from the police department. In West Los Angeles, influential citizens knew how to get results. Partridge's first phone call had been to the Commanding Officer of the West Los Angeles Area Detective Division—Fey's boss. Why go up the chain of command when it was so much easier to go down it?

William Partridge singed Lieutenant Mike Cahill's ear. How come the police department couldn't have a patrol car sitting in front of the Partridge house twenty-four hours a day to stop something like this from happening? And why would anyone break into a house and just steal a Christmas tree? It was almost insulting. Didn't the thief know how much Partridge had paid for the paintings on the walls of the house, or the jewelry nestled in Mrs. Partridge's jewelry box? And what was Lieutenant Cahill going to do about it?

Cahill knew exactly what he was going to do about it. He was going to get Detective Fey Croaker to give the case her personal attention.

Fey was perplexed to find herself personally investigating a run-of-the-mill burglary.

Initially she had expressed her dissatisfaction to her boss. "You've got to be kidding me, Mike. In case you've forgotten, I run the homicide unit. What happens if we get a couple of bodies laying in the chalk while we're out chasing a tree thief?"

"I didn't say I wanted your unit to handle Partridge's case, Fey. I said I want you to handle it. Personally."

"What did you do, check your list to see who's been naughty or nice, before deciding to give me this little gift?"

"That's not fair, Fey. You know that the entire squad room has been decimated by this flu epidemic. I would have assigned this case to the burglary unit supervisor, but Bill Sanders is out spewing up his guts and running a hundred-and-two degree temperature, and so is every other detective supervisor except for you and me. Hell, half of the squad detectives are under the weather, and the other half are almost overwhelmed with the extra work." Cahill sat forward earnestly, leaning on the edge of his desk. "Come on, Fey," he said with a cajoling inflection. "You can handle this assignment standing on your head with one hand tied behind your back and a ten-second penalty delay. After all, how hard can it be to find some Grinch who stole a Christmas tree? Just follow the trail of pine needles."

Fey sighed unhappily in resignation. "Don't try and butter me up. I'm too old for that line. What you're really saying is it's down to either your butt going out to handle this or mine."

"Exactly," Cahill said with a smile. He settled back in his chair. "And you know what they say, *RHP*."

"I know, I know," Fey said standing. "Rank has privilege. Fine, I'll take care of it, but don't expect a Christmas card from me this year."

★ ★ ★ ★ ★

Fey was somehow able to soothe Partridge's ruffled feathers, despite his verbally expressed disappointment that Cahill had sent a woman to handle the case instead of a real detective. The proverbial trail of pine needles, however, led nowhere. There were no witnesses to the burglary, nobody who saw anyone driving away with the Partridge's tree tied to the roof of a car or van, and no clues to why only the decorated Christmas tree had been stolen and all the beautifully wrapped Christmas presents ignored.

Fey's comment that Santa must have taken the tree back up the chimney when he left was greeted with silence. She made a mental note not to make any more jokes if she could help it. If she wasn't careful, Partridge would start insisting she put out a crime bulletin on a white bearded fat guy in a red suit and eight tiny reindeer. Time to call up a segment on *America's Most Wanted*.

Fey's first theory on the case was that somebody who disliked the Partridges had stolen the tree simply to be nasty. That theory, however, didn't narrow the suspect base down by much. Nor did it hold up when two days later another tree was stolen.

This time, the victims were a family in the exclusive Pacific Palisades area. Fey caught the call as she was returning from lunch and rolled to the scene while the uniformed officers were still taking the burglary report.

The victims' residence was a well-cared-for mansion with a porticoed entry that shamelessly ripped-off *Gone With the Wind*. Mr. and Mrs. King, however, were no Scarlet and Rhett. Disgruntled and bad-tempered, their anger over the loss of their Christmas tree made Partridge's appear mild by comparison.

It was the third King, though, for whom the term pain-in-the-butt had been coined. Little Amanda King was a brat of the first order and screamed constantly from the second Fey stepped through the door to begin her investigation. It didn't take long for Fey to start planning ways to abandon Amanda on 34th Street and begin praying for a miracle that would get the child's photo on a milk carton.

Over Amanda's wailing, the Kings expressed their displeasure with a police department that couldn't protect fine upstanding citizens from predators. It was an outrage. Didn't Detective Croaker realize that the stolen tree had won the community's prestigious Martha Stewart tree decorating contest?

"The what?" Fey had asked, causing all three Kings to look down their noses at her in shock and disdain for her ignorance. How could Fey, a woman, not know who Martha Stewart—Yuppie earth goddess—was?

The Kings' impression of the police department was not enhanced when, despite Fey's best efforts, no clues to the evil tree thief's identity or whereabouts were unearthed. No scent of fallen pine needles to follow. No trail of broken bulbs or Christmas ornaments.

The following day, Fey found herself the target of squad room humorists. Her desk was covered with pine needles and a stuffed Grinch, wearing teeny-tiny handcuffs, was sitting in her chair. A note was pinned to the Grinch's chest—*DEAR FEY, HOPE THIS CHRISTMAS THIEF HASN'T BEEN CAUSING YOU TOO MUCH TROUBLE. LOVE, SANTA.*

Fey appeared to take the good-natured ribbing in stride. After all, she didn't have much choice. She had certainly dished out her own share of pointed barbs over the years. However, even though she didn't show it, the jibes got under her skin. Perhaps it was because it was Christmas—a time of year Fey dreaded. She hated the jealousy she felt directed at everyone who had special people with whom to share the blessings of the season.

Even when she'd had a family, it hadn't been one that made Christmas anything special. But Fey no longer had a family, and refused to impose herself on friends. The best she could hope for on Christmas day would be a turkey pot-pie shared in front of the television with her two cats. The more likely scenario, however, was a fast food burger on the way to a typical Christmas homicide—a turkey carving knife sticking out of the chest of a relative who'd criticized the cranberry sauce.

With all the extra work caused by the flu epidemic, her job hadn't even left her enough time to open Christmas cards let alone send any. Because of that, she had little sympathy for the Partridges and Kings of the world whose lives of leisure had been disrupted by something as seemingly petty as the theft of fancy trees.

"Are you getting anywhere with the tree theft cases?" Mike Cahill called out to Fey from his office.

"I'm working on it, boss," Fey replied.

"Well, you better work harder because the story has just hit the papers with case number three." Cahill brandished a copy of the local *Independent* newspaper in the fist of his right hand. The front page bore the headline, *THE THIEF OF CHRISTMAS*, followed by a detailed story covering each of the first two cases and a third case in which the thief had stolen a tree that was to be the focus of a tree lighting at a local, upscale shopping center.

Cahill continued his broadside. "Get your reindeer's butts over to the Century Heights Mall and find out what happened to the tree and why they went to the papers first instead of us."

Fey had slipped into her jacket, slid her gun into its shoulder rig, and was heading for the door before Cahill had finished bawling at her.

Cahill's parting shot, "Tomorrow is Christmas Eve, Croaker! I want this case solved before Christmas, or it'll be your goose that gets cooked!" reached Fey's red-tipped ears as she was flying down the stairs.

Fey quickly found that security officers from the Century Heights Mall had made a police report on their missing tree, but the paperwork had not made its way through the system yet. The story reached the papers first through a reporter who had been on the scene to cover the tree lighting.

Fey knew the reporter, Kathy Gold, as she also covered the police blotter for the *Independent*, and found out that she had pulled the story of the other stolen trees from the police department's *daily occurrence sheet,* which was a reporter's bread-and-butter information source.

Neither the mall security personnel nor Kathy Gold could add anything to Fey's clues closet. One moment the tree had been in the middle of the mall parking lot, and the next it was gone.

"Where did the tree come from?" Fey had asked the mall's head of security, Terry Donovan.

"I think we got it from a different tree lot than usual this year," Donovan told her. "There's a new place called Santa's Tree Lot at the corner of Wilshire and Federal. It's a nice place. The trees are real fresh and a good price. You should get your own tree there. They give cops a good discount."

"That's the last thing I need," Fey said. "A tree of my own for somebody to steal."

As she left the mall without stopping to do any Christmas

shopping—not that it would be difficult to pick up a catnip mouse and a can of kitty treats at the last second—Fey realized her time was getting short as Christmas Eve was rapidly approaching. Fey didn't much care that Cahill wanted the case solved before Christmas. That was only to stop his own chestnuts from roasting on an open fire. But Fey knew in her heart that she had to solve the case before then or the thief of Christmas would melt away and disappear like Frosty on a hot day. Whatever was going on had a yuletide deadline.

With desperation leading to inspiration, Fey pulled out her cell phone as she drove. Punching in the homicide unit's number, Fey was relieved when Monk Lawson answered the line. Monk was Fey's number two and could be relied on to always support her.

"Monk, it's Fey. I need a favor."

"What do you need?"

"Pull both reports on the Christmas tree thefts and see if the officers wrote down where the victims bought their trees. If the information isn't there would you call the victims and find out?"

"No problem," Monk told her. "But it sounds as if you're grasping at straws."

"I don't have anything else to grasp," Fey said. "You come up with something on this for me and I'll jingle your stocking big time."

Monk laughed. "Promises, promises."

Fey smiled as she disconnected and tossed the phone on the passenger seat of her car. Monk was one of the few men she could rely on not to take her sense of humor too seriously.

Thinking that she was probably wasting her time, Fey turned her detective sedan out of the mall parking lot and headed for Santa's Trees.

Santa's Tree Lot took up a vast corner of undeveloped ground owned by the Veteran's Administration Hospital. Situated in the middle of the snooty Wilshire district, developers would have killed their own mothers to have a shot at filling the corner with high-rise office buildings. The government, however, had steadfastly refused to sell or to move the veteran's hospital that kept a steady flow of the disenfranchised shuffling through the area.

Outside of Santa's Tree Lot, a man in a shabby wool overcoat and tennis shoes with no laces scuffed his way back and forth in the eighty-degree December heat. He wore a sandwich placard board over his shoulders and rang an old-fashioned school bell with his right hand. The front of the sandwich board proclaimed the evils of celebrating Christmas with pagan images. The sandwich board's back placard was graced with a roughly drawn Christmas tree surrounded by a red circle with a red line through the middle across the tree.

Now, there's a clue, Fey thought. *Who in the name of Christmas is that character?* She keyed her radio microphone and requested a patrol unit to the location to complete a field interview card on the bell ringer. *Hey, you go with what you can get,* Fey gave rein to another thought as she pulled into the tree lot.

Before she exited the car, her cell phone rang. Fey picked it up to find Monk on the other end of the line.

"I don't know if you're damned good or damned lucky," Monk told her.

"I'll take being lucky any time," Fey said. "What do you have?"

"Both the Partridges and the Kings bought their trees from Santa's Tree Lot."

"Yes!" Fey said. This was her first sniff of a break. "Did they have the trees delivered or pick them up themselves?"

"Delivered," Monk said. "A guy in a stake-bed truck dropped the trees off on the same day they were stolen."

"Thanks," Fey told her number two.

"Anything else?"

"Yeah. Patrol is filling out an FI card on a 5150 who's protesting using Christmas trees as pagan images in front of the lot. Can you get a hold of the info and see what you can come up with on the guy?"

"No sweat."

"I'm going to interview the lot owner and then I'll be back to the station."

"Don't step in any reindeer droppings."

"You know, if reindeer really can fly, our cars are in a lot of danger."

Fey disconnected on Monk's laughter.

Wenceslas Good was an unsmiling cadaver of a person who looked as if he should be molesting sugar plum fairies instead of selling Christmas trees. Despite his appearance, Wenceslas turned out to be a congenial host. Within short order of producing her police identification, Fey found herself installed in Wenceslas's trailer office with a mug of hot apple cider in her hand and Christmas carols assaulting her ears.

Wenceslas agreed that he sold the tree to the mall. After checking his delivery records, he further agreed that trees from his lot had been delivered to both the Partridge and King homes. He was at a loss, however, to explain why anyone would steal a Christmas tree. They didn't have any extended value, and there was certainly no black market for them.

Fey asked if all three trees had possibly come from the same tree farm. Wenceslas shook his head and informed her that his trees came from several different farms in the northern part of the state. The Partridges' and the Kings' trees had come from one farm, but the tree at the mall had come from another.

Wenceslas called Alf Atnas into the office and introduced him to Fey. Atnas was a small, heavy-set man with twinkling eyes and a white goatee. He reminded Fey of a midget, beatnik Santa Claus—Maynard G. Crebs crossed with the North Pole.

Alf could shed no light on the tree thefts, but Fey was sure he was holding something back. It was as if he was enjoying a huge private joke at her expense. As she thanked Wenceslas for his hospitality and turned to leave, Fey thought she saw Alf lay his finger alongside his nose and wink at her.

Back at the station, Fey found Monk waiting for her with a mountain of computer printouts.

"Good news or bad?" she asked.

"It depends on how you look at it," Monk replied.

"Give it to me straight."

"Okay. The crazy in front of the tree lot is Christopher St. Nicholas—better known as St. Nick."

"Get real! I expect better from you than juvenile humor."

Monk chuckled. "I'm not pulling your chain here, boss. That's his real name. He had it legally changed last year when he got out of the joint."

Fey perked up. "Prison?"

"Yep. He's on parole for burglary. Did two on a five stretch for breaking into residences and stealing—" Monk paused dramatically.

"Not Christmas trees," Fey said. "I'm not buying it."

Monk shrugged. "It's almost as good. Christmas presents. He used open windows to gain entry and then scooped up whatever was wrapped and under the tree."

"A burglar who liked to surprise himself."

"I talked to the district attorney who handled the case. She said that St. Nick, or Rudolph Redding as he was known then, pled hardship in court—said he was an orphan who never had Christmas growing up. He had a rap sheet longer than a fire hose, and the court didn't buy the sob story. The judge slammed him for five years, but he was a model prisoner—found religion inside—and the parole board kicked him loose."

"And now he's out trying to stop people from buying Christmas trees."

"Everybody has to have a hobby."

"Yeah, but is he zealous enough to steal trees from people who buy them?"

"I don't know, but if he is, he certainly knows how to pick his victims." Monk hefted the sheaf of computer printouts. "I checked out William Partridge and David King. Both are notorious scrooges. Partridge runs a sweat shop for garment workers and King is a major slumlord."

"I knew there was something about those people I didn't like," Fey said.

"Yeah, but how does the Century Heights Mall fit into the picture?"

Fey thought for a second. "Wasn't there something in the paper the other day about the corporation that owns the mall closing down a camp for underprivileged children that was funded by another corporation that they recently took over?"

"Now that's cold."

"Yeah, but does any of this get us any closer to solving the case?"

Fey relieved Monk of the computer printouts, thanked him for his efforts, and carried everything back to her desk. After filling her coffee mug, she sat down at the computer and began looking for information on Wenceslas Good and Alf Atnas.

Wenceslas checked out easily, but there didn't seem to be any information on Atnas. That bothered Fey. Everybody is in the computer somewhere, and she should have been able to come up with something to give her a background on the Santa's Tree Lot deliveryman.

After several hours of frustrating effort she decided to throw in the towel for the night and took herself off for a laced coffee at The Blue Cat. She decided what she needed was a hot shower, a good night's sleep, and a fresh perspective in the morning. What she didn't need was her beeper going off and the watch commander telling her another tree had been stolen.

After leaving The Blue Cat, Fey made a beeline for the station. When she arrived, however, she found the situation had gone from bad to worse. Not only had one tree been stolen, but another report had also come in. Fey rolled to the scene of the first theft of the night to find mass confusion.

One of the patrol officers came to speak with her.

"What's the trouble?" she asked.

"The victim can't tell us what happened."

"Why not?"

"He's a deaf mute."

"A deaf mute?"

"Yeah. He can't talk or hear."

"I know what deaf mute means!" Fey flashed her eyes angrily. She was tired and wanted to be done with this nonsense. "Is he illiterate as well? He can't be if he's living in this place." The house was a mid-size residence in Cheviot Hills. OLD MONEY in capital letters.

"I don't know."

"Then give him a piece of paper and see if he can write down what happened. Do you even know what his name is?"

"He's been silent, of course, since we got here, but he gave us an ID card that shows his last name as Knight."

"Okay, okay. Just get him to write down what happened and find out where he bought the tree."

After a few minutes of frenetic activity the uniformed cop came back and gave Fey the news that the tree had been delivered earlier in the day from Santa's Tree Lot.

Okay, we have a pattern here, Fey thought once she had the information. *But what am I supposed to do with it?*

There was even more confusion at the next victim's residence, an expensive condo along West LA's border with Beverly Hills. The Halls, returning from an evening out, had walked in on the thief and almost caught him.

"I would have had him if he hadn't decked me with this bough of holly," Mr. Halls told Fey brandishing the offending decoration. He had an insignificant scratch across his forehead.

"Did anyone else see the thief?" Fey asked.

"No," Halls said. "My wife ran to a neighbor to call the police when we realized there was somebody in the house. I confronted the thief myself."

Fey gave the wound on Halls's head a closer scrutiny. It looked suspiciously self-inflicted. Halls's false bravado did not impress her.

"What did the thief look like, Mr. Halls?"

"He was a big guy. Must have been six-foot-five and two-hundred-and-fifty pounds. I know big when I see it, you know—I'm a wrestling promoter—but I wasn't about to let the jerk get anything else."

"So, all he took was your Christmas tree?"

"Yeah. For all the good it will do him. Thanks to me, he didn't get any of our good stuff."

"Even after the thief viciously decked you with the bough of holly, he didn't bother to take anything but the tree?" Fey had trouble keeping the sarcasm out of her voice. She didn't believe Halls's description of the suspect for a second. The man was all bluff and bluster.

"Okay, Mr. Halls," Fey said. "These officers will finish taking a report from you."

"That's it? You're just going to take a report? I've been assaulted and injured, and all you're going to do is take a report?"

Fey turned full on to Halls and put her face in close to his. Her voice was low with menace. "I'll let you run your little charade about being assaulted, so you don't lose face in front of your family and neighbors, but if you push your luck, I'll have you down at the police station faster than a cookie disappearing down Santa's gullet. Once I have you there, you will rapidly confess to lying about being assaulted, and I will book your cowardly butt for making a false police report. Am I making myself clear?"

Halls was clearly shaken. "Yes. Yes. All right. Thank you."

Fey backed off. "Merry Christmas, Mr. Halls," she said pleasantly.

More bad news awaited Fey when she returned to the station.

"You're not going to believe this," Ruth Kopitzki, the watch commander, told Fey. "The fire alarm in the jail went off. I went to check it out along with the front desk officers. It turned out to be a false alarm, but when everything returned to normal, we saw somebody had stolen the tree from the station lobby."

Fey hung her head in resignation, but then began to chuckle. "Only in Los Angeles," she said. "Nowhere else in the world could this happen."

"I'm sorry, Fey."

"I take it nobody saw anything?"

"Nothing."

"No reindeer? No sleigh? No tiny elves?"

"Nope."

"No fat guy in a red suit?"

"Nope, the Chief wasn't here tonight."

'Twas the day before Christmas and all through the cop house not a creature was stirring not even a louse.

"I want you to know I appreciate you all coming in to work today," Fey told her assembled crew. "But there doesn't seem to be any other way to crack this case."

The five detectives who made up Fey's homicide unit were gathered around her desk. Arch Hammersmith and Rhonda Lawless—better known as Hammer and Nails—were both dressed all in black, making no concession to the Christmas season. Abraham Benjamin Cohen—better known as Alphabet, sat in his desk chair. His partner Brindle Jones held a fashion model's pose on a corner of the desktop. Monk Lawson leant back against a file cabinet listening to Fey.

"We've got six stolen trees. All of the victims, including the police department, obtained their trees from Santa's Tree Lot on Wilshire. The only other thing the victims—except for the police department—have in common is that they are rich and have displayed unpopular behavior throughout the year."

"Are you trying to say, they've been naughty not nice?" Alphabet asked.

"Exactly," Fey said, nodding in his direction. "I don't know what the point was for stealing the tree from the station lobby—unless it was simply to rub our noses in the mess—but the other cases are pretty cut and dried. Partridge runs a sweatshop under almost inhuman conditions. David King is a major slumlord. The corporation that owns the Century Heights Mall closed down a camp for underprivileged kids. Despite his handicaps, it turns out that Knight runs a series of nursing homes accused of substandard care. Knight remained silent, taking the fifth, during civil action brought against him."

"And Halls?" Rhonda Lawless asked.

"He's also a real sweetheart. He claims to be a wrestling promoter, but he's under investigation for embezzling funds and not paying his wrestlers."

"So, the one abnormality is the theft of the tree from the station lobby," Monk said. "Do you think it was a copycat theft?"

"At this point, I don't care," Fey told him. "The only strong lead we have is Santa's Tree Lot, and that gives us two possibilities. First, Christopher St. Nicholas, a.k.a. Rudolph Redding, convicted Christmas burglar and current Christmas tree protestor. Second, Alf Atnas, the Santa's Tree Lot delivery person. He has no history in the computer, and has been to all of the houses involved when he delivered the trees. He also delivered the tree to the mall and to the police station."

Arch Hammersmith spoke. "You want us to stake out these characters and to see what they get up to when they think nobody is looking?"

"Got it in one," Fey said.

★ ★ ★ ★ ★

Alphabet and Brindle teamed up to cover Christopher St. Nicholas, but the boring routine of his protest march in front of Santa's Tree Lot was only matched by the boring routine of his Christmas Eve dinner at Denny's, followed by his participation in a league tournament at a local bowling alley, before returning to his rented room for a long winter's nap.

Alf Atnas proved much more entertaining for Hammer and Nails, however, as he led them on a merry, slow motion chase all day as he delivered last minute trees hither and yon.

"Do you think he's on to us?" Rhonda asked Hammer at one point during the day.

"Either that or he's the most careful driver I've ever seen," Hammer replied. "I mean he never misses a turn signal, he stops completely for every stop sign, and never drives over thirty-five miles an hour. It's as if he thinks a whole platoon of motor cops are lurking around every corner."

"Perhaps he wants to make sure we don't lose him," Rhonda said.

"Now there's a thought," Hammer said. "I wonder exactly what he's trying to prove."

Later in the evening, Hammer and Nails were waiting outside Santa's Tree Lot when it closed down for the final time. Fey and Monk had joined the duo and were staked out in another car on an opposite corner. They watched as Wenceslas Good paid Alf from a roll of cash, shook hands, and wished him a loud Merry Christmas.

Alf was on foot, making him difficult to follow in the cars. Fey took a radio and fell into step a block behind her quarry. Monk hopped into the back of Hammer and Nails's car, which moved slowly, block by block, as Fey reported her rate of travel.

Alf appeared to be totally oblivious to Fey's presence. He

never once looked behind him, nor did he vary his pace.

From her position behind him, Fey watched as Alf approached a large red truck and unlocked the driver's door.

Fey turned her back and spoke into her radio. "Move up. He's got wheels—an enclosed red truck. I'm not close enough yet to get the license plate." There was excitement in her voice.

"Is the truck big enough to hold the trees?" Rhonda's voice came back over the radio.

"You bet," Fey said. She turned back to look at the truck. "Holy Christmas! He's gone. Get up here, now!"

The red truck was indeed gone. Fey had not heard it start up or drive away, but nonetheless it was gone. Fey was standing in the street where the truck had been parked when Hammersmith pulled the detective sedan to the curb with a screech. Rhonda scrambled into the back seat of the car next to Monk so Fey could sit in front.

Sliding into the passenger seat, the others could see that Fey was holding a small, gaily wrapped package with a large red bow.

"What is it?" Monk asked, as Hammersmith pulled out in the direction the truck must have gone.

"I don't know," Fey said. "It was on the curb where the truck was parked."

"How could he simply disappear?" Hammer asked with exasperation.

"I don't know that either," Fey told him. "I turned my back to speak into the radio, and when I turned around the truck and the suspect were gone."

"This is nuts," Hammer said, his logic driven mind unable to grasp anything that didn't fit into logical probabilities.

"Are you going to open the package?" This from Rhonda.

"I don't know if opening it is a good idea," Monk said. "Maybe it's a bomb."

"I don't think so," Fey said, and quickly untied the ribbon. She tore the paper from around the box, and then carefully opened the lid.

"Well?" Rhonda demanded.

Fey turned the box over and shook it. A single piece of paper fell into her lap. She picked it up and looked at it.

"It's a list of addresses."

"Addresses?" Hammer questioned.

"Yes. Five of them."

"Addresses for what?"

"At a guess, I'd say they were the addresses where we'll find our missing trees."

"This is too weird," Hammer said. He had been looking up and down side streets, but could find no sign of Alf Atnas or the red truck.

"What do you want to do?" Monk asked. "It's getting late."

"I want to play the hand out and see where it takes us," Fey told him. "Hammer, head for *The Hood*. That's where the first address on the list is located."

The Hood is about as close to a ghetto as anyone could find in the West Los Angeles area. Tucked into the southeast corner of the division, *The Hood* was two dozen blocks of run-down apartment buildings crammed together like impacted and rotting wisdom teeth. It was a haven for gangs and drug dealers, but was also home to many families and individuals without the monetary means to find better accommodations. In short, *The Hood* was a social worker's nightmare.

The first address on the list led the detectives to a small house situated on a patch of ground reclaimed from the abandonment around it. A small lawn was well tended, and simple flowers and bushes grew along the front walk. There were a number of lights on in the house and a dozen neighbors stood outside the open front door.

Hammersmith parked the detective sedan at the curb, and all four detectives exited and carefully approached the house. The faces of the people surrounding the open front door of the residence showed a certain wonderment. As the detectives approached, the faces looked at them, but for some reason did not change to express the suspicion, or hatred, or fear that the police usually engendered in the neighborhood.

Fey continued to approach the open front door with her compatriots behind her. The sounds of Christmas carols emanating from cheap speakers reached her ears, and she could also smell apple spices in the air. Her normal response to put her hand on the butt of her gun in similar situations was for some reason held in check.

At the door, the detectives were greeted by a thin black woman wearing a well-worn, but clean dress.

"Come in. Come in," she said, beckoning with one hand. "Come and see the tree."

"I don't believe this," Fey said, as she stepped inside.

The small family room was furnished with thrift store originals, but was clearly immaculately clean. Pictures of relatives and graduation photos of children were framed and hung on the walls with obvious pride.

The focus of the whole room, however, was a blindingly ornamented Christmas tree. The tree was heavily flocked and filled with white lights, golden swans, and shiny teardrops. Around the base of the tree sat six youngsters ranging in ages from four to twelve. Their eyes were wide with awe as they listened to an older man, sitting in an easy chair, reading to them from a Bible about the birth of Christ.

Sitting in a matching easy chair, a youngster perched on his knee, was an even bigger surprise for the detectives.

"Mr. Partridge? Is that you?" Fey asked.

William Partridge turned his head to look at Fey and smiled. "Hello, Detective Croaker." His voice was mild and benevolent.

"Are you okay?" Fey asked. This was certainly not the man she had dealt with earlier—the iron boss who ran a sweatshop.

"I'm fine, detective. Actually, I'm better than I have been in a long time. I don't know what's come over me. I've just called for my wife and family. They're coming down to join us."

"Here?"

"Yes. Why not?"

Fey didn't have an answer.

"How did you get here?"

Partridge turned his face to look at Fey again. "Why the message from your department, of course."

"What message?"

"One of your officers called and said to meet you at this address to recover my missing tree."

Fey caught Monk's eye. He shrugged and looked away.

Hammer and Nails stood in the front doorway. They also shrugged when Fey looked at them.

"I take it this is your tree," Fey said to Partridge.

Partridge looked at the children on the floor around him. They were all looking at him, their grandfather having stopped reading for the moment.

"It's the tree from my house, but I would say it belongs to all of us here," Partridge said.

"How did the tree get here?" Fey asked.

The woman who had greeted them at the door answered.

"It was here in the room when we returned from church. It was just here, lit up bright as daytime."

At that moment Partridge's wife and two young boys arrived at the door. An older black woman, clearly the family grandmother, came out of the kitchen carrying a tray of mugs filled with steaming apple cider.

"Here we go," she said. "Now everybody take a mug and granddad will finish reading from the Bible."

Fey took a step back. "Let's go," she said to Monk and the others. "I don't think we're needed here."

Four more addresses later and the detectives were still stumped.

"I wouldn't have believed it if I hadn't seen it for myself," Fey said.

"Me either," Monk said, and the other detectives all murmured in agreement. They had been joined by Alphabet and Brindle at the second address after Fey called off the fruitless stakeout of Christopher St. Nicholas.

The scene at the house where Partridge's tree had been found was matched at the four other locations. The three Kings, with Amanda blissfully silent, had been found with their magnificent tree in a downtown tenement, surrounded by the residents, eating cookies and singing carols. Like Partridge, they seemed changed by the experience, as if the sourness had been wrung out of them. The hostility that would normally be engendered by such a confrontation was totally missing.

"I didn't think I believed in miracles," Rhonda Lawless said. "But I don't know what else to call what we saw tonight."

The mute Mr. Knight had received a message on his deaf-phone from *Detective Croaker* that led him to a speech therapy school for children that was in dire financial straits. His Christmas tree was the centerpiece of the school's common room, and Knight himself was found, fingers flying, happily signing away to the school's administrator. Apparently, Knight would soon be providing funding for the school's continuance.

The tree from the mall was located at the fourth address on the list—the camp for underprivileged children that the mall's corporation was closing down. The camp leader told Fey he had received a call earlier in the day that the camp was going to be kept open. He didn't know where the tree had come from, but it was certainly much nicer than the scraggly artificial one the camp had been using.

"How are we going to clear these cases?" Monk asked. "We don't have a suspect in custody."

"I don't think that's going to be a problem somehow," Fey told him. "All of the property has been located and I don't think anyone will want to pursue this even if we did have a suspect. We'll do a multiple follow-up listing what we know about Alf Atnas and clear all the cases *Victims Refuse to Prosecute*. I'll make sure Cahill signs it off."

The last address on their list led the detectives to an orphanage where the wrestling promoter Halls was found surrounded by a number of his clients. Halls's tree was smack dab in the middle of a tiny wrestling ring erected in the orphanage's central room.

Halls's clients were playing with the kids and acting with surprising benevolence toward Halls himself. When questioned, they stated Halls had seen the error of his ways and had started kicking loose the money he owed them. Like Halls himself, they had all received messages from *Detective Croaker* to meet at the orphanage to recover the tree. The tree of course remained, as did the wrestlers and their promoter.

"It's all a saccharine bunch of humbug," Hammer said. "And I don't buy into it for one second."

"You don't mean that," Rhonda said to him putting her hand on his arm. "It was pretty special out there tonight."

Hammer shrugged. "No I don't mean it, but I have to keep my image up."

"I don't think any of us can explain it," Fey said. "Let's just accept it as a miracle and go home and get some sleep."

"What about the tree from the station lobby?" Alphabet asked.

"Who cares?" Fey said. "Five out of six isn't bad."

Driving home, Fey began to feel just the slightest bit sorry for herself. Monk had his family. Hammer had Nails. Who knew what was going on with Alphabet and Brindle, but there was some spark there. But who did she have? Nobody. It was Christmas, and she had nobody who gave a damn.

Pulling into the driveway of her townhouse, she closed the door on her car and suddenly picked up the sounds of her cats meowing. It was as if they were more excited than normal at her return. She could see both feline figures perched in the front window looking at her. They were outlined by a light she couldn't remember leaving on.

Her heart started to pump harder in her chest and she set her purse down on the car hood. Taking out her gun, she approached her residence carefully and checked the front door. No signs of forced entry. She worked her way around the house and checked the back door. It was secure.

Using her keys, she unlocked the door and slipped inside, keeping low. Moving through the kitchen, she heard the cats alternately meowing and purring. They obviously were not in distress. Nor were they hiding from strangers.

An odd scent caught her nose. Not odd, just not usual for her house.

It was the scent of pine.

Fey lowered her gun, stood up, and walked into her living room.

Marvella and Brentwood rushed forward to greet her and rubbed around her legs. Twinkling lights on the tinsel-draped branches of the Christmas tree from the station lobby welcomed her home.

There was a card on the tree. Across the top were the words, *Hold up to a mirror to read the rest of this message.* The remaining words looked like gibberish—*EVITCETED, SAMTSIRHC YRREM.* The card was signed *ATNAS.*

How in the world had Atnas got the tree into her house—let alone the trees to all the other locations? How had he stolen the trees in the first place? How had he led so many nasty people to a change of heart? How had he disappeared in the red truck?

Fey held the note up to the mirror over her bar. She stepped closer for a better look. The gibberish was now readable—*MERRY CHRISTMAS, DETECTIVE.* It was Atnas's name at the bottom of the note, however, that grabbed her attention.

In the mirror it now read *SANTA.*

*In the mid-eighties, **The Saint Mystery Magazine**
was revived for a half-dozen issues before suffering an
ignominious demise. While it existed, I was asked to write a series of
non-fiction tales based on true police
incidents in which I had been involved. While
The Saint Mystery Magazine folded before the
commissioned stories were published, I was fortunately
able to find another home for them in publisher/author Wayne
Dundee's excellent **Hardboiled** publication.
Concrete Killer was published in **Hardboiled #9** in
1988. The setting is West Valley Division (as opposed to the West
LA Division where I am now assigned).
The time frame is 1979. I was still working uniformed
patrol, and was about to experience a career blunder
like no other. Seeing as I still managed to move
from patrol to detectives in West Valley Division, the long lasting
effects were obviously not devastating.
But at the time . . .*

CONCRETE KILLER
A Blaine Pope Story

During the career of every police officer, no matter how competent he or she may be, there will come a time when the normal flow of police work becomes a high farce—a time when the police officer will feel as if they are standing on a street corner wearing nothing but their gun belt and a smile. It took three years, and a knife wielding maniac's refusal to come down off a car roof, to prove I was no exception to the rule. Years later, I can see the humor in the situation, but at the time . . .

On the day of the fateful incident, two circumstances conspired to set the scene for my downfall. The first was related to police department policy, but the second was of my own making. In the late 1970's, many big city law enforcement agencies were coming under pressure from civil rights groups and the media for the ever-increasing number of police-involved shootings. As a result, city officials and top police brass became far more concerned with their public image than with the lot of the cop forced to make the split-second decisions involved in any shooting situation. During roll-call training sessions, it soon became clear that if a suspect was shot as the result of police action, the involved officer was going to be considered guilty of violating the department's shooting policy until it could be proven differently.

This situation led to numerous non-lethal options being put forward as alternatives to shooting a suspect who posed a threat to an officer's life. It was just my luck that the day of my embarrassment was chosen as the perfect opportunity to test several of those hastily conceived options under actual conditions.

I had come on duty that day immediately after an all-night drive, returning from a department-sponsored relay race across Death Valley (this event is still run today as the Baker to Vegas Relay, in which over a hundred law enforcement teams compete each year). Assigned to day watch, I had tried to arrange to take the shift off, but manpower minimums were down and my request was denied. Subsequently, as the result of my own determination to run in the race, I stumbled into roll call dead-tired, bleary-eyed, and dressed in a rumpled uniform.

The day's patrol started off quiet enough, and after two or three stops for coffee, I began to suspect I might make it through to the end of watch. My partner, Bones—so named because he was so skinny he had trouble keeping his seat down in the theater—had taken pity on my condition, agreeing to drive while I slouched down in the passenger seat.

However, with its usual bad timing and immediacy, the radio crackled out the information that an officer was in foot pursuit of a suspect who had just stabbed the officer's partner with a hunting knife. The location of the incident was two blocks west of our current position. To get there, Bones whipped an illegal U-turn while punching the gas and emergency lights at the same time.

It took two minutes of running with lights and siren to reach the unit requesting back-up. As we pulled in behind it, we could hear the wail of an ambulance and other police units descending upon the area. Lonnie Barker, a short but muscular officer was talking rapidly into his patrol unit's mike. He had removed his uniform shirt and wrapped his tee-shirt around his forearm where it was stanching a flow of blood.

I jumped out as our unit slid to a stop. I ran over to Lonnie as he was giving a suspect description to the RTO in communications. The adrenaline coursing through his system was making him sound out of breath. "—male, Caucasian, long blond hair, six-foot-two, one-hundred-and-ninety pounds, twenty-five to thirty years. He's wearing blue Levi cut-offs, hiking boots, no shirt. He's armed with an eight-inch hunting knife. He's incoherent and combative. Last seen running south on Wilbur Avenue toward Ventura Boulevard with my partner in pursuit." Lonnie stopped talking and took a deep breath. The RTO *rogered* the information and began to rebroadcast it for all concerned units.

I took Lonnie by the shoulders and made him lie down on

the backseat of his unit. I checked his wound and found a deep gash about three inches long. No arteries appeared to be severed, however, so I covered the wound again and began to apply steady pressure. *Where the hell was the ambulance?*

"What happened, Lonnie?"

"The guy is a psycho, or something, Blaine. He was taking his clothes off in front of the elementary school, but when he saw us, he started trying to climb a telephone pole. I grabbed hold of him, but he pulled a knife out of nowhere and cut me good. Danny hit him with his baton, but the guy didn't even feel it. He just dropped to the ground and took off running with Danny chasing him."

"Okay, man. Just relax," I said. "The ambulance is here. Bones and I will find Danny and back him up." I moved out of the way to let the paramedics take over, and trotted back to Bones who was listening to the police band in our car.

"Danny and the suspect are in a gas station around the corner on the boulevard," he told me. "The guys in the fire station on the opposite side of the street spotted them and called it in."

"Anybody there to back him up yet?" I asked.

Bones threw the car into gear. "Help is on the way, but we're closer."

"Then let's go nail this asshole."

A classic Mexican stand-off would be the only way to describe the situation at the gas station when we arrived. The station was rather large, spreading over the entire southwest corner of the intersection where it was located. On its west border a row of cars was parked, pointing outward from a low three-foot-high wall, which separated the gas station from the blank side of a two-story apartment building. On top of the middle car—a brand new, black Cadillac—stood the suspect brandishing a wicked-looking knife and an impressive expanse of exposed chest muscles. Surrounding the car, just out of stabbing distance were a sergeant and two uniformed patrol officers who had beat us to the scene. All of them had their batons drawn, but nobody was taking any chances on moving in.

Danny Harris, Lonnie's partner, was sitting in the passenger seat of the sergeant's unit with the door open. I went over to talk to him as two more responding units and another sergeant's unit pulled in.

"You okay?" I asked.

"I should have shot him, Blaine." Danny's voice was very matter-of-fact, and he was staring off into space. It scared me a little. "He stabbed Lonnie and he tried to stab me. I was an idiot. I tried to take the knife away from him, tried to talk to him as if he was a reasonable human being. I should have just shot him, but I kept thinking about coming up in front of the review board and trying to justify to all those Monday morning quarterbacks why I had used a gun to handle a suspect who was only armed with a knife." He looked up at me with suddenly questioning eyes.

"It's okay. You did the right thing," I said, trying to soothe him.

He turned his head away as if I had disappointed him somehow. "No. I didn't," he said. "I should have shot him when he stabbed Lonnie. I should never have given him the chance to stab me while I played hero. What good would I be to Frannie and the kids with my guts washing down the gutter?" His voice was altogether too calm.

My attention was diverted when Sergeant Stanton tapped me on the shoulder. We walked to the front of the car.

"He'll be okay," said Stanton with a nod of his head toward Danny. "Just needs a little time to pull himself together. He really did do the right thing."

"The right thing for who, Sarge? Himself and his family? Or the right thing for some political seat warmer with a bunch of fruit salad on his shoulder who's worried about the department's press image?"

"Don't bust my chops, Pope. You know how the game is played. We've got bigger problems right now—like how're we gonna get this dirtbag to jail before anyone else gets hurt."

I realized Stanton was right. Part of the policeman's lot is adapting to the mood changes of a fickle public. Currently, they were telling us to cut down shooting incidents where there were alternatives. With the present situation, we still had a few options to trot out. I asked Stanton what he wanted me to do and found myself assigned as the *designated shooter*.

This was a fairly new innovation at the time. In essence it meant that if things went to hell and we were forced to shoot the suspect, then I alone would have the responsibility for putting him down instead of every officer on the scene clearing leather. It was a good tactic, avoiding potential crossfires and unnecessary shoot-em-ups. It was also a weighty obligation.

I retrieved the shotgun out of my unit and took up a position to the right of the car the suspect was standing on. At the moment he seemed to be taking pleasure in the dents his heavy boots were making in the car roof. At Stanton's order, I was holding the shotgun pointed downward alongside my leg instead of the standard port-arms position—an attempt at maintaining a low profile.

The scene itself, however, was beginning to take on a circus atmosphere. Now that tempers had cooled and we knew Lonnie was going to be okay, it was easier to see the lighter side of the situation. The gathering crowd of onlookers was definitely amused. Here was one of the world's most efficient police forces being held at bay by a looney-tune with the IQ of a fence post. The worst was yet to come, though, in a comedy of errors to rival any Keystone Cops caper—a comedy in which my own contribution would be the crowning achievement.

From my stationary position, I observed the arrival of the division's police brass. This was a turn of events guaranteed to add to the confusion. I also spotted the arrival of the press cameras, destined to gleefully record the coming events.

A grim-faced Lieutenant Bendix exited his car and approached me. "Are you the designated shooter?" he asked gruffly.

"Yes, sir," I was still polite to brass in those days.

"Well, we've decided not to shoot the suspect even if he comes down from the car roof and gets away."

"What?" I said, the idiocy of Bendix's statement stunned me. Before I could say anything further, Captain Drover, who had approached me from the other direction and over-heard Bendix's order, stepped in.

"Don't be ridiculous. We can't let the suspect get away. If we were to let him escape and stab another citizen, we'd be civilly liable." Drover turned to me. "Pope, you stay prepared to shoot, but only as a last resort." Nobody appeared to care that the suspect had already stabbed one police officer and tried to gut another. Apparently, cops are as expendable as cannon fodder.

Just then, the suspect decided to start a rain dance on the car roof. I jacked a shell into the chamber of the shotgun and pushed the safety off. The noise made by my actions is unique and unmistakable. It even penetrated the suspect's drug addled brain, calming him immediately. I pushed the safety back on.

From behind me, I heard a sergeant using his car radio to put in a request for two tasers to be sent to the scene. At the time, tasers were the latest high-tech shooting alternatives. These early versions looked like large flashlights. They fired twin barbs connected to the taser's powerful batteries by long thin wires. Once a barb was imbedded in a suspect, enough voltage was set loose to knock even the most violent psycho on his butt long enough to get the cuffs on. Tasers are now in standard use, but this would be the first time many of us would get the chance to see them in action. We were all anxious to judge the results.

While waiting for the tasers, however, two enterprising young officers decided to take things into their own hands. They commandeered a thick length of rope from the gas station's service bay, and each took an end. With it stretched between them, they raced down opposite sides of the Cadillac and tried to knock the suspect off his perch.

The total result of this action was to allow the suspect to show off his skipping skills. The public audience roared their appreciation, and the television cameras rolled merrily along. There was no second effort.

Wanting to keep the show going, the suspect suddenly jumped from the roof of the Cadillac to its hood and back. I took the shotgun's safety off again and waited for him to calm down. In actuality, I was glad of a little movement. Standing still for over an hour, combined with no sleep, was having the effect of attaching heavy sandbags to my eyelids. I shook myself alert, and when the status returned to quo, I put the shotgun safety back on.

The tasers arrived in a flurry of activity. Two sergeants, who had been trained in the taser's use, took up positions off to either side of the Cadillac's front grill. They aimed the tasers at the suspect, who formed the third point of their human triangle.

Just as they fired, however, Mother Nature decided to get

in on the farce by kicking up a stiff breeze. The taser barbs blew wildly off course. None hit the suspect. The set shot by the first sergeant blew across to bury themselves in the second sergeant. The second sergeant's taser barbs stuck firmly into a by-standing officer. Both the sergeant and the officer lighted up like Fourth of July pinwheels, flopping to the ground unconscious.

It was a remarkable performance, proving how effective the tasers could be—if only they hit the right target. The crowd was shocked into a hush, which was shattered by laughter as the two policemen began to dazedly regain consciousness. Stronger methods were definitely called for.

The fire department was summoned, but refused to squirt the suspect off the top of the car with their hose. "What about their civil liability if the suspect fell and got hurt?" they wanted to know.

Far from discouraged by their first attempts with the *jump rope,* the two officers responsible for that debacle decided to try something else. Without telling anyone, they dragged a fifty-pound bag of dry cement they had found lying around to the roof of the apartment building behind the Cadillac. Their plan was to drop the bag onto the Cadillac and knock the suspect off. There was speculation later that they planned to actually *knock off* the suspect, who had embarrassed them previously.

Their weighty solution, however, crashed harmlessly through the Cadillac's rear window. The surprised audience convulsed with laughter, the television cameras whirled, and the newscopters circled. Not even P.T. Barnum could have put on a better show.

With each new barrage of tactics, both authorized and unauthorized, the officers surrounding the Cadillac sought any opening to take the suspect down. Every move they made, however, was thwarted by the ferociously slashing blade that had become an extension of the suspect's arm.

The general feeling among the officers was to throw caution to the wind, go in with nightstick flailing, and beat the suspect to a pulp. But with the press so readily in evidence, this would have caused a public relations disaster. The brass vetoed even the suggestion of mass force, and kept the officers present on a tight rein.

The suspect's mother turned up after recognizing her son when a live news bulletin broke into her favorite soap opera. She told us the suspect's name was Donny Lee Younger. He was a good ol' boy from Tennessee who had recently been dishonorably discharged from the Marine Corps. He had a local rap sheet for violence and possession of the crystalline drug PCP, which was clearly flowing through his veins currently. Danny had been right. He should have shot the bastard.

Mrs. Younger was brought out to the front of the Cadillac to try and talk to her son. Her appeal was met with angry screams and a stream of urine, which ran down her son's leg and puddled in the newly customized dents on the Cadillac's roof. I pushed the shotgun's safety off.

We were three hours into the standoff, and new ideas were getting scarce. Tear gas had been ruled out. Mother Nature was still up to her breezy tricks and we didn't want everybody but the suspect acting like the mother of the bride. SWAT (Special Weapons And Tactics) had been contacted, but they were tied up with a hostage situation in another division. A small net had been located, but nobody could figure out a way to get it over the suspect successfully. To top everything off, the bat signal was out of order. Still, where there's an idiot, there's a way.

To say the least, I was dog-tired by this time, and frustrated with the whole situation. My legs ached, my spine was cramping, and my right hand, which held the shotgun, was going to sleep. I wished fervently for somebody to do something, anything, to put an end to the ordeal.

Remember the homily about being careful what you wish for as you just might get it?

I flexed my right hand to get rid of the pins-and-needles, and the shotgun exploded with the sound of Armageddon. I stayed rooted to the ground, but the shotgun was torn from my grasp and leapt ten feet into the sky. Everyone else on the scene jumped at least half that distance. Donny Lee Younger was as startled as anyone else.

The shotgun pellets blasted a hole in the concrete of the gas station's slab next to my foot, missing my toes by millimeters. The pellets ricocheted, following the surface of the concrete (not bouncing up as bad movies would have you believe) and shredded the right front tire of the Cadillac.

As Donny Lee took a startled step to steady himself on the tilted car, he slipped in a pool of his own urine. Crashing to a landing on his back, his arms were flung away from his body, and the force of the tumble knocked the knife from his grasp.

Confusion reigned as policemen, wielding handcuffs and well-concealed baton jabs, flashed in on their target.

For the press, the show was over. They had been enchanted by the build-up, but disappointed by the abruptness of the final curtain. True, there had been a shooting, but there had been no blood. The only casualty was the gas station's concrete slab.

The nightly news was kind to me stating, "the situation was resolved when an unknown police officer accidentally discharged his shotgun into the ground." The police shooting review board was not as kind. They knew who I was.

"No," I told them, "I have no independent recollection of how my finger came to be inside the trigger guard instead of alongside it."

"Yes," I said, "it was my sergeant who ordered me to hold the shotgun alongside my leg instead of at port-arms."

"No," I explained, "I didn't know the safety was off. I'd had it on and off so often during the course of events I'd lost track."

"Yes, I was lucky I didn't blow my fool foot off."

The review board talked to me sternly and gave me a two-day suspension for improper handling of a firearm. It didn't matter that I was following orders, or that the situation resolved itself as a direct result of my actions. Two day suspended. Without pay. Period. Paragraph.

Not everyone, however, was devoid of a sense of humor. On returning to work after finishing my *bad time,* I was greeted by a hand-lettered banner strung across the roll call room proclaiming *Welcome Back, Concrete Killer.*

Ah, the stuff legends are made from.

Squeeze Play, the second of the fact-based stories
originally written for **The Saint Mystery
Magazine**, was actually the first to be published
in **Hardboiled**. It appeared in
Hardboiled #3 in 1985.
*The actual incident the story is based on occurred on
New Year's Eve 1980, shortly after I'd been
assigned as a detective trainee in West Valley Division, and definitely required a change of undershorts
after it came to a close.*

SQUEEZE PLAY
A Blain Pope Story

New Year's Eve in a big city police department's detective
bureau is much the same as in any other type of business—everybody wants to get away from work and get on with party
time. During the morning, I'd made a few half-hearted inves-
tigative calls to pass the time, but the effort had been a lost
cause. Around noon, Captain Johansson took a big step forward in employee relations by telling everyone they could go
home early if somebody volunteered to stay behind and answer the phones until end of watch.

Now, if you've ever been in any branch of the military, the
first thing you learn is never volunteer for anything, so I
couldn't believe it when my partner, Tommy Harrison, a
jaded two-tour veteran of the Vietnam fiasco, indicated he
and I would hold the fort. I didn't have time to argue. No

sooner were the words out of Tommy's mouth than the squad room was transformed into a Sahara of empty desks and lonely chairs.

I actually didn't mind. Rather than risk drunk drivers and exorbitant New Year's Eve prices, Tommy and I had planned to spend the evening at his home with our wives, so there were no big preparations to be made. Getting off at our usual time wouldn't interfere at all.

Tommy and I had been partners on the sex crimes detail for over a year. He had twelve years on me age-wise, but to look at him you would probably still place him in his early thirties, which was my domain. He was built tall and lanky, his handsome features marred only slightly by an almost feminine chin. By contrast, I top out at six-foot and fill a stocky frame, which I constantly struggle to stop from becoming a chubby one.

We were good friends both on and off the job, although at times we fought like an old married couple—the unstoppable force meeting the immovable object syndrome. Fortunately, neither of us held a grudge. Together we solved a lot of crimes and threw a lot of villains in jail.

The phones stayed fairly quiet all afternoon, the calm before the evening storm, which would thankfully be a problem belonging to the uniformed troops. To kill time, Tommy and I drank endless cups of coffee and dragged up old war stories while we dealt with the few minor problems which cropped up—a mother who wanted her son arrested for not taking out the garbage (she was 64, he was 40), and a man whose ex-wife was constantly breaking into his new Porsche and coaxing her Saint Bernard to defecate on the driving seat.

"Did you hear the one about the guy who comes running up to the front desk at the police station and wants to report a dead cop lying naked in the alley?" Tommy asked as the clock ticked over to end of watch.

"Yeah," I said getting up to grab our jackets off the coat rack on the other side of the room. "The desk sergeant asks the guy, if the dead man is naked then how does he know it's a cop, and the guy replies, 'because he has a hard-on and coffee pouring out his ears.' "

Tommy chuckled, even though it was his own joke, and scooped a long-fingered hand down to silence the phone which had started ringing again. I looked at my watch. It was five minutes past end of watch. Answering the phone was just asking for trouble. With a jacket in each hand, I walked back to where Tommy was mumbling monosyllabic affirmatives into the phone. He rolled his eyes and covered the mouthpiece of the phone with his palm.

"I can't believe this," he said exasperatedly. "It's the FBI. They've got an informant who's told them some guy named Jackson Shaw has just checked into the Hopkins Hotel down on Ventura Boulevard. Apparently Shaw is a big-time burglar who's planning on capering tonight while all the high-rollers are out celebrating."

A candle flickered dimly somewhere in the dank recesses of my memory. "Wait a minute," I said. "I think Freddie Ames was working a case on a suspect by that name. Tell the FBI we'll give Freddie a call and get back to them."

Tommy talked back into the phone for a minute or two before hanging up. I was looking Freddie Ames's phone number up on the detective's roster.

"The FBI want this turkey for transportation of stolen property across state lines," Tommy said.

"So, why don't they deal with him?"

Tommy shrugged. "They claim they don't have any agents to spare because it's New Year's Eve. They also said they had

Shaw pinned down six months ago in a house they'd staked-out. However, even with a couple of forty-five-autos shoved in his face, Shaw put four agents in the hospital and got away."

"Sounds like someone you'd want your daughter to bring home for dinner," I mumbled. I was still trying to find Freddie's number amongst the mass of erasures and strikeovers on the phone roster.

"You haven't heard the best news," Tommy said. "Apparently, this gorilla played center for the San Diego Chargers before he got cut from the team for injuring too many of his own teammates during practice."

I swore and dialed Freddie's number quickly. I just knew we were going to get stuck taking on this animal. The thought didn't please me in the least. Freddie answered on the fourth ring.

"Hello."

With that one word alone, I could smell the alcohol fumes down the phone wires.

"Freddie? This is Blaine Pope at the station. Damn, man, how much have you had to drink already?"

"Honest, officer, only two beers." That meant he was soused to the gills. *Two beers* was the answer given by every drunk driver when asked the same quantitative question.

"I know it's no good asking if you're in any shape to come in and give us a hand," I said accepting the inevitable, "but I need the skinny on this Jackson Shaw character you've been chasing. An FBI snitch has got him bedded down in one of the local hotels."

"Down on the boulevard, I bet. High-class joint like the Hopkins," said Freddie quickly. Perhaps he wasn't as far out of things as he wanted me to believe.

"You got it in one."

"Look, watch your ass with this guy. He's bad news all the way around. He hits big houses south of the boulevard in the Encino-Tarzana area to the tune of seventy or eighty thousand dollars a week. He's based out of Palm Springs. Travels up here in leased Cadillacs. He capers, burns the stuff off fast to a local fence, and then heads back to his own turf. He's a real crazy, even brings his current lady along sometimes to give her a thrill." Freddie stopped for breath before continuing. "I've got him made on prints, and there is a copy of the warrant underneath my desk blotter. I think the FBI also has warrants out for him, as do six or seven other jurisdictions. Be warned, this guy is not going to go to jail without a fight."

"What does he look like?" I asked with my stomach sinking down to somewhere around my toes.

"There's a mug photo clipped to the warrant, but it doesn't do him justice. He's about six-foot-eight, two-hundred-and-eighty pounds, ugly as the south end of a north bound mule, and mean enough to hunt grizzly with a switch." Freddie liked to show off his Kentucky origins. "Oh, there's one other thing. He carries an automatic machine pistol with him at all times, and he's aching for the chance to use it."

No wonder the FBI didn't have anybody free to send out. It's tough dodging bullets when you're wearing a blue suit with white socks and brown wingtips.

Half an hour later, Tommy and I were in the locker room slipping on bulletproof vests, checking the loads in our service revolvers, and strapping backup weapons to our ankles. I took a lead-weighted sap down off the locker shelf, hesitated, moved to put it back, and finally slid it into my rear pocket where it nestled with comforting reassurance.

Since talking with Freddie, we had tried, without success, to get some help in taking Shaw down without a fuss. Narcotics was out of their office. Vice had their own problems. And uniformed patrol was running a skeleton crew and could only loan us one unit on the condition we kicked them free by midnight. I felt like Cinderella. The bottom line was the New Year's Eve celebration. Everyone who could, including the station cat, had taken the night off.

There was no way to turn a blind eye to the information on Shaw. And since there was no one else to pass the buck to, Tommy and I were elected without even wanting to be nominated. We called our wives and told them we'd be home as soon as we could.

Tommy called the FBI back and got the license number and description of the car Shaw was supposed to be driving. Like Freddie had surmised, it was a leased Cadillac registered to an agency in Palm Springs. We briefed the patrol unit assigned to us and they hit the street to try and get a fix on the wheels in the area of the hotel.

Gearing up to go after a dangerous suspect is not exactly rare in our line of work. Each time you do it, though, there is still a funny sense of your own mortality. Will this be the time I get hurt? Will this one get me killed? Will this be the time I blow somebody away?

I checked to make sure my gun cleared easily from my shoulder rig, and caught up with Tommy as he headed out the door. Our car was a plain, four-door, green Plymouth. It had black walls and an antenna farm on the roof which spilled over onto the trunk. It was about as low profile as Muhammad Ali.

The Hopkins Hotel was in a class well above the commercial sameness of the Holiday Inn or the Hilton chains. By the time we pulled into its parking lot, the patrol unit had scored by locating Shaw's car. It was next to the curb just west of the hotel, but still in view of the front doors. We told the black-

and-white to stash itself out of sight while Tommy and I went in to check the hotel register.

The night-duty clerk recognized us from past contacts and was more than willing to help out. We didn't tell him who we were looking for. He wasn't above tipping a suspect off if he thought there might be a few bucks in it for himself. Instead, we commandeered the register and checked the listings ourselves. There was no Shaw registered in the hotel, but in room 218 there was a George Bernard with a notation of the license plate number to Shaw's vehicle. George Bernard. It was disgusting. A con with a literary sense of humor.

I wanted to tackle Shaw head on in his room, but Tommy thought we should stake out the Cadillac and take Shaw down when he hit the street. We talked it over and I quickly came round to Tommy's point of view. There was no telling what we would come up against going into a room blind. At least on the street we would have a clear view of the action and room to maneuver.

The only thing against a stakeout was the waiting. Waiting. We do a lot of that. Waiting for suspects. Waiting for snitches. Waiting for cases to be filed. Waiting to testify. Waiting for juries to make up their minds. Waiting for payday. Waiting for clues to jump into the clues closet. To pass the time we played mind games. One of us would name a historical figure or event, and the other one would relate everything he knew about the subject. We would pick a color (blue), and then alternate naming related subjects (Blue Boy, Bluebeard, Blue Moon) until one of us was stumped. We played for quarters. After two hours Tommy was two-seventy-five up. I was beginning to get antsy.

Our car trunk yielded up a slim-Jim, and I pressed our luck by popping the lock on Shaw's car door. Under the front seat there were three handguns and a rifle. In the glove box a stash of cocaine. I unloaded the guns quickly, put them back, and tossed the ammo down a convenient storm drain. The cocaine stayed put. I'd get to it legally later.

Back in the police car, I poured a cup of lukewarm coffee and went back to waiting.

By 11:30 p.m., we were bleary-eyed and butt-sore. We had coffee coming out our ears and the caffeine was making us irritable. In the middle of this mental lull, a gorgeous blond, dressed to the nines, and a geeky looking guy in a tux walked out of the hotel. Tommy whistled under his breath. Both of us watched the wide stretch of satin-clad thigh that exposed itself every time the blond took a step in her side-slit, black sequined dress.

Simultaneously, we both sat bolt upright when the geek started to unlock the passenger door of Shaw's Cadillac. There was no way this idiot was Shaw, and there was no mistake about the car we were staked on. The Caddy was our only tangible link to Shaw, and as the geek started for the driver's side, we knew we couldn't let it drive away.

A couple of short sentences into the radio brought the black-and-white into action. With red lights on, it pulled in behind the Cadillac. The uniformed officers efficiently got the geek and his pin-up companion out and onto the sidewalk. Tommy and I walked over and identified ourselves.

On closer inspection, the girl was still good looking, but there were the beginnings of hard lines around the edges of her young face. In her purse was a .22 auto with pearl grips, and enough speed capsules to fuel a moon shot. She was seventeen, a runaway who appeared to have worked her way into the criminal high-life. She exuded a jaded sexiness that had no correlation to the tight-sweatered innocence I remembered in the girls from my high school days.

The geek was yelling about his rights, his lawyer, and a civil suit. Tommy told him he had two choices—shut up, or have his lungs pulled out through his nose. The geek shut up.

Neither the geek nor the blond would admit to knowing anyone named Shaw. Both refused to waive their rights, and would not give permission for us to search the car. The part about their rights didn't matter. We already had more than enough to book them without needing any further statements from them. Permission to search the car could be overcome by impounding it and getting to the guns and dope with a legal inventory check. Shaw was still the outstanding factor, however, which was aggravating and scary.

Suddenly, I heard Tommy yell out, and felt the wind take a forced vacation from my lungs as he knocked me to the ground. Creation was eradicated by the chatter of automatic gunfire and the sound of the windows in the Cadillac and the police car exploding like so much shattered crystal. Was it real or was it Memorex? It was all too real. I looked up from the gutter and saw the huge figure of Shaw crouched in the hotel lobby doorway slamming another clip into a machine pistol which had been hidden on a sling under the folds of his light topcoat. Somehow my revolver made the trip from shoulder rig to hand without conscious thought. I brought it up to fire, but the desk clerk and another guest popped up directly behind Shaw. My shooting background was now full of innocent targets. Since my name wasn't Annie Oakley, I held my fire and rolled under the Cadillac as Shaw let rip again.

This time, however, there was only the crack of a single bullet. I came up on the far side of the Caddy and saw Shaw struggling with the machine pistol's mechanism. The damn thing had jammed on him.

I leveled my gun over the trunk of the car and yelled,

"Freeze, asshole!" at the top of my lungs, but Shaw paid no attention. Instead, he tossed his gun down, slipped out of his coat, and took off running.

I had a clear shot at him, but visions of the next day's headlines—POLICE SHOOT UNARMED MAN—streamed through my head. It wouldn't matter the now unarmed man had just tried to blow us away. I swore, shoved my gun in its holster, and started to give chase. Tommy was also running along with me, but I couldn't shake the feeling we were about to have our heads handed to us.

Racing up Ventura Boulevard, we dodged through incoming traffic, praying the uniforms from the black-and-white were calling for backup. Shaw was pretty fast over the first hundred yards, but then the distance and his size began to take their toll. We began to close rapidly. Next to me, Tommy put on a sprint. Reaching out a long arm, he tapped the right heel of Shaw's flying feet. This caused a crossover effect, and Shaw sprawled to the ground in a tangle of legs.

Traffic screeched to a halt, swerving in all directions, as Tommy jumped full-length on to Shaw and immediately tried to apply a chokehold. Shaw was too quick for him. Screaming like an enraged bull elephant, Shaw pushed himself up to his feet and shook Tommy off like a minor irritant.

I had my lead-weighted sap in my hand and swung it with a vengeance at Shaw's collarbone. Shaw bobbed when I expected him to weave, however, and he took the brunt of the blow across his forehead. The total effect of the blow was minimal other than to make Shaw mad enough to plant an anvil shaped fist directly into my chest. I went down hard, the world dancing a head-spinning tango to the beat of distant police sirens.

With blood pouring from his forehead, Shaw began to run

again. Before he'd taken half-a-dozen steps, he bounced off a slow moving Volkswagen and ricocheted back into Tommy's arms. All the techniques taught in the police academy for subduing hostile tactics were immediately forgotten. This was street fighting at its ugliest—head butting, eye gouging, biting and bone breaking.

I dragged myself off the tarmac and leapt onto Shaw's back. I threw my right arm around his almost non-existent neck. Using my left palm, I slammed his head as hard as I could to shift his chin into the crook formed by my right elbow. Within a second, I locked up the chokehold by grabbing my left shoulder with my right hand, laying my left arm across the back of Shaw's neck, and grabbing my right shoulder with my left hand. I now had Shaw's neck in a vise grip and started to squeeze shut the carotid artery supplying blood to Shaw's pea-sized brain.

Bellowing, Shaw reached back and tried to tear me loose. I desperately buried my face into his left shoulder and cinched my legs around his waist. I was playing a bizarre piggyback game called *squeeze or die*. Tommy was trying to take every advantage of Shaw's diverted attention. He threw jab after jab into the granite expanse of Shaw's exposed solar plexus. When this achieved no visible result, Tommy reared back and let fly with a vicious side-kick that blew out Shaw's right knee, and sent all of us crashing to the ground again.

I hung on for all I was worth. As squad cars began sliding to a halt all around us, I squeezed the chokehold with every ounce of strength I could muster. I felt Shaw's body give the twitch that begins the dance we call *the chicken*—an involuntary St. Vitas boogie preceding unconsciousness brought on by a chokehold. Shaw's bladder voided, and I was disgusted to feel his hot wetness seeping through the material of my trousers and onto my legs. I released the chokehold and rolled Shaw's unconscious bulk over for Tommy to handcuff.

When he returned to the land of the living a few minutes later, Shaw was still the same pleasant addition to the human race he'd been before having the piss choked out of him. The neck stretching hadn't improved his attitude. His hands were cuffed behind him. His legs were secured with a department-approved hobble. He was surrounded by hulking, uniformed officers just itching to get in a couple of licks. Yet he was still defiant. Still angry at the world and all it had to offer. Before he could cause more problems, Tommy and I picked Shaw up like a large, smelly, cursing, piece of luggage and stowed him in the back of a black-and-white. A uniform put the car into gear and pulled into traffic headed for jail. UPS couldn't have done a more effective shipping job.

With the excitement over, Tommy and I sat on the curb. We examined our torn clothing and scuffed shoes. I felt as if I was going to puke—too much adrenaline still coursing through my body. I was bleeding from a wound on my arm that looked like teeth marks.

Tommy looked at his watch and put his arm around my shoulders. "Happy New Year, partner!"

Shaw was booked for attempted murder of a police officer. The District Attorney's office later added several counts of assault with a deadly weapon, nine counts of first degree burglary, and various weapons charges. A *no bail* injunction was imposed. A week later at the preliminary hearing, the attempt murder charge was dropped as part of a plea bargain involving the remaining charges. Shaw was sentenced to ten years in the state penitentiary. He served five years before gaining parole.

He is on the streets today.

THE HARDBOILED STUFF

Quint and the Braceros *was nominated for the Private Eye Writers of America's Shamus award in 1984 in the category of Best Short Story of the Year. It did not win. However, according to the publicity spin mavens, the book cover hype of "Shamus Award Nominated Writer" works almost as well as "Shamus Award Winner."*

The story itself was sparked by two criminal factors —the lack of crime reporting by victimized illegal aliens, and unsubstantiated reports of marijuana harvesting farms in Northern California staffed by slave labor.

*Ramon Quintana, along with a number of other lead characters from my short stories make an appearance en masse in my Fey Croaker novel **Tequila Mockingbird**. While writing that novel, I found I needed a roster of characters to staff a private security agency run by Ethan Kelso, a secondary character from another unconnected novel (**Chapel of the Ravens**). Rather than reinvent the wheel, I put a call out for all my old short story friends who appeared without delay to take up the challenge.*

QUINT AND THE BRACEROS
A Ramon Quintana Story

★ **Dialog translated from Spanish is indicated by the following style of qoutation marks: < >**

I was petrified with fear. Hell stretched out before me in an abyss of living terror which sent my stomach lurching in panic. Hell was a pit. A pit five-foot deep and four-foot wide, with a lashed bamboo grate to lock across the top. Once in the pit you could neither stand nor lie down, just crouch in muscle-cramping despair.

I'd been in a pit like this before. In Vietnam. Now, naked and beaten, almost unable to move, I remembered swearing then that nobody would ever, ever, put me in a pit again. I'd sworn to die first.

Fueled by the steel tension in his thick arms, the huge hands of Paco Avila forced my shoulders further and further over the lip until I started to scream.

<Un millar muertes son la verdad de terror.>

The truth of terror is a thousand deaths. For me the first death had paid a visit three days past.

They don't make buildings like the Bradbury in LA anymore. Today all they do is upchuck some chrome and glass monstrosity for Hollywood to use in its next space epic. In a town where you'd be hard-pressed to find a building over fifty years old, the Bradbury will eventually make way for progress too. Until then, though, my office sits on the third floor, left side, next to the bathroom. I've got a single window overlooking *Little Tijuana* at Broadway and Third, also a desk, a chair, a small icebox and a couch. It's not much but I'm comfortable. Sort of.

It wasn't often big money walked into my office, but Luis Benjamin Rojas was definitely big money, in capital letters, with some extra zeros thrown in for skeptics.

I didn't know him at first. College was a long time ago. But, since the big man had pushed open the door marked *Ramon Quintana Investigations*, I figured he was looking for me and not for the latrine next door. At least I hope so. My desk already had too many unidentified stains on it.

"You look tired, Payaso," he said.

Part of it was the old nickname that made me take a closer look inside the hand-tailored suit and the two-hundred-dollar-shoes. Nobody had called me a clown in a while. However, it was the rich baritone delivering the name that dropped the penny for me.

"Luis! I hardly recognized you!" I swung my legs off my desk and stood up to embrace him. "The last time you called me Payaso I kicked your butt all over the playing field."

He laughed in the series of short grunts I remembered well. He plunked down on the worn flower-pattern spread across my couch.

"I think you're a bit confused about who kicked whose butt," he said with a grin. "Maybe you'd like another go-round right now for old times sake?"

Seeing how I was still five-foot-five to his six-foot-two, it didn't seem like a good idea. My machismo isn't as easily riled as it used to be.

"How about a beer instead?" I asked.

Luis nodded, and I took a couple of bottles of Carte Blanca from the icebox. I popped the caps with an opener screwed to the desk above the trash can. Laziness, the mother of invention.

I handed a bottle to Luis. "I'm sorry the accommodations don't run to a glass."

"De nada," Luis said, raising the frosty bottle. "Your health." He drank deeply and then glanced critically around the room. "Madre de Dios, Quint! What is the son of one of the richest men in Mexico doing in a hellhole like this?"

And here I was thinking this was going to be a nice visit.

"What's the matter, Luis? You don't like my decorator?"

117

Luis shook his head. "Still the same old Payaso. Always ready with a snappy comeback."

It was an old habit. When you're a dwarf cactus in a land of redwoods, a one-liner hits harder than your right cross.

"You had everything, Quint, a prestigious family, the best of educations, connections, money—a green-card you didn't have to lie or risk your life for. What more could you want?"

"About ten inches of tall and a way to do something for all the others who don't have everything."

Rojas looked at me for a silent second and shook his head again. "I don't think I've ever met a man with as much guilt as you. I'd have thought all the idealism would have been kicked out of you by now."

"Yeah, I'm sure you'd think far more of me if I'd followed you into *La Familia*, or whatever the current term is for the Mexican Mafia. Then I could have the flashy clothes and diamond pinky rings too. No thanks. I like to sleep nights."

"There's always a place for you back in the fold, Quint."

I finished my beer and threw the bottle into the trash basket with more force than intended. "I was never in the fold, damn it. My father was a dope peddling, corrupt government stooge, just like his father before him. I have the right to break the mold."

There was a strained silence as I watched Luis visibly try to get his temper in check. I didn't much care whether he did or not. I'd heard all his arguments before. I opened another beer.

"Do you know about what happened to Antonio?"

"Just what I've picked up from the street. He had good grades going into college. Instead of the athletics and beer busts, which were our forte, his style ran more to student activism. I heard he was spending the summer in the San Ignacio Valley vineyards, working with the migrants who still haven't received the gospel according to the United Farm Workers Union. I also heard he got himself badly beaten for his efforts." It came out harsher that I'd expected and I felt slightly uncomfortable.

Luis glared at me and then downed the rest of his beer. I waited patiently.

"I've often thought Tonio should have been your brother instead of mine." He started quietly. "You were always the one with the causes and ideals, the one who couldn't let well enough alone. You went to Nam when the rest of us were taking student deferments. You turned your back on your father's contacts when you could have asked for anything you wanted. Tonio was like that. I love him, but I've never understood his choices." He sighed deeply and watched a trickle of condensation roll off his beer bottle onto the hardwood floor.

"At least he had a chance to make choices. That's a better deal than most of our kind."

Luis nodded slowly and then said something in a voice so low I had to ask him to repeat it. "Antonio is dead," he said. "The doctors have him hooked on life support machines but his brain is dead. He's never coming back." There was a depth of emotion in his voice I'd never heard before. "I want to find out what happened to him. I want you to find out, Quint. Somebody has to make things right."

I felt cold inside. "That's police work, Luis," I said eventually. "I'm not a hit man. Not even for friends."

"I'm not asking you to kill anybody. To the police, Antonio is just another case of Mexican vs. Mexican, no humans involved. Unless the case is handed to them on a platter they won't bother with it."

"And you want me to provide the platter? Why? Don't you have people available for this kind of thing?"

"I have to keep my own doorstep clean. To involve my

business associates would show me in a position of weakness. I can't afford that. I need you."

I looked at the stack of bills sprouting from my in-box. "Things are too tight for charity work, Luis. I get two-hundred-and-fifty-dollars a day, expenses, and a thousand-dollar bonus upon successful completion." I had no doubt he could afford it.

The sun was shining like a debutante in June as I walked across the University campus to the student union building. According to the University brochures, some of the greatest scholars in the world had strolled along the pathways I was following. What the brochures failed to mention was a lot of losers, anarchists, and degenerates had also traveled the same routes, albeit to different destinations. The student union was a huge circular building dedicated to some long obscured alumnus. The center of the building housed a large cafeteria and even larger auditorium. Six corridors sprouted from the heart of the structure like spokes of a wheel.

I followed my nose and, as usual, ended up hopelessly lost. Eventually, I asked a pretty coed for directions and received a look of disdain when it turned out I was standing directly across from my destination. I should carry around a hole to bury myself in.

The door I wanted was slightly ajar and bore a hand-lettered sign announcing the presence of *La Razas Unitas*. The races united, I thought as I pushed the door fully open and stepped inside. A nice sentiment, but who really cared anymore? Sometimes it seems as if there are far more sociologists than bandwagons for them to jump on.

My entrance startled a dark-haired girl who was rooting through a box of books and papers in one corner of the poster-covered room. It was a typical editorial office for a slightly radical college magazine. Che's visage was represented alongside Malcolm X, Eldridge Cleaver, and everybody's favorite, Lenny Bruce. To keep a balance there were also photos of Bobby Kennedy and Martin Luther King.

"Moving in or out?" I asked.

Large luminous eyes glanced at me from a pleasant face with strong Mexican bloodlines and prominent cheekbones which bespoke a trace of Castilian Spanish. "Out, I'm afraid. Can I help you?" Her voice was strangely accentless, untouched by even the play tough Spanish of the LA streets.

"I'm looking for Lupe Calvera," I said hopefully. "My name is Ramon Quintana."

"I'm Lupe. Tonio's brother called to say you might come by. You were lucky to catch me."

Luis had told me Antonio was the editor of *La Razas Unitas* and had gone to San Ignacio on assignment for the magazine.

"Do you think you could help me carry these out to my car?" Lupe asked, indicating two boxes packed to overflowing. "I have a seminar in half an hour and we have to clear the office by this afternoon. We can talk on the way."

"What's happening?" I asked. "A change of causes?"

Lupe looked at me sharply, and I smiled to take the bite out of my words. It didn't appear to work.

"In a way," she finally conceded. "Tonio's beating has changed a lot of things. He was the force behind the magazine. Without him there doesn't seem to be anything to hold the rest of us together. But I don't appreciate you laughing at me. Didn't you ever believe in a cause?"

I took a beat to think by bending down and picking up the two boxes. "Maybe a long time ago," I said. "Maybe I still do.

I don't know. I've always believed causes are important."

"Even lost ones?"

"Especially lost ones. They're the most important to believe in."

"Why?"

I shrugged. "How can a cause be truly lost as long as someone, somewhere believes in it?"

"Is finding out what happened to Tonio a cause?"

"It's just the kind of thing I do, Miss Calvera, and I don't like being laughed at either."

The girl looked me in the eye for a second and then smiled. "Touché, Mr. Quintana."

"Make it Quint, okay? It's easier. Can we get going? These boxes are getting heavier than our philosophizing."

"Oh, I'm sorry." Lupe looked concerned and hastily picked up the last box before heading out the door.

"What can I do to help you?" she asked as we walked.

"You can start by telling me what Antonio was doing in the vineyards."

Lupe was walking fast, and I was having trouble keeping the huff out of my voice.

"It's an old problem really. Most people think all Latin crop pickers are illegal aliens. The reality is, however, that most of them are *braceros*—legally hired migrant workers. Their history stems back to when America first started hiring Mexican workers to supplement a domestic workforce that considered itself above such menial tasks."

I was familiar with the social commentary, but we were walking up a flight of concrete steps towards the parking lot and I didn't have enough breath to comment.

Lupe wasn't having the same airflow problems. She had the capacity for large lungs, and talked right along. "Now, though, some of the braceros are beginning to think they're also above picking produce. Some of them have started working for growers looking to cut costs by bringing in illegals at substandard wages. The braceros control and bully the illegals, forcing them to work under horrendous conditions, keeping them in line with the constant threat of exposure and deportation."

"It doesn't say much for the conditions they came from if the illegals are willing to stay and put up with the situation," I said.

"One cause at a time, Quint."

We reached Lupe's car. It was one of those foreign mini-pick-ups that look like an adolescent car that hasn't decided what it wants to be when it grows up. I placed my load gratefully on its tailgate. I tried to be casual about the deep breaths I was taking.

"What did Antonio hope to accomplish?"

"Immigration laws are changing all the time, but it's almost impossible to get the illegals to realize they actually have some rights. Tonio planned to spend the summer helping to educate some of them."

"I bet that made him real popular with the growers and the braceros."

"I know it might seem a ridiculous thing to attempt, but there was something inside Tonio that made him take on impossible causes."

I understood that, even if his brother couldn't. "Did Tonio have any contacts in San Ignacio?" I asked.

"Yes. There was a bracero named Umberto Galves who was sympathetic towards our cause. He'd worked with Tonio before in several union movements."

"Have you heard anything from him since Tonio's beating?"

"Nothing, but perhaps I could help you find him."

"That would look a little odd. A migrant worker arriving at the vineyards in a new pickup truck with a beautiful escort. Somehow I think it would blow my cover."

"You mean you're going to work in one of the vineyards?"

"I'm going to get hired on. Sometimes those are two different things. Detective work is nothing special really. You backtrack, you stir the pot, you wait to see what happens. If nothing does, you backtrack a little further and start all over again. Locked rooms, puzzles, hidden clues and drawing rooms full of suspects are for books, not real life." I paused, thinking for a second. "Where was the last place you heard Tonio was working?"

"The Lantana Winery. It was the third vineyard he'd visited. While he was at the others, we heard from him pretty regularly. But that stopped when he stared at Lantana. It was like he disappeared. Two weeks later he was found in the fields beaten into a coma." Lupe looked at me. "Lantana's head bracero is a man called Paco Avila. He favors large knives and likes to crush things with his hands."

"Sounds like a fun guy," I said.

Why is nothing easy?

Californians refer to it as Steinbeck Country. A green, fertile expanse of state pride which starts at some indistinct point north of LA, and runs out somewhere around San Francisco.

In the middle of it all is Monterey County, which encompasses the Los Padres National Forest, Salinas, Cannery Row, the Carmel and San Ignacio Valleys, and some of the finest vineyards in the world.

I stood outside the entrance to the Lantana Winery and watched two hundred or so migrants snipping bunches of small white grapes off gnarled vines. It's never out of the ordinary to see women and children working as migrants, but from my estimation over ninety percent of the pickers in the vineyard fell into that category. Odd.

Back in LA I had traded my linen three-piece for a baggy pair of khaki pants, a blue workshirt, and a battered Levi jacket. I had a wide brimmed hat to keep the sun off my neck, and ran the risk of wearing scruffy but good quality boots. I figured I could always say I stole them. It would fit the stereo-type.

Hitching rides up the coast and sleeping rough had helped to get the scent of the city off me. It was the type of thing most people don't think about. If you turned up in the fields smelling of smog and Ivory soap, you were definitely going to wrinkle somebody's nose.

Wiping my face with a large red bandana, I trudged up the dirt roadway to the winery buildings. Nobody paid much attention until one of the overseers spotted me and waved a stout wooden club.

<What do you want,> he asked me in rapid Spanish.

<I am looking for work, Senor. I was told to try here,> I replied in kind.

He looked me over quickly. <Do you have a green card or a work permit?>

I looked silently at the ground. The bracero laughed.

<All right. Come with me. Mr. Lantana likes to see any new help.>

The bracero turned back towards the field and yelled out some instructions to a counterpart before leading me toward an adobe-style ranch house. On the way he laid the flat of his club across the back of an old man who wasn't working fast enough. It took all my effort not to take the club away and stick it to the bracero where the sun don't shine.

At the back door he let himself in. I followed him through

to a sitting room occupied by a heavy-set older man with Italian features.

"Senior Lantana, this man wants to hire on."

Lantana looked up at me from under bushy, silver-gray eyebrows, made a rumbling noise deep in his throat and then spat with accuracy into a brass cuspidor. An honest-to-God brass cuspidor. I'd never seen anything like it.

"You speak the English, Jose?" he asked me.

I stared at the bracero and ran the brim of my hat through my hands.

"His back is still wet from crossing the Rio Grande, Senor," the bracero told Lantana. "He has no papers, like the others."

"Good. Okay, Chico, let him start today and let Paco know we have another couple of dozen ready for him."

That was an exchange I only half understood even though I did speak English. However, my ears perked up at the name Paco.

As we started to turn away, Lantana spoke loudly.

"Hey! You know why they don't let Mexicans be firemen?" he asked. "Because they can't tell Jose from hose-B." He laughed uproariously at his own joke until he started to hack violently. He rumbled deep in his throat again but, instead of spitting, he suddenly grabbed his chest and fell heavily into a padded armchair.

"My pills, you ignorant spic," Lantana wheezed at Chico, who jumped towards a jumble of knick-knacks on the hard-wood mantel above a cold stone fireplace.

From behind the collection of plaster animals and photographs, Chico extracted a vial of nitroglycerine heart pills. He shook one out and handed it to Lantana, who quickly slipped it under his tongue.

A couple of seconds passed before Lantana's color

returned and he waved us out of the room. I looked back once and saw Lantana returning the vial to its resting-place on the mantel. Borrowed time, I thought, one day the pills wouldn't do the job and Lantana's life would be balance due.

Chico gave me all of ten seconds to throw my battered rucksack onto a filthy mattress on the floor of a barracks-like building. He then hustled me out towards the grapevines.

Looking around on the way, I saw my new sleeping quarters were aligned with two other buildings of similar purpose. There was also a square structure in front of the barracks, which Chico told me was where the braceros slept. There was also a row of outhouses, which proved the extent of sanitary conditions. The far end of one barracks building had been turned into a kitchen, with long tables set under canvas sheeting stretched between crooked poles. It could have been worse. It also could have been a whole lot better. Where are you when we need you, Cesar Chavez?

I was given a sharp paring knife, a definite threat to my fingers, and was set to loading cardboard boxes with the fruit of the vine.

The work was backbreaking and monotonous. It was not made easier by the presence of the club-wielding braceros, who allowed no talking among the migrants and few water breaks. Infractions were dealt with harshly. Wonderful conditions for a promised dollar-an-hour.

We loaded the full boxes onto a battered pickup, which delivered them to another winery building where the wine-making process started. It was a tidy, if brutal, operation. I would have loved to get a look at the business books, though, to see if the efficiency computed into the dollars needed to maintain the winery in the plush custom observed at the main house.

At dusk we quit for the day and were allowed to shower

under ice-cold hose pipes behind the barracks. The smell of menudo wafted from the kitchen, and the sullen mood of the migrants lifted slightly as children played in the compound and conversation was allowed.

Bottles of cervesa were set out in ice-filled tubs—the cold beer clearing dust from parched throats.

I was still puzzled by the overwhelming lack of male migrants. I mentioned it in conversation, but received only blank stares in return. One woman, a gnarled, weather-beaten veteran crop picker, told me in a whisper to get clear of the winery while I still could, but she froze up and hurried away when she caught one of the braceros staring at us. I wanted to ask about Tonio, but there was a strong element of fear in the compound holding me back.

Most of the evening meal was eaten in silence until a battered clapboard truck pulled in with a swirl of dust. Several new braceros climbed out, but it was the driver who grabbed my attention.

His attitude showed he was the head hombre, and his size backed his undisputed claim. The fat gene had been present at his conception, but so had the muscle and girth genes that give brute strength. A full Zapata mustache drooped in grizzled fashion from the sides of his mouth, and the beer bottle he immediately grabbed from the ice tubs disappeared in his fist. I watched Chico hurry over to talk with the new arrival, and knew instinctively I was looking at Paco Avila.

For the most part the braceros ignored us, and as the evening wore on most of the migrants made for their beds. A few of us remained up, huddled around a fire in a trashcan and listened to the plucking of an old guitar. I'd planned on making a closer examination of the other winery buildings. However, before I could slip away, Paco and a couple of his friends stepped into the picture.

Gathered around the square building of their sleeping quarters, the braceros were laughing loudly and drunkenly. The old man I had seen Chico striking earlier was being used as a lackey to ferry beer and other menial tasks. He was assisted by boots, shoves, and verbal abuse, most of which was demeaning but harmless, until Avila brought out a large bullwhip and cracked the dirt between the old man's feet.

The migrant howled in pain and fell as the tip of the whip exploded like a rifle shot again, this time in the area of his groin. Avila let out a whoop and delivered another blow. This one drew a split of blood across the victim's forehead.

The guitar next to our fire stopped playing, but that was the only sign of reaction from the migrants around me. Most turned their faces from the old man's plight. All of them ignored it.

I couldn't.

Lost causes aren't lost as long as somebody, somewhere believes in them.

I rose silently to my feet and covered the ground between the trashcan fire and the braceros' barrack in smooth, rapid movements. I didn't think about what I was doing, I just did it.

Avila's broad back was toward me. His whip was pulled back to deliver another lash when I leapt on him. Throwing my legs around his waist, I locked my feet at his belt buckle and jammed the bony part of my forearm hard across his Adam's apple. With the flat of my left palm, I slammed the side of his head, dropping his chin into the crook of my elbow, locked up the choke hold, and began squeezing off the blood to Avila's brain.

Like an angry bull in rut, Avila began to thrash around. I knew if he pulled me off I was a dead man. I squeezed down on his carotid artery. As Avila fell to the ground with me underneath him, I felt the wind whoosh out of my own lungs.

I held on until the bullish body on top of me began to flop about like a freshly killed chicken. A wet warmth soaked my socks as Avila's bladder let loose. Finally, I dragged myself free and backed the other braceros off with the demented stare of an adrenaline high.

I helped the quivering old man to his feet and moved away towards the migrants' barracks. As we passed Avila's inert body, I could see his chest rising and falling slightly. The old man spat his contempt, and I dragged him shuffling away before the spell of inaction over the braceros broke.

<Why do you do this?> the old man asked when we got back to the trash can fire. The other migrants had disappeared like snowflakes on a hot chimney. <You must get out quickly before that puta recovers. You should have killed him if you wanted to live.>

I didn't comment but instead asked him his name and how long he'd been working at the winery.

<My name is Tejone Marvilla. I have been here for three months.>

<What is going on here, Tejone? Where are all the men?>

<The braceros come and take them away in the truck when there is enough of them. They leave the women and the families and tell them to work hard if they ever want to see their sons, fathers, and husbands again.>

<Where do they take them? Why haven't they taken you?>

<I am too old to be of use to them. They took my sons, but leave me here to use for jest.>

Tejone then asked his own question.

<You are not a migrant. What do you want here?>

<I'm trying to find out what happened to a young man. His name was Antonio Rojas and he came here to help the migrants.>

<I remember him. He was like you, unafraid to stand up to the braceros. They took him away with the other men. A few days later, we found him beaten and entangled in a grapevine. It was obvious he was badly hurt. The ambulance came for him but it was hopeless. It was a warning to the rest of us.>

I looked toward the braceros' barracks and saw Avila being helped to his feet. <We better get inside,> I said.

<No! You must leave! Avila will take you with the others and then you will never escape.>

<Tell me what they are doing with the men.> I already knew Tonio had been beaten almost to death. I had to find out why before I could put it on a platter for the police.

Tejone looked at me sadly. <I cannot tell you. I am scared for my sons.> He looked at the ground. Suddenly he grabbed the sleeve of my work shirt, with the desperation of fear in his grip. <Please, Senor, if you find them, help them.>

I put an arm around his bony shoulders and we went inside.

I had expected trouble from the braceros, but after I had been on my mattress for two hours without retaliation I felt a little more secure. Around me the migrants slept a dreamless sleep of ignorance, innocence, and fear in equal measure. The sickly cloying smell of heated sweat hung in the air, and a claustrophobic fist wedged against my chest.

As silently as possible, I made my way out of the barracks. I gave the braceros' hut a wide berth and moved quickly toward the winery buildings. The three main buildings were set in the same positions as the original adobe and clay structures built when the first grapes had been planted generations before.

Inside, from what I could see through dust-smeared windows, were all the traditional winemaking effects—vats, presses, casks, and soaked oak barrels. One building was maintained as the winery's own bottling operation. It was an ancient process made modern, only of interest to a winegrower, seller, or connoisseur. Nothing for the wino, whose only interest was sucking down the final product, or for the nosey P.I. trying to make a buck.

The fourth building was more up my alley. It was a recent structure made from wood with a palm thatched roof. Large and rectangular, it was a rural farmer's dream barn minus the red paint.

I didn't really need to hoist myself through an open window. Once close to the building the smell told me what was inside. But what the hell, curiosity only killed the cat, not his owner.

The inside of the barn was as functional as its exterior. The bare walls did nothing for the decor, but the long extension cords connecting the heat lamps suspended from the ceiling rafters did add a rather avant-garde touch. It was the long racks of drying marijuana, though, that gave the building its true ambiance. Surrounded by the heavy scent of the cannabis, I felt like a lone deodorizer strip in an incense factory.

I knew marijuana was still California's number one cash crop. It was clear Lantana was not about to be left out of the gold rush. I wondered if anybody ever joked with him about selling *no dope* before its time.

I took a closer look at one of the plastic wrapped *dime lids* and found the dope to be a finely groomed, almost seedless end product. California has always been on the cutting edge of drug technology, and I had no double the *THC* content in the leaves would be as high as any from South America or Hawaii.

The French are not enjoying the backlash from the current batch of award-winning Californian wines, but at least they are slightly civilized. When Colombian dope profits start to tumble, there'll be a hell of a lot more than noses put out-of-joint.

I wasn't sure exactly what I was going to do about my discovery. I figured I'd get away from the winery, clear my head from the contact high I was getting inside the barn, and try and plan things from there. I now had a rough idea about where Tonio and the other male migrants had been taken. If I was right I was going to need police help.

I was scooted back across the window ledge into the cool dark outside. My eyes were not functioning well after exposure to the heating lamp lighting in the barn. As a result, my plan collapsed along with my kidneys.

A searing deep bruising pain thunked across my lower back as somebody tried to swing a baseball bat through me like Reggie Jackson aiming for the bleachers. I screamed in agony. My mouth filled with dirt as my lips scooped the ground, and my body flopped around like a fish on a sandbar. Heavy boots, too many to count, added to the party and being alive became a lost cause.

Not even I cared anymore.

I might have given up on living, but unfortunately it hadn't given up on me. I came to consciousness abruptly, only to have my head slammed against the rusting bed of the braceros' pick-up truck as it jolted over a deep rut. I was confused and disoriented, vaguely aware of the packed bodies around me, and very aware of the icy cold that penetrated my bones to the marrow.

I was naked except for a rough burlap sack some saint of mercy had thrown across my fetal curled shape. My swollen eyelids refused the command to open. When my head was slammed into its metal pillow again, I agreed with them and shut everything down for the duration.

Don't believe the lies you hear about *things* being darkest before the dawn. When Paco Avila's meaty hands pulled me out of the truck it was dawn out, but *things* were still pitch black and getting blacker.

I wasn't caring too much about *things,* but instinct turned my body over to take the brunt of the drop from the back of the truck on my shoulders and not my head. Still, the jolt was enough to jar my eyes open. This time they refused to close.

Paco laughed at me. He started dragging me across the rough ground of what appeared to be a forest encampment. From my unelevated position, I could see wooden benches filled with men of all ages sitting listlessly as they stripped the serrated leaves from long stalks of marijuana plants.

The braceros here had traded their clubs for machetes, and stood over their captives with insolent bravado. There were no amenities anywhere. It was obvious the captives ate, slept and worked exactly where they were sitting now. The stench of the shallow latrine pit overpowered even the pungent aroma of cannabis. This is what Tonio had found and tried to escape from. The living hell of a slave labor camp somewhere in the Californian mountains. I had the serving platter now, but I didn't want it anymore.

I screamed when Paco detoured through a bramble patch that tore shreds of skin from my back and shoulders. He laughed some more and dragged me back for a second helping. Some remote part of my brain, which refused to accept the pain, was busy recording everything around me— the open air cooking pits, the lean-to shanty for the braceros, the two eight-foot towers staffed by guards with automatic rifles, the haystack piles of harvested marijuana, and the huge storehouse of the trimmed and packaged finished product.

I also noted the staggered shapes of *smugglers posts,* irregular lengths of two-by-fours pounded into the ground and equipped with jury-rigged trigger mechanisms, which fired a lethal dose of shotgun pellets when the trip wire snagged. In the dark the posts would keep hijackers out and slaves in.

Then I saw the pits. There were six of them in a row. I started to kick and scream and fight with everything I had inside me. It wasn't enough.

Paco bunched his fist and paralyzed my legs by slamming them like a demented judge demanding order in the courtroom. As he began forcing my shoulders over the lip of the pit, I raked at his eyes with my fingernails. He roared in pain and retaliated by punching my mouth back through time. Blood spurted from my lips. It splashed across the filthy "white of his tee-shirt, and then I was sliding head-first into the pit. My neck popped violently as my head hit bottom.

There was a loud crash as Paco threw the bamboo grate across the pit's opening and locked it down. Tears ran up my face, and I felt something akin to madness settle over me.

Vietnam was my first introduction to lost causes. Ideals such as patriotism, justice, and humanity ceased to exist in the reality of fear and survival. In my quest to prove something to myself, which has become intangible with time and experience, I became part of Delta Red. The unit was a five man, Long-range Recon Patrol, which was dumped into Quang Tri Province. Our orders were to kill as many Vietcong as we could before we died.

By the end of our first day, three members of Delta Red were dead. Two died by booby-trap, one by his own hand. That left just Click-clatch Charlie and me.

Charlie was the biggest man I've ever known. He stood 7'2" and was an easy 300 pounds of wire-twisted muscle. His skin was as black as a whore's heart. He was also a psychopathic killer. That's why I liked him. He kept me alive.

I don't know why he liked me. It could have been something to do with the disparity in our sizes, or because I helped him out when we'd been in boot camp together. It could also have been just a quirk of his warped psyche. I'd opt for the quirk if you pinned me down on the matter.

For the next month, we killed more Cong that I could remember. Day and night, we waited in ambush before exploding into violence, I don't think we ever slept. Through all the horror there was the odd *click-clatch* sound of Charlie chewing a double-edged razor blade. It was a habit he'd picked up when light bulbs fell into short supply.

Eventually the inevitable happened. Jungle fever seeped into our brains and we stumbled into a Cong camp by mistake. We found ourselves POWs. We were duck-marched to a prison camp and thrown into the punishment pits over which the guards urinated.

For three days I heard no sound from Charlie's pit. I thought he must be dead, and I wept for him. Then I wept for myself because I was still alive.

When I first heard the familiar *click-clatch* of a chewed razor blade again, I thought I was hallucinating. Suddenly Charlie's low rumble reached my ears.

"Are you alive, Quintana?" It was almost the longest sentence I'd known him to construct.

I was too scared to reply in case I broke the spell of the dream. Instead I scrunched my face against the pit's cover and squinted through the darkness. I watched as Charlie's thick fingers forced a razorblade through the bamboo lashings of the grate and then tore it back.

His big, grinning face peered down at me from what seemed a great distance. I tried to say something, but all that came out was a strangled whimper. I tried to move, but couldn't. I looked up at Charlie, watching as he popped the razor blade back in his mouth (*click-clatch*). He then reached down with one hand to pull me out of the hole by my neck.

In the middle of the compound the bodies of our VC captors lay in a ragged line. Each had a large bamboo stake driven through their sternum, pinning them to the ground like so many insects. The other prisoners in the camp were wandering around in various states of confusion, some trying to get things organized, others almost catatonic.

Looking at Charlie, I realized his back was curved in a grotesque hump. I managed a smile, and he smiled back. *Click-clatch.*

"How did you do it?" I asked.

The reply was only *click-clatch.*

With no effort, Charlie threw me over his shoulder and moved into the jungle with a long, sure-footed glide. *Click-clatch. Click-clatch.* For two days I heard nothing but *Click-clatch, click-clatch.* And then we came to the edge of a clearing around an American camp. Charlie came up silently behind the sentry, scaring the poor bastard out of twenty years growth, and sent him for help.

When the sentry left, Charlie laid me on the ground, wiped the sweat from my face, kissed me on the forehead, smiled once, and moved back into the jungle. *Click-clatch. Click-clatch.* It was the last I ever saw of him, except in my nightmares.

In this new pit, my ears rang with the sound of a chewed razor blade. I wished Charlie was there. Without him, I knew I was lost. But he was there. *Click-clatch. Click-clatch.* The sound pounded between my ear in time to my pulse, driving me to survive. To do something. To live.

I fought my way to an upright position and dug my fingers into the soft soil walls surrounding me. It was dark outside again, and I realized I'd been wallowing in despair for almost the entire day. I worked my fingers up and down, scrabbling them through the dirt until I came into contact with two granite stones large enough for my purpose.

Remembering to breathe for the first time in what seemed like hours, I relaxed for a second. Then, holding one stone as flat as possible against the wall, I smashed it again and again with the narrow end of the other rock. In my confined space the sound was dulled and did not travel. Eventually the rock broke like a split log, showering the floor of the pit with sharp, jagged shards.

I picked up the largest splinter and went to work on the rope which lashed the pit's bamboo cover together. My hands started to bleed and my arms numbed, but the noise of Charlie's razorblade kept my cutting pace. *Click-clatch, click-clatch*. Finally, the rope parted.

I crouched, panting in high gear, close to freedom but without the energy to gain it. *Click-clatch* went Charlie in my head, and I made my move. Pushing my way through the bamboo grate, I pulled myself out of the pit into the night and lay in agony as my spine straightened out.

Dawn was about two hours away. When my vision cleared I was relieved to see I had drawn no attention from the sleeping braceros, or from the migrants sleeping by their benches. There was a guard at the entrance to the camp, but he too was curled in sleep at his post.

Right then and there I was back in the jungle. I was running on empty, but somehow still running. I hit the sleeping guard hard and fast. I damn near broke the branch I'd scavenged over his head.

Working quickly, I stripped his clothing and stuffed his undershorts in his mouth. I tore his shirt into ribbons to bind his hands and feet. His pantaloons and sandals became my property as the spoils of war.

Next stop was the braceros' pickup truck. The keys were in it. I briefly considered jumping in and making a run for it, but two things stopped me. If I did make it to safety, I doubted I would ever be able to find my way back to the camp. Secondly, I had some real misgivings about trying to convince anyone of my story in time to do something. Instead, I decided to bring the mountain to me.

I tore one of my pant legs off at the knee with the help of a machete I'd taken from the sleeping guard. I tore the material into thin strips and used them as a makeshift fuse, which I pushed into the pickup's gas tank. I left about two feet of material dangling down the side of the truck. I lit the end with a match from the pocket of my new pantaloons. I then jumped into the pickup, cranked the engine over, and gave my giant Molotov cocktail wheels.

I didn't know how long the fuse would take before the flame dropped into the gas tank, but it didn't seem to matter. I floored the gas pedal. The truck leapt across the compound. Fighting the manual steering over the rutted ground, I crashed through the braceros' lean-to, scattering bodies in all directions.

Paco's bulk was in the middle of the melee. I chased him since he was running towards the storehouse of drying marijuana, my intended destination. When he veered off, I kept going straight ahead. I finally jumped clear of the truck before it crashed through the wooden wall of the storehouse structure.

There was a sudden quiet after the crash, and I thought perhaps my fuse had gone out. Suddenly, though, there was a concussive *wahuuuuuump!* that blew flames through the palm thatched roof and turned the storehouse into the biggest marijuana joint in the world.

A thick column of smoke tunneled into the sky, and I knew

it wouldn't be long before the Forest Service fire watchers came for a look-see. Meanwhile, I had a more immediate problem.

Above the noise of the yelling braceros and migrants, I heard the grunting of an enraged animal. Turning around I stared into Paco's mad eyes which glinted sharper than the machete in his right hand. He stood still for a second, and then charged toward me.

I turned and ran.

I still had the guard's machete with me. When I saw the irregular heights of the *smuggler's posts* only a few feet away, I turned back violently, swinging the heavy knife in a deadly figure eight motion. The first swipe tore across Paco's chest. The return slash took both his hands off at the wrists.

I had literally disarmed him, but his momentum carried him forward. He crashed into my battered body, which crumpled under the collision. I fell backwards, Paco's screaming louder than my own. I felt the tautness of a trip wire depress under my back.

The shotgun blast sounded like a cap gun in the middle of a fireworks display, but the back of Paco's head disappeared anyway, leaving only my screams to fill the void.

The Forest Service was on the ball and their first recon of the smoke tunnel was followed by the arrival of water-copters, fire units, ambulances, and the Sheriff's Department.

I told my story again, and again, and again, ad-infinitum. By the next day, they were convinced enough to take a trip out to the Lantana Winery.

When we arrived the workers were back in the fields and the marijuana I had discovered had disappeared into the great morass.

I wasn't too surprised.

Lantana himself denied all knowledge of the slave camp. He said if it did indeed exist, then it was the work of Avila and the other braceros without his knowledge. Lantana winked at me behind the deputy's back.

The Sheriff investigators at the scene told me they had no evidence to tie Lantana to the slave camp, and I should consider myself lucky I wasn't up on charges in connection with Avila's death. After all, the camp had been closed down. What more did I want?

I told them I wanted justice for Tonio and the others. They said I'd had all the justice I was going to get. I didn't tell them they were wrong.

I rode back to the Sheriff's station in silence. I said goodbye to my escort and walked over to Lupe Calvera's sport mini-truck and climbed in on the passenger's side. I'd called. She'd come. I'd talk to Luis later. Much later.

"Did it go as you expected?" Lupe asked.

"Yeah," I replied grumpily.

"A lost cause?"

"Maybe not," I said with a small smile.

I took the vial of nitroglycerine pills I had palmed from the top of Lantana's fireplace mantel out of my pocket. I held it up to the light and squinted at it. I wiped my prints off the amber glass, and tossed it out the window into the bushes.

***The Man Who Shot Trinity Valance** started
with the title. I keep a journal full of plot
ideas, character names, interesting quotes, and titles that strike me
as having particular resonance. When Max Allan Collins (creator
of the excellent Nate Heller
historical private eye series) asked me to contribute
a short story to a Mickey Spillane edited anthology called **Murder
Is My Business**, I jumped at the
opportunity. The theme of the collection was to revolve around hired
killers. Opening my journal in search of
inspiration, the title **The Man Who Shot Trinity
Valance** immediately set my creative process cranking.
Like many of my short stories, **The Man Who Shot Trinity
Valance** contains a kick in the denouement. This one, however,
was particularly fun to write.*

THE MAN WHO SHOT TRINITY VALANCE

A Trinity Valance Story

Trinity Valance was a master assassin, one of the best in the game. The word on the street, for those who concerned themselves with such things, was that her prowess was second only to the enigma known as Simon.

Ever since the thrilling rush of completing her first crude hit, Trinity knew she had found her true calling and she adopted the cover name of Starlight. As her reputation grew, it rapidly became clear killing was something at which she excelled. But for Trinity, excelling wasn't good enough. She had to be the best. To this end, Simon became an obsession with her.

Twice the two assassins had crossed swords while competing for the same open contract. And twice Simon had snatched the kill from directly in front of Trinity's proverbial gun sights. Even in her anger, Trinity sensed Simon had been playing cat and mouse with her, showing his disdain for her techniques of killing from a distance—through the use of booby traps—while he killed up-close and personal. Personal enough to feel his victim's fading heartbeat. But while Simon's figurative laughter taunted Trinity, his true identity eluded her.

Trinity took pride in achieving letter-perfect executions with a trademark touch of flair or panache. She developed a delicious knack for choosing an intriguing location, or a difficult time when the victim was surrounded by a crowd, or a situation where both the trigger and the mark would be on the move when the hit went down, or anything else that would add to the challenge and heighten the rush.

However, even though she planned each of her hits down to the finest detail, Trinity still felt Simon was always a step ahead of her, mocking her, constantly letting her know she wasn't quite good enough to be the best—to be considered Numero Uno.

As Trinity soaked in the bathtub, hot water channeled a thin, sensual canal between swells of full breasts turned lobster red by the heat. Tendrils of blond hair, having rebelled at being confined in a bun on the top of her head, hung limp with the steam rising off the water.

Running a soft sponge down her body, she glanced up at the 8 X 10 glossy taped to the fogged bathroom mirror. *Tonight,* she thought, *tonight the kill would be different.* Tonight, she would be inside the kill zone and all of her senses would be alive with the thrill. But the biggest rush would come in snatching the mantle of superiority from Simon's goading shoulders.

Trinity accepted this new assignment immediately upon the successful completion of her last score. Normally, she would have taken a break before making her next move, but this time she had been instantly infatuated by the face of her target. It was as if there existed a link between the executioner and her intended victim—a link that ran beyond mere fate and into the erotic.

The features in the photo were hollowed almost to the point of being considered gaunt. The sharp cheekbones and neatly clipped beard served only to emphasize the pointed chin and cadaverous cheeks. The eyes peering out from below heavy brows, however, seemed to hold a Santa Claus twinkle that was immediately betrayed by the cruel line of the lips. Trinity considered the sparkle in the eyes was really nothing more than a trick of the photographer's flash, whereas the draw of the lips perhaps exposed a true glimpse of the inner man.

Whenever she looked up at the photo, she felt the butterflies of anticipation change their direction of flight as they fluttered through her stomach. For the first time a contract was becoming very personal, touching her for some reason at the core of her sexuality. She longed for the kill, lusted for the sexual release of it, and knew this time she needed to be close enough to touch, smell, and taste the target—to feel the tingle in her loins when she pulled the trigger.

In the bath, her fingers were drawn inexorably downward across her abdomen as she closed her eyes and opened her mind to the fantasy.

Professor Royce Kilpatrick rested his large boned hands

on the padded steering wheel as he guided the snowy white Lincoln Towncar through the heat of the desert that was Las Vegas. He had always admired his hands. He stared at them now as he drove, drawing comfort from their perfection. The tendons and veins running across their backs looked almost sculpted. His long fingers had character etched into each individual knuckle and smoothly polished fingernail.

He knew in the Old West hands like his would have been referred to as gambler's hands—hands best suited to dealing or double dealing cards, shuffling, cutting, nimbly and invisibly snatching cards from the bottom, middle or top of the deck—hands that could make you rich or make you dead, either option being better than poor. Royce cherished the image because he was by nature a gambler and cards were his natural vice.

He took one of his long-fingered hands off the steering wheel to smooth his beard across hollowed cheeks. His job as a professor of English at the University of Nevada Las Vegas didn't pay nearly enough to cover the style of living he strived to maintain. Items like the leased Towncar and the expensive clothes covering his body did not come cheap, and they were well beyond his professor's salary. Still, there were other ways to make money.

Recently, however, his losses had been higher than usual. His touch for the cards had deserted him. He knew it would only be a short while before he got back on track, but until then he knew he had to keep hustling—not just with cards, but with the dice, the sports books, the ponies, or even how hot the temperature would be the next day. Experience had taught him if he could get enough balls in the air, something would come through. He secretly loved the rush he got from it all. Anything that smacked of a game of chance pumped his blood like a fire hose turned on full blast.

He'd been in gambling trouble like this once before—way in over his head, watching out for leg breakers at every turn, living life on the cutting edge—but that time he'd scammed his way to safety riding a fixed horse race that gave the bookies a bath, and had given him enough ready cash to pay off his markers, renew his lifestyle, and begin to work his way back into the hole again.

Royce had been one of the small fish in that scam, a bottom feeder who sucked up a diamond by pure luck, and as such he'd been ignored by the heavy mob who were sent after the players who pulled the coup. Royce figured it was because he was a sharp operator. The truth was the big boys knew he'd be back. There was no way somebody like Royce stayed away. And there was no way he'd get away again. If he'd been honest with himself, delving beyond the arrogant facade of education that he used to keep his students in line, Royce would have realized that this latest streak of bad luck was taking him down a long tunnel where the light at the end was nothing more than an onrushing train.

Every once in a while a worry would sneak into his conscious mind, but it was more a worry about finding a casino that would still let him play than about the markers piling up like a child's block tower. If the thought of how much he owed ever battled through his defenses long enough to be recognized, he shoved it casually aside. They didn't kill anyone over being in debt. They wouldn't kill the golden goose. If he were dead, how the hell would they ever get their money? How the hell would he ever get even again?

Nah, the big boys wouldn't kill you for just being in debt.

Would they?

The first time Royce saw the intriguing blond in the hot

red convertible was in his rearview mirror as they entered the outskirts of Las Vegas. The red convertible pulled to the left and blasted past in a flash of color. All Royce could see was a mass of flying hair and a glimpse of a red choker around a long elegant neck. Watching the blond, Royce felt primal male instincts move within him, as if he were an old lion intrigued by a lioness from another pride.

Off the highway and driving along the strip heading for downtown, he saw the blond again. There were faster ways to get to the downtown area of Vegas, but Royce enjoyed driving along the strip with its crush of tourists and its flashing lights coming to life in the early evening dusk. The strip never failed to energize him, to build up his anticipation for the evening ahead—lover's foreplay. Stopped behind the limit line at a traffic light, Royce heard an engine revving quietly next to him. Looking over, he was surprised to see the red convertible and its beautiful occupant.

In profile, without her hair blowing in the wind, he could see that she was a classic beauty. This time, he could see the blood red choker matched the color of both her lipstick and the perfect fingernails that tapped a beat across the black steering wheel. Even in the deepening dusk it was easy to see the color perfectly offset pale, flawless skin.

As if she knew Royce was staring at her, the blond turned her eyes toward him, smiled briefly in acknowledgement of her own beauty, and then left him standing flatly at the light as she accelerated away. A horn sounding from behind him brought Royce back to reality and he fumbled to pull away from the light himself.

The evening did not start out well for Royce. The first two casinos he entered had security moving immediately. Royce knew all about the overhead cameras and other techniques used by the casinos to keep undesirables at a distance and to make sure the majority of the chips stayed on the right side of the table.

In the Empress, Royce was frozen out immediately at the cashier's window when he tried to exchange a chunk of ready cash he'd picked up earlier in the day from a hot tip on a horse in the fourth at Hollywood Park. He had a cash-and-carry deal with the bookie he'd used for the bet, and it was one of the few resources he hadn't tapped out.

Now, at the Empress's cashier window, he was approached by the floor manager who told him he would have to make a payment on his credit line before he would be allowed to play further. The cash burning a hole in Royce's pocket wouldn't go very far if he tried paying off debts at this point. He had to parlay it, make it into a sizable chunk before he paid off on past miscalculations. And to do that he had to get on to the tables.

At the Golden Nugget, Royce got as far as sitting down at the blackjack table before trouble brewed. He was three hands into the shoe—two wins and a loss—when he saw Benny Harrington moving toward him. Royce felt a stab of panic lance through his chest. If ex-Mr. Universe Benny Harrington was around, then his twin brother Billy Harrington, also an ex-Mr. Universe, couldn't be far behind.

Benny and Billy were a tag team of leg breakers. They enjoyed their work. For them, a gambler past his credit limit was a rawhide chew bone to be abused by two bull mastiffs in a tug-of-war. Royce scooped his chips from the table and fled. It wasn't cool, but it was smart.

There was something more to the unpleasant start to the evening, however. Ever since the blond had roared away from him at the traffic light on the strip, Royce had found thoughts of her popping in and out of his mind. Royce never had much trouble seducing women, as several of the female staff and female student body at the university could attest, it was just that sex never did as much for him as gambling. For some reason, though, the brief glimpses he'd had of the blond had set his hormones racing. As a result, unrequited sexual lust was taking the shine off the usually arousing prospect of the slap of the cards.

Royce managed to get into a poker game in the Pacifica, but he soon ran through the majority of his collateral and was forced to withdraw when no credit was forthcoming. Making his way back to the center of the strip, he entered the Citadel casino. He hadn't been in the Citadel for a while and hoped he might find a friendlier reception there. He decided to try his luck and approached the cashier's window to see about extending his credit line.

"No problem," said the clerk, after consulting her computer screen.

Surprised, Royce quickly drew out a thousand dollars in chips before the clerk changed her mind or realized the computer had made a mistake. With a bounce in his step and an immediately growing confidence, he made his way to the playing floor.

And then he saw her.

A brief flash of blood-red around a long, pale neck.

He brought his attention back to the craps table and saw the blond from the red convertible as she placed a stack of chips on the green baize. The shooter fired out the dice to the admiration of the small crowd who "ooohed" and "ahhhed" over the result. The blond was cool as the stickman pushed a stack of chips in her direction.

Royce felt a stirring as he took in the blond's complete package—white sequined dress over red seamed hose and blood-red high heels. She was broader through the shoulders than most women, as if she had been a competitive swimmer at some time, but slim and flat through the hips. She was tall, just below six-foot, and her legs seemed to go on forever.

As he watched the blond, Royce's pulse rate increased in anticipation. Never one to turn down a long odds proposition, he made his way over to the table and into an open position next to the blond. She looked at him and smiled. It wasn't a dazzler, full of perfectly capped teeth and Pepsodent, but it was more of a seduction, a mocking acceptance of Royce's motives for standing where he did.

"Hello," he said, in response to her look.

The blond nodded casually and returned her attention to the table. She took several chips from the stack in front of her and placed them on the baize. Without hesitating, Royce placed his chips next to hers.

Even before the shooter rolled the dice, Royce felt his luck click back into place. It was almost a physical sensation, a trilling of the nerve endings. The dice tumbled and bounced, but Royce didn't even bother to watch them. He knew he was going to turn up a winner. Double sixes showed, and there were Royce's chips sitting sweetly on the number twelve next to the blond's.

As their winnings were pushed across the table, the blond looked at Royce again.

"It appears as if I'm good luck for you," she said.

"It certainly does," he replied.

The blond extended her right hand. "Trinity Valance," she said.

Royce took her hand. Like her disposition it was cool and dry, her fingers lingering in his grasp for the extra second that determines the difference between friendly and sensuous. "Royce Kilpatrick," he said.

"And a fine Irish name it is, too," said Trinity. Her voice

was throaty with promise, the sound of silk sliding down a willing thigh.

Royce laughed. "And your name?" he asked. "Any relation to Liberty Valance?"

"Let's put it this way," Trinity said, her heart pounding at being this close to her quarry. "The name of John Wayne is never mentioned at any of my family reunions." She smiled, and this time it was a dazzler.

This is it. The thought raced silently through Royce's mind and rapidly became a belief. *Lucky streak city.*

The rest of the evening and night passed in a whirlwind. There was no game that could not be bowed before the combination of Royce's skill and Trinity's luck. They laughed, touched, and gathered in their chips—intimate strangers riding a bullet train.

Trinity was thrilling to the sensations of being so close to a man she was about to kill. She had known of Royce's gambling problems and had arranged on her own account for the extension of credit to Royce at the Citadel. She was extremely pleased with the way she had picked Royce up while leaving him with the feeling he was the one doing the picking.

The cat and mouse overtones of the whole hit appealed to her making her feel vibrant and sexy. For her, death had become so close to sex in so many ways that she understood why the French referred to orgasm as "the little death."

From the gaming tables, Trinity deftly moved Royce away and into a darkened lounge in one corner of the vast casino. It was just after midnight, and the room was populated by couples swaying to a live samba beat across the dance floor.

Royce knew he was being led, but was loving every second of it. Under normal conditions, he would have stayed at the tables as long as he was winning, a slave to the drug of gambling that always promised the next score would be the big one—the one that would give you enough "screw you" money to walk away for good. But nobody ever did, because there was not enough "screw you" money in the world to keep a true addict away from the rush of the risk.

Royce also knew the current circumstances weren't normal. Trinity Valance was a wild card that could make every hand a winner, and her spell was stronger than any game of chance. Somehow she had turned up in the hand he'd been dealt and Royce could do nothing but play her out. Moving into his arms, Trinity guided Royce onto the dance floor. The beat had become slow and sultry, the lighting a subdued hue of blue tinged with red edges. The combo on the small stage unknowingly caught up in Trinity's seduction.

As she leaned against the wiry muscles of the body next to her, Trinity's breath took on a ragged edge, and she truly realized for the first time why Simon had always laughed at her. He had always known the intensity of life that came from making death personal, the power of being right there next to the target and knowing you could snatch his very breath away any second you desired.

Trinity leaned hard into Royce, her lips next to his ear. She nipped his earlobe hard with her small white teeth, and when he didn't pull away she whispered, "I have a room upstairs."

He squeezed her tightly, and by mutual consent they moved off the dance floor, out of the lounge, and toward the elevators. Alone, inside the small box-like projectile, Trinity wrapped herself around Royce. Their mouths met, lips full and open, tongues intertwining and darting away as if they were birds executing a mating ritual. Royce's hands moved up to cup Trinity's braless breast. Her nipples were already as hard as nail heads, and she moaned through their kiss.

They broke their clinch as the elevator doors opened and moved with the speed of desire down the long corridor to Trinity's room. She fumbled to unlock the door as Royce ran his hands all over her from behind, biting at her neck and eliciting a jealous, "Disgusting!" from a pair of passing matrons.

The couple tumbled into the room and fell onto the deep pile carpet. They pulled at each other's clothing, animal passion taking over from human compassion. Naked, except for the blood-red choker around Trinity's neck, they made a half-hearted move for the sheets and comfort of the turned-down bed, but didn't make it. Still on the floor, they embraced—killer and quarry—their metaphysical beings separated only by the physical barriers of skin, bone, and muscle. Blood red nails scrabbled against taut back muscles. Long fingers entwined in masses of blond hair. Pelvic movements sought each other and joined in a ritual as old as animal-kind.

The heat and the passion burned brightly from one completion to the next, and the next, until Royce lay exhausted, his eyes closed as he savored the last lingering sensations of his giving. Beside him, Trinity breathed deeply, trembling on the edge of consciousness.

In time Royce drew himself up, and Trinity heard him enter the bathroom and close the door. There was the rush of water as the shower came to life. Deep within her, Trinity felt the quiver of the final orgasm that she had been holding back, nurturing, denying herself the pleasure of its release until the right moment.

Pulling her legs underneath her, Trinity stood up and moved in naked beauty to the bed. Leaning over, she pulled open the bedside table and withdrew her gun. She checked the load for the hundredth time and turned toward the bathroom.

In a soft voice, she crooned the perverted mantra from which she took her work name. "Starlight. Star bright. First star I see tonight. I wish I may, I wish I might, kill myself a man tonight."

Silently, she twisted the bathroom door handle and pushed it inward to be met by clouds of steam. Blood was screaming through her veins bringing her closer and closer to the ultimate climax with every passing millisecond—the gun in her feminine right hand becoming the ultimate extension of male sexuality.

Simon. Simon. Simon was right. Every fiber of her being trembled.

She moved forward, slid open the opaque shower door with a violent shove, and thrust her gun hand into the billowing steam.

For a moment her orgasm froze as she stared into the empty stall, and then she felt the ice-cold ring of a gun muzzle as it pressed into the back of her pale, swan-like neck. Above the noise of the running water, she heard the gentle laughter that had haunted her dreams.

Royce's voice seemed to reach her from a long way off. "Simon says, you lose."

Her orgasm and the assassin's gun at her neck both shattered time and existence together.

The following Monday morning, Trinity Valance ducked out of her humanities class at the University of Nevada Las Vegas and made her way quickly across the campus quad to a scheduled meeting with Professor Royce Kilpatrick. At the Student Union, she stepped through the open double doors and saw him waiting for her in front of a large portable bulletin board. Standing next to him was a small petite blond who was scribbling violently in a shorthand notebook.

"Trinity! Over here," Royce called out, waving when he spotted her.

When she was close enough, he drew her to him with an arm around her shoulders and introduced her to the smaller blond.

"This is Lynn Berkster," he said. "She's a reporter for the local rag."

The two women nodded at each other in the assessing way that instant rivals have.

"It seems," Royce continued, oblivious to the antagonism, "that the university's staff have been causing the usual ruckus over our annual Killer tournament. Lynn has come out to cover the action. I was just showing her the obituary board."

Royce, alias Simon, took his arm away from Trinity's shoulders and turned to examine the board behind them. "You see, Lynn," he said in his best professor's mode. Trinity noticed the reporter wasn't impressed, raising Lynn several notches in Trinity's estimation. "Trinity is proof that women can be very good at this game. This was her first tournament, and she took second place. I was really amazed."

Trinity cringed. *Amazed,* was he? She was going to amaze him all right. The fact that he had beaten her was bad enough, but his chauvinistic, condescending attitude was far too much of a goad to swallow. She refused to be considered second best.

The bulletin board held twenty 8 X 10 glossies. Royce's picture, a duplicate of the one that had been taped to Trinity's bathroom mirror, was at the top with Trinity's right below it. All the photos except Royce's had the word *deceased* stamped in red across the subject's features.

"Killer is simply a role-playing game acted out on a life-size scale." Royce continued his lecture. "It's harmless. A modern version of cowboys and Indians, or James Bond versus the bad guys, for adults using confetti bombs, or starter pistols, or other harmless devices. Each player chooses a secret identity and then is given an assignment to assassinate another one of the group who is also trying to assassinate another player. Once a hit has been successful, the killed player turns his assignment over to the player who bumped him off. In this way the tournament is a virtually self-destructing circle leaving only one player to be the top assassin at the end of play. Participants only know the code names of the other players but not their true identities. Neither of us knew the other was involved in the role playing when the tournament started. Part of the role playing game, however, is using your own devious methods to discover the other players. That way you can bump them off before they get a crack at you."

Oh, you smug bastard, Trinity steamed silently. Her stomach churned thinking about what a fool she'd been. She thought she was leading her target along when all the time the target was leading her, smirking at her, laughing up his sleeve at her.

Royce had learned her true identity, and then played with her—watching as she prepared to *assassinate* two of her Killer targets and then beating her to the punch by *assassinating* them himself. She was embarrassed by the memory of how she'd been manipulated, and humiliated by the way she'd fallen for Royce allowing her to learn of his real-life gambling problems in order to lure her into his web. Damn! She was angry.

"Players also don't know how close to the top of the obituary board they are getting," Royce continued his explanation. "That side of things is run by a gamemaster who oversees all the action and is the final judge when rulings are needed. In order to keep players from learning their competitor's identities too easily, the gamemaster keeps the obituary board a secret until the end of the tournament.

"This year, I took the code name Simon and came out numero uno. Trinity, here," Royce patted his rival, "was known as Starlight. She did a fine job, but wasn't quite good enough to beat the best." He laughed softly, and fingers of anger and humiliation again wrapped themselves around Trinity's spine at the familiar, taunting sound.

Berkster looked up from her notebook long enough to pose a question. "The university staff is worried not only about a game which could be construed as morally repulsive, but also about a player who might blur the line between fantasy and reality. How do you feel about that proposition?"

Royce laughed softly again. "Come on. We're all adults here just having a little fun. There are worry warts everywhere who still think rock-'n'-roll will destroy the world, that children's cartoons will pervert the masses, and that superhero comic books will corrupt the next generation. All of them are full of hot air. Playing Killer no more distorts the line of reality than playing Battleship, or reenacting historical battles with tin soldiers. I'll tell you what, why don't you come along to the celebration beer bust tonight and talk to some of the other players? You'll see that Killer is no more harmful than swallowing goldfish, cramming students into a phone booth, or any other college fad."

"That's what they said about college hazing," the reporter replied. "But, I'll come and talk to the others." She stuffed her notebook away.

"Good," said Royce. "We'll see you there." He put his arm around Trinity, but it was obvious his sexual antenna was pointing in another direction.

"Oh, just one thing," Trinity said breaking away from Royce. "You might need this for protection." From her purse she withdrew the starter pistol she'd used in the Citadel's hotel room and tossed it to the reporter with a grin.

Smiling, she moved back into the curve of Royce's arm. The purse she'd slung back over her shoulder was only slightly lighter. It was still comfortably weighted by the bulk of the brand new, fully loaded, .38 caliber Smith and Wesson nestled inside.

For Trinity reality and fantasy did blur on occasion, and soon she would show everyone who was really the best. Numero uno.

Number one with a bullet.

*The vision of Ebenezer Scrooge as a tormented private
eye gave rise to this stream-of-consciousness
updating of the Dickens's classic, **A Christmas Carol**. My
warped enjoyment of mixing metaphors and
stabs at **Moby Dick** and other classics should also
be apparent.
Ebenezer was also privately published by **Mysteries To
Die For** as a Christmas gift for customers in 1995.
It contains my favorite "bad" simile in the line
referring to a femme-fatale, who is attired in a dress made
entirely of tiny silver bells—"She tinkled as loudly as a
young boy in the morning." In writing, you are
told to "kill your darlings," but some simply refuse to die.*

EBENEZER
A Hardboiled Christmas Carol

Bob Marley was dead to begin with. I don't know why
that thought entered my head, but it may have had something to do with the radio station playing reggae on Christmas
Eve.

I was in my office in the Star Building overlooking what
had once been a thriving amusement park called Jungle Land.
It was now deader than disco, and had been for years. Where
Jungle Land once stood, there was now a monstrosity that
housed not only city hall, but also a huge concert auditorium,
a dinky concert forum, and a rat warren of other offices. A
typical story of city officials getting together to waste sixty-

five million tax dollars on the effort, all in the name of culture.

The structure was a four-story building in a city where only two-story structures could be built. It was a cubist, architectural eyesore, in a city where all other buildings were required to have a Spanish-style motif. So, it was sixty-five big ones spent for an edifice that broke every standard the city had ever established. It wasn't even decorated for Christmas.

The way this project had been ramrodded through the city council, I wouldn't doubt there's a body or two doing the concrete boogie in the foundation. Intimidation and greed can move mountains a hell of a lot quicker than faith. Somebody ought to start an investigation. But not me.

No. Not me.

I'm a private eye, but my heart isn't in the game any more. I'm an ex-cop, an ex-husband, an ex-altar boy, and an expert at self-delusion. I hadn't had a client in a month, my rent was overdue, my heart had a hole in it, and I was down to my last fedora. So much for a merry Christmas. Bah humbug.

I milked the last of the bourbon bottle into a tooth glass and swilled the swallow down. I looked out the window at the Christmas lights in the surrounding hills and despised each and every one.

The door to my office swung open and a dame stepped in. Trouble always starts with a dame. This wasn't just any dame, mind you. This was a dame named Tricksy Spillane —more trouble than a bitch in heat at a dog show.

Tricksy had been my last partner before I was bounced from the force a couple of years prior to retirement. She was a looker with legs that went straight down to Hades, blond punked-out hair, and a libido that was kinkier than a permed afro.

She swayed over to my desk one hip at a time on spiked

heels that defined cruel. The rest of the voluptuous package was wrapped in a gray trench coat. The collar was turned up and the belt cinched tight at her almost invisible waist. There was a soft tinkling whenever she moved as if she was an android and some of her parts were loose. In Tricksy's case, however, it was probably just her morals.

"Merry Christmas, Ebenezer." Her voice was honey over a three-day growth of beard—throaty and full of prurient promises. It brought images of torch songs immediately to mind.

"Bah humbug," I said.

"Sounds as if you've got a bad hairball there, Ebby baby. Maybe you should be drinking Petromalt on the rocks instead of that rot-gut you've got in your hand."

"Go scrooge yourself," I said, setting the bourbon glass down on the desk with a bang. "What do you want coming 'round here anyway, Tricksy? Can't you see I'm busy celebrating?"

"Busy wallowing in self-pity is more like it."

"What do you know about anything? Get lost, why don't you?"

She hitched one of those marvelous hips up onto a corner of my desk, leaned forward and placed the palms of her hands flat on my blotter. The view down her trench coat was more than enough to make a grown man cry. I brought my eyes up to her face. Her baby blues were smirking at me, knowing they'd caught me looking. She breathed deeply and the tinkling noise made itself heard again.

"I'm on my way to a party, Ebenezer, but I wanted to stop by and give you your Christmas present." She undid the belt at her waist and the trench coat fell open. Underneath was a silver chain mail dress with little silver bells everywhere. It was cut low on top and short on bottom to save on weight.

There were two things that appeared to be holding it up and they were both pointed at me.

"You expecting an assassination attempt?" I asked.

"Humor was never your strong suit, Ebby."

"No. C&R is more my style. Polyester and rayon. You can't beat it, and it's a lot lighter than chain mail."

She shimmied her gorgeous shoulders and the chain mail and bells tinkled louder than a young boy in the morning. "But it doesn't wear as long, and it doesn't feel near as good with nothing on underneath it."

I swallowed. "There is that," I agreed.

She twitched the trench coat closed, disappearing all that lovely, chain-wrapped, feminine flesh and treated me to one of her rare smoky laughs—an aphrodisiac for the ears.

"Ebenezer, you were once a good cop, but you allowed yourself to be hoisted on Romeo's petard." She reached into one of her trench coat pockets and pulled out a fresh pint bottle of bourbon. She hefted the bottle in her hand, as if judging its weight, and then set it in the center of my blotter. "The facts were clear," she said. "Romeo was a dirty cop. He got what he deserved."

I shook my head at her, feeling the cold in the pit of my stomach. This was something I didn't want to get into. I felt as if I was a tiger looking at a staked goat. The tiger knows it's a trap, but it has to eat the goat anyway.

I looked at the bottle and licked my lips. "Romeo was my partner before you were, and what he got was dead. Whoever did it is still out there running around when he should be worm food. Tonight the bastard is probably swilling wassail, eating plum pudding, and counting visions of sugar plum fairies. So, it ain't such a merry Christmas, if you ask me."

"Stop it, Ebenezer. You want to blame everyone but yourself for your troubles. You ended up in this dump trying to follow the trail to Romeo's killer. You did everything you could, but in the end all you hit was a brick wall. You were making too many waves. Making the department look bad. Telling everyone that if Romeo was crooked, there had to be somebody higher up more crooked than Romeo had been."

I shrugged, feeling renewed anger. "Internal Affairs did a whitewash. It was a typical damage control action—fry the little fish, but let the shark keep swimming."

"So you claim, but there was never any evidence."

I shrugged.

"You couldn't let it go, though, so they found a way to make you look like the drunk you are, and you ended up out on your ear."

I didn't need this stuff. "Romeo was the worst of cops and the best of cops. He may have been on the take, but he was there when I needed him—"

"Yeah, yeah, yeah. I heard this all before, Ebby. He saved your worthless life. So what? He's dead and buried."

"He was my partner. I owe him. You of all people should know what that means."

Tricksy smiled and stood up. "Yeah, I know what that means." Her voice had softened. "You were my partner also. You taught me a lot, when I was still wet behind the ears. I owe you."

"What does that mean?"

"It means that while you've been sitting on your sorry butt scratching both your groin and a living by peeping in keyholes, I've been using what you taught me to dig up Romeo's killer."

I felt my bowels clench.

She smiled again. Thin-lipped this time. She knew she'd hooked me but good. "I know who killed Romeo."

I felt a sweat break out on my forehead and my heart was

pounding my ribs hard enough to break them.

I finally forced out the one important word. "Who?"

"I'm going to give you a chance to figure it out for your-self, Ebby," she said. "I owe you that much. But it's going to be up to you to do the right thing."

"Why the games?" I asked.

"Why don't you just hang around and have a drink," she said, ignoring my question. "Maybe it'll give you some inspi-ration. Think about things, Ebby. See if there isn't a way for you to square your past and change your future."

She started to walk out of the office, tinkling all the way.

"Wait," I said.

She turned and, just like Santa in the story, she lay a finger alongside her nose. "Merry Christmas, Ebenezer. Keep up the good fight."

She rose up the proverbial chimney before I could stop her. But then again I wasn't sure that I wanted her stopped. I'd learned a long time ago that playing with Tricksy was like playing with a flame-thrower—sooner or later you were going to get burned. She was a good detective. One of the best. I'd trained her good, if I do say so myself. Maybe too good. If she'd found out who killed Romeo and could prove it, then the trouble that had gone before would be nothing compared to the coming storm.

I reached forward and picked up the bottle she'd left on my desk. The seal was already cracked, so it wasn't as fresh as I had imagined, but who was I to deny Tricksy a swig or two off the top. I sat there contemplating the bottle. I tried not to think about the glad tidings Tricksy had brought my way. Well, I had my visit from an angel. Now, all I needed was a visit from three wise-guys to make my Christmas Eve com-plete. If I'd had a manger handy, I'd have crawled in and gone to sleep.

164

EBENEZER

★ ★ ★ ★ ★

When the cuckoo clock on my wall chirped one a.m., Tricksy's bottle was three quarters empty—even from an optimist's point of view. I didn't remember falling asleep, but then they say your memory is always the second thing to go.

I jerked my head up from the desk when there was a loud clatter in the hallway outside my office. My door swung open and somebody ducked their head to enter.

"Santa?" I asked.

"Call me Ishmael," the black giant said, in a voice that Mickey Mouse would have envied. This guy was going to be a whale of a lot of fun.

"I'll call you whatever you want," I said, thinking of the old joke about what you call a six-hundred-pound gorilla. "But as I remember, the last time you and I did the nightstick and handcuff two-step, you were called Tiny Tim. What's with this Ishmael stuff? You become a converted Muslim or something all of a sudden?"

The giant smiled and what office light he wasn't blocking glinted off a gold front tooth. He looked around the office. "Ain't much," he said.

"You a critic for Decorator's Weekly now? You don't like the furnishings then make like a tree and leaf."

"How 'bout a drink for an ol' friend?"

"You were one of my informants. You ain't never been a friend. What do you want?"

"Come on, we be goin' for a sleigh ride."

"I'm not going anywhere."

Suddenly, Ishmael had my collar in one of the meat hooks he calls hands and I was upright and heading for the office door. My head was swimming and I realized that the bottle Tricksy had left behind had been doctored. I'd been slipped a mickey as easily as a john trying to pick up a Singapore whore.

165

I don't remember the sequence, but the next thing I knew we were in Ishmael's sled—a convertible Caddy that had seen better days. The cold wind cleared my head, but my body felt too heavy to move. I could only hope I'd heard right and we were going on a sleigh ride and not a slay-ride.

The Caddy was light blue with dark blue trim. There was also something familiar about it.

The streets were deserted at that time of night and it didn't take us long to drive to the small strip of shops where Romeo had been gunned down in a drive-by shooting. It was up at the top end of the same boulevard on which the Star Building was located, but the shops here were set back from the street. There was a bookstore, a couple of hair salons, a nail clip joint, and tux shop.

I knew now why the Caddy was familiar—the guy who blew Romeo's brains out had been driving one just like it. A drive-by shooting using a Caddy convertible. Who says crooks can't have class?

The windows of the stores in the little strip mall were like blind eyes staring into my soul. I don't mind telling you I was scared—feeling more like Halloween than Christmas.

Ishmael pulled the Caddy over and parked under one of the spreading oak trees that lined the sidewalk. Actually, it was not just one of the spreading oak trees. It was *the* spreading oak tree. The one under which Romeo had died.

"What are we doing here?" I asked.

"Consider me the Ghost of Christmas Past," Ishmael said. "Christmas day, one year ago, Romeo be catching the bullet train right here at this stop."

"So tell me something I don't know." I looked out at the sidewalk and imagined I could almost see the remains of the chalk outline where Romeo's body had fallen. I felt sick. Romeo, Romeo, why for did thou die here, Romeo?

"You always be tellin' me I was your best snitch. Ain't that right, Ebenezer?"

"It's still Mr. Ebenezer to you, punk. But yeah, you was a good snitch. If you couldn't get the information by asking somebody, you'd beat it out of them. Pretty effective."

"But you're gone now, Ebby, and I still gots a jones to feed."

"Ain't Tricksy taking care of you? I passed you on when I was bounced."

"Detective Spillane, she's a nice lady. She don't talk mean like you, just dirty. She even pay more than you did."

"Then she's a fool."

Ishmael C-clamped my throat back against the headrest. "Don't you be talking bad about Detective Spillane, you hear?"

"Yeah," I barely managed to croak.

"She bin askin' questions 'bout who killed Romeo—"

"I already asked all the questions," I said, after Ishmael gave me my throat back. "There aren't any answers."

"There be answers," Ishmael said. "They just ain't the ones you want to hear. You know who killed ol' Romeo. You just don't want anyone else to know."

"What are you talking about?" I wanted to ask, but my head started to swim again and things went a little blank.

When the haze cleared, I was sitting propped up against the glass door of the bookstore. Ishmael didn't seem to be anywhere around. I peered through the glass and saw a soft light on in the bookstore's back room and it drew me like a moth to the flame.

Things were getting mighty weird. Whatever Tricksy had slipped me in that bottle was bringing on the paranoia big time.

I clawed my way to my feet and freed my forty-five from under my left pit. The butt of it in my hand felt as warm and familiar as a lover's breast.

The address on the glass door was 2-B. Maybe I could run, but I couldn't hide. If I left now, the past would just catch up again later. 2-B or not 2-B? That is the question. Whether it is better to suffer the cruelties and self-recriminations of a coward, or to take up my forty-five against whatever sea of troubles lay ahead and by charging straight-ahead defeat them.

Stream of consciousness was not another of my strong suits. I pushed open the door and bulled in hard and fast. I took the corner into the back room like a whirlwind and was brought up short by a classy looking dame munching on milk and cookies.

"Ah, Ebenezer," she said, in a calm voice. "I'm so glad you came. It's Christmas time in the city, you know? And I'm just checking my list to see who has been naughty or nice."

"Isn't that the big fat guy in the red suit's job?"

The dame laughed. "Oh, don't be silly." She took a huge scroll off her desk that said SANTA'S LIST in big letters at the top. She started unraveling it as if she were a kid playing with a toilet roll. "Now, let me see here. Ebenezer? Ebenezer? Hmmmmmm." She slid on the pair of reading glasses that had been bouncing on her remarkable pulchritude, held there by a chain around her neck.

"Ah, here it is. Ebenezer." She squinted just a little. "Oh, my."

"Oh, my?" I asked.

She turned to me, brushed the forty-five away, and walked into the main part of the store. I felt foolish holding the gun. I slipped it back under my pit for safe keeping and followed the dame. She turned on another low light at the front desk.

"Oh my?" I asked again.

She was studying the list again under the light. "Oh, my. Oh, my. Oh, my!"

This was getting monotonous.

"Can we cut to the chase here?"

"I'm surprised at you, Ebenezer. You have been a naughty boy."

"Who are you? My mom?"

"No, Ebenezer, I'm the Ghost of Christmas Presents."

"Give me a break. And don't you mean the Ghost of Christmas Present?"

"Ebenezer, you little dickens. You always were a nit-picker."

"Used to sell those nits by the bushel load. Made for a good off-duty income."

"Yes, it certainly did."

"Hey, I was only joking."

"No, you weren't, Ebenezer. The nits you picked were everybody's little secrets. Cops get to know lots and lots of secrets. They get to know all the skeletons in all the closets, where all the fabled bodies are buried."

"It goes with the territory. You find out stuff, you make an arrest—"

"Ah, Ebenezer, but that's where you became a naughty boy, isn't it. Instead of arrests, you started making blackmail demands. No, no toys for you from Santa anymore. Just a lump of coal at the bottom of your stocking. You crossed the line, Ebenezer. Naughty, not nice."

I felt grim. This broad was getting under my skin. It sounded like she knew too much for her own good, and mine. My forty-five was hanging heavy in its holster. "Make your point," I said.

"The point is that Romeo wasn't the dirty cop. You were.

Blackmail is such a sordid little sideline. Romeo was on to you, wasn't he? Partners are close, very close. You couldn't keep something like blackmail hidden from him forever."

I felt as if I was sweating blood. My head was starting to sway and fear was crawling out of my gut like an evil specter. "You don't know what you're talking about!"

"Oh, yes I do, Ebenezer. It's all here on Santa's list." The dame held up her scroll. "All the naughty and nice things everyone does. I check it twice and then forward a copy to St. Peter."

I gave the dame a quizzical look.

"What?" she asked. "You didn't know Heaven subscribed to our mailing list? Absolutely. Helps to keep the lines down at the Pearly Gates if St. Peter already has St. Nick's list. There's a lot more riding on this naughty or nice stuff than just a new red bike or a lump of coal."

"Give me that list," I said. I reached out to grab it, but the big dark opened up again and I fell in.

When I came around again, I was back in my office sitting behind my desk. I thought maybe I was looking in a mirror, but then I'd never installed a mirror in the client seat opposite my own. I closed my eyes and shook my head, but I was still there when I looked again.

"What are you selling?" I asked. "Gold, frankincense, or myrrh?"

"You don't look as if you could afford much, boy," my mirror image said to me. "In fact, you look like Hades."

"If you're me," I said, "then I don't look that bad."

"I'm you, alright, but I'm you before you became what you are now."

"Run that by me again. Ain't you supposed to be the Ghost of Christmas Yet to Come, or some such nonsense? I mean, let's keep the story straight."

"There may be no Christmases yet to come for you, Ebenezer. This might just be it."

I stared into my eyes and knew what I was telling myself was true. I reached out for the remains of Tricksy's bottle with a shaky hand.

"You drink too much," I said to me.

"What are you? My friggin' conscience?"

"Exactly."

"Whoa," I said, taken aback despite myself. After a second, I found the nerve to ask, "What about Ishmael and the weird dame with the list?"

"All parts of you, just like me."

"Get outta here."

"Ishmael is the brute in us come to the surface, the terror that helped us face down scumbags without succumbing to fear."

"And the dame with the list?"

"We were a good cop, because we are anal-retentive. Always had her around to take care of the details."

Mirror image or not, real or imagined, Mr. Conscience was faster than I was. I went for my forty-five, fear running my every emotion, but he was there first and snatched the gat away.

"Come, come, Ebenezer. It's Christmas Eve. Is this any time for gun play?" He threw the gun on the desk in front of me. I went to grab it, but it was suddenly heavier than an anchor.

"What do you all want from me?"

"Redemption, Ebenezer. Redemption."

I started to cry. "There is no redemption. I killed him. My partner. Romeo found out about what I was doing—the blackmail. I couldn't let him tell the world I'd crossed the line, so I drove by and shot him like a punk in the street. I planted evidence. Made him the bad guy . . ." I blubbered on and on, the words flowing out of me in huge waves, gasping for breath between tears. "But nobody knew. Nobody knew. Just me."

"Santa knew," Mr. Conscience said. "He knows who's been naughty or nice."

"There is no redemption for what I've done," I said to me again.

"There is always redemption. There is always forgiveness. Especially, on Christmas Eve."

I looked at the weapon on my desk. "What do you want me to do? Smoke my gun?"

"That's no way to gain redemption," Mr. Conscience was talking again. "There has to be atonement."

"I can't carry this burden anymore," I said, yanking at the gun trying to pull it free from the desk.

"Ebenezer, calm yourself."

I stopped my frantic tugging. There was something, something from the part of me that hadn't turned rotten.

"Don't fight yourself anymore, Ebenezer. You know what is right. You've strayed from the path, but you still know what is right. You can still be forgiven—can get yourself back on the nice list—get a red bicycle for Christmas."

I sat back slowly in my chair and closed my eyes.

It was cold up on the roof. I was sitting at the base of the bright neon star that topped the Star Building. Could there really be redemption, I wondered.

I'd had alcoholic blackouts before. I'd even seen the creatures brought on by the DTs. But I'd never experienced anything like the hallucinations that Tricksy's bottle of bourbon had delivered.

EBENEZER

I looked at the neon star. It was Christmas. I loved obvious symbolism.

Next to where I was sitting there were the two items I'd brought with me. My forty-five and my portable phone.

Two choices.

Naughty or nice.

A red bicycle or a lump of coal.

Redemption through confession and atonement. Or having St. Peter displeased when he came to my name on his copy of Santa's list.

I'd been a nice cop once. I was a naughty ex-cop now.

Could there really still be a chance to get back on the right side of the list?

When I made it, the choice wasn't really that hard.

I picked up the forty-five and snuggled the tip of the barrel up against my temple.

I always did have a flair for the dramatic.

I held my pose for a second and then slid the magazine out of the gun butt, flipped out the bullets, and scattered them like hard raindrops over the edge of the building.

I watched them fall and listened to them ping off the concrete so very far below.

I walked back to the neon star and picked up the phone.

I dialed the number of the detective squad room. I knew it by heart.

She answered. I knew she would.

"Hello, Ebenezer," she said.

"Hello, Tricksy."

"I was beginning to worry," she said. "I thought maybe I'd overestimated you."

"How'd you like to come over?" I asked. "I have something to tell you."

"I hope it's more than Merry Christmas."

173

"Bring your handcuffs," I said and hung up. Tricksy was kinky enough to like that last part.

I looked out across the city. Christmas lights twinkled with promise in the false dawn.

Merry Christmas, I said to myself, beginning to unwrap the gift of redemption. *And to all a good night.*

For me, stories begin in several ways—a plot
twist, an intriguing title, or a character taking life as my creative
muscles engage in intercourse. **Derringer** *began with the character*
of Blue MacKenzie, a
burned-out, ex-CIA agent, turned body building private eye, but
the problem in starting with a character
is finding an appropriate plot in which to involve him.
Blue MacKenzie had been in my head for a long time
before a case I was investigating in real life showed me
the possibility of a bizarre little twist. When reality didn't
follow the twist, I realized Blue MacKenzie could.

DERRINGER
A Blue MacKenzie Story

When the end of your life stares at you from the business end
of a gun, the barrel opening appears bigger than creation. If
you expect to survive, you have to get beyond the fear of
death. You have to tear your attention away from the tun-
nel-size opening and focus on the real threat, the finger on the
trigger. If you neutralize the threat on the trigger, then the
gun is useless. It is something only a professional can do, but
then I've survived being on the wrong side of a gun enough
times to be considered a pro.

This time, however, it was going to be a tough call. The
threat with his finger on the trigger was an amateur, and
looked about as stable as a lemming heading for the nearest
cliff.

★ ★ ★ ★ ★

Three days earlier I had been throwing the heavy iron around when Lacy called across the gym floor and told me Max Venables was on the phone. I finished the set of dead lifts I was working on and picked up a towel to wipe the sweat out of my eyes.

"Tell him I'll call him back," I groused, upset at the break in concentration.

"He said it was important," Lacy persisted.

Max is an entertainment lawyer and a close friend. Whenever he has a chance, he sends a client in my direction. In the entertainment business everything is important. Even bowel movements can become media events.

"I'll still call him back," I said.

Lacy shrugged her shoulders in resignation and glided back to the phone on the reception desk. I noticed the gains she was making with her calves. Lacy hasn't been pushing iron long, but she's blessed with a natural, physical aptitude.

She turned up at Derringer's Gym, which I own, about a year ago. Since then, she's turned into one of the sport's fastest rising stars, and has become an irreplaceable assistant. Her business and managerial abilities make it possible for me to help people, such as Max's clients, when the mood takes me.

I hit the weights again, blitzing my back muscles, isolating each one and really blasting it with weight, striving to obtain maximum geometric development. I did twelve reps of dead-lifts with a 445 pound bar, and then flowed straight into two sets of hyperextensions. For the next hour, I worked my lats, my traps, and the small muscles across the top of the shoulders. I finished off with a set of ultra shrugs that had me seeing stars. I was so wasted I could barely keep my head up, but my erectors felt like two steel pythons running up either side of my spine.

I showered in my small apartment over the gym, and changed into an old pair of Levi 501's, a plaid work shirt, and Tony Lamas. I slipped my two-inch derringer into the holster sewn inside my left boot and called Max . We agreed to meet in an hour at Yesterdays. Lacy stuffed some checks and order forms under my nose. I signed them while watching two dozen sweaty bodies battle with their pain threshold on the main floor. I told Lacy where I was headed, and bobbed out the door for the fifteen-minute drive to the restaurant.

I'd started lifting weights when I was fifteen. At seventeen, I won the title of Mr. Junior Universe. At eighteen, my weightlifting career was curtailed when Uncle Sam sent me to Vietnam and introduced me to something else at which I was good—killing.

Two tours and uncountable LURP missions later, the war ended and the CIA picked up my option. For the next five years, I plied my violent trade throughout the Pacific until the stress caught up with me and brought on a total physical and mental breakdown.

I can talk about it now, but at the time I thought it was the end of my life. I was pulled out of the field, given a small pension for services rendered, and stuck back into the real world of civilian life, a life I had forgotten existed. At twenty-five, I was a burned-out shell with nothing inside.

Somehow, I found a solitary spark buried somewhere, and began to put myself back together using the only thing that meant anything to me—bodybuilding. For a while I was as happy as a pig in poop. I bought Derringer's and found escape pumping up my 6'3" frame with a 58" chest, 23" arms, 29" thighs, 20" calves, 34" waist, and 275 pounds of various other muscles. After a year, though, I began to feel something was missing.

The need for the hunt had come alive again. I fought it until, with the help of a psychiatrist, I came to accept it as a part of me, and realized I might be able to use it for the right reasons for a change.

The CIA sniffed around for a bit, but I sent them packing in no uncertain terms. Instead, I posted a twenty-five-hundred-dollar bond, passed a civil service exam, and hung a private investigator's license behind the door of my bathroom.

I didn't advertise my services, but picked up work from old contacts who still operated in areas that provided a need for an independent investigator. Since then word-of-mouth has brought more than one client around to drop his troubles on my doorstep.

The LA weather was acting as if it had no idea it was winter. I had the top down on my Mustang and found the short drive to meet Max invigorating. Yesterdays is one of my favorite watering holes. It has a dozen or so tables on its second-floor balcony that overlooks the Westwood street scene. When I entered, I found Max and another man already sitting in the far corner.

"Hello, Blue." Max stood up and extended his hand. Tall and rapier thin, he was dapper in the pinstripe of his conservative dark blue suit. Before taking over his father's law firm, Max had been my field control for two years in the South Pacific. On occasion, I wondered just how completely he'd put away his cloak and dagger.

He gestured to the man sitting next to him. "Blue, meet Harry Stein, owner of Nightsong Records." Ever the gentleman, he gestured back towards me, "Harry—Blue MacKenzie."

Stein stood and I shook his hand, he seemed impressed by my size, which I don't like to see happen. It makes clients think you're going to break heads rather than use one. At one time Stein had probably been in fair shape himself, but there were too many businessman's lunches and not enough workouts under his belt now.

"Harry has a problem you might be able to help him solve." Max came right to the point after we were seated and I had a sweating bottle of Harps in front of me.

"Have you ever heard of Nightsong Records, Mr. Mac-Kenzie?" Stein asked. When I shook my head, he looked at Max as if to say I should have at least made out as if I'd heard of his company, if only to soothe his ego. I didn't tell him to call me Blue.

Max covered smoothly as always. "Have you ever heard any recordings by Charity Ross?"

"Sure," I replied. "She has a current country-rock crossover hit called *Moonwatch*. The critics are having a field day calling her the new Crystal Gayle." I rapidly made the mental connections. "I take it Nightsong Records is Charity's recording label."

Stein smiled, revealing two gold teeth. "That's right. Charity has been with Nightsong since the start of her career. She's now the mainstay of our catalogue." Stein suddenly looked uncomfortable.

"The fact of the matter is," Max cut through the garbage, "after twenty years in Nashville, if it wasn't for Charity Ross, Nightsong Records would have to close the studio doors."

Stein turned a bit purple at Max's bluntness, but didn't deny the observation.

I waited a beat, sipping beer. When Stein didn't offer anything further, I pressed on. "Aside from having all your eggs in one basket, and that egg being number three with a bullet on both the country and rock charts, what other problems do you have?"

"She's gone," Stein said morosely. He was staring at his

half-empty glass, and idly making wet rings on the table.

"Gone?" I looked at Max, and then back at Stein. He finally raised his eyes to meet mine.

"She disappeared over a month ago with her next CD only half finished. A week later, I received a letter from her asking me to forward her mail and her residuals to a post office box in Los Angeles. I sent her several letters imploring her to get in touch with me and let me know what was going on. The only reply I received was a short note telling me not to worry and again asking for me to forward her checks."

"Wouldn't her checks go through her agent?"

"I'm her agent as well as her producer. And if I don't get her new CD in the stores before Christmas, I might as well forget being around to celebrate New Year's. I held back her residuals, but didn't get any response. Last week, I decided to fly out to find her, but I don't really know where to start. The post office says she hasn't picked up her mail in two weeks, and that was my only lead."

I thought for a moment. "Does she have any other money that she can access?"

"An accountant handles her cash flow and the movement of money within her investments. It was one of the reasons I was surprised she asked for her residual checks to be forwarded directly to her. Normal procedure is for everything to be handled through her accountant. In day-to-day life, she really has no need to handle paper money."

I tried to conceive that kind of existence.

"Frankly, I'm at my wit's end, so I've had to resort to something I dislike. I'm taking Charity to court to get her to honor her contract and finish her CD."

I looked at Stein in amazement. "You can't be naive enough to think you can get a civil case through the courts in time to get a CD on the stands for Christmas."

"No, I'm not that naive, but I'm not without influence. With a little string pulling, I've arranged for a preliminary hearing of the case in Nashville next week. I want you to find Charity and serve her a subpoena. I don't expect the court to resolve anything, but if I can talk to Charity face to face, I know I can get her to come back willingly. Max handles some of my west coast dealings. He seems to have faith that you can help."

I glared at Max. This wasn't my kind of thing. However, I owed Max several favors. "Does Charity have any friends in LA?" I asked.

"A few friends in the business, naturally, but I've checked with them."

"How about relatives?"

"Her mother and sister are back in Nashville. Her father left the family a long time ago, before Charity started singing. All her other relatives are still in Texas where I discovered her." The last declaration was said with a touch of pride.

"Did she say anything to anyone before she left?"

"Not word one. She left the studio late on a Friday night after a really good session. Saturday, we had dinner with friends and she was full of enthusiasm for how the CD was coming along. I called her Sunday night, but there was no answer. On Monday, she just didn't show up for the studio session."

"How about a boyfriend or a lover?"

To my surprise Stein actually blushed. "Charity and I have been close for quite a while. There was no one else for either of us. It's one of the reasons I can't understand her taking off. I'm worried sick."

The blush made me like him a bit more, but I still couldn't help wondering if he was more worried about his lover or his nest egg.

"My fee is five hundred dollars a day plus all expenses. You'll get an itemized list. I'll want a week's retainer, refundable if my fee doesn't run that high. If that's agreeable, Max will write up a contract for you to sign."

"Thank you," said Stein. Max smiled weakly at me.

"I also want the P.O. box number Charity gave you, a copy of the subpoena, a stack of publicity stills, and a number where I can reach you."

Max had anticipated me and handed over a thick manila envelope.

"Please hurry, Mr. MacKenzie," Stein implored me as I stood up.

I didn't bother replying.

On the way home, I picked up a copy of Charity's *Moonwatch* CD at the local music mart. Upstairs in my room, I put it on the stereo, and a throaty voice began to drift softly from my speakers. I dug into my small collection of CDs. My personal taste runs more to Tom Waits or Jimmy Buffet, but I had been given a copy of one of Charity's earlier CDs as a gift. I finally found it and pulled it out.

The picture on the cover showed a blossoming young girl with rose-petal skin wearing a full-length skirt topped with a peasant blouse. A yellow ribbon wove through her waist-length, blond hair, which was blowing wildly in the wind.

The photo on the current CD was a shocking contrast. Charity's hair was now bobbed in a short, almost punkish style, her body had become a woman's and was poured into a skin-tight, black jumpsuit. Her eyes were filled with a kind of hollow hunger, which she hadn't known existed when the first photo was taken.

Her voice had changed too. The new sound reaching my

ears was rougher, sexier, even a bit cynical, but also seemed to be struggling to meet the demands of her new image. It had happened to countless others before her. Charity was just another victim of fame, demand, adulation, and manipulation. I thought again about a lifestyle where you never handled any of your own money.

I waited until the CD ended before picking up the phone and jabbing in the number for the Postal Inspectors, the security branch of the mail service.

There is really nothing mysterious about detective work. All it requires is a simple recipe of two parts common sense blended with equal measures of perseverance and luck. While simmering the basic ingredients over a world-weary flame, you add a pinch of cynicism and a dash of toughness. The most important step comes just prior to serving when the whole concoction is stuffed into a wrapper of intelligence and sprinkled liberally with contacts—the one ingredient you can't leave out when baking a detective. Knowing where to go and who to talk to is what separates the detective from his employer. It's what he gets paid for. It's the reason Harry Stein had no idea where to start, but I did.

When the phone connected, I asked for Sally Swain and was placed on ignore while somebody tried to find her. I'd met Sally at a bodybuilding contest six months earlier. Since that time, she had changed from a voyeur to an actual fan of the sport.

"Howdy, stranger. Staying hard?" she asked when she came on the line.

"I'm still throwing the iron around if that's what you mean."

"You know it isn't."

"Does your mother know you talk dirty?"

"Who do you think taught me?"

"It's more than my life is worth to answer that one. Listen, I need a favor."

"I'll be right over."

"Whoa, girl. Cool your jets. I only want you to find out the owner information on a P.O. box number."

"What's in it for me?"

"Dinner at Milano's?"

"Followed by a session of pumping iron back at your place?"

"We'll see what develops."

"You are so wishy-washy sometimes. Okay, okay, give me the box number."

I did so and Sally returned me to the ignore button while she looked up the information on the office computer. After ten minutes of listening to elevator Montovani, her sunny voice came back on the line.

"This sounds like something right up your alley. The box is registered to Barbarians Inc. in Westlake." She rattled off a street address almost quicker than I could copy it down. "Remember," she said. "Drinks, dinner, champagne, dancing, more champagne, and then back to your place to see what comes up." The itinerary appeared to have expanded somewhat.

"I'll call you."

"Sure you will—next time you need a favor."

When I hung up the phone the receiver was smoking. Sally scares me to death.

I'd heard of Barbarians Inc. before. Instead of advertising in reputable muscle magazines, they promoted themselves on the back pages of comic books, true detective tabloids, and soldier-of-fortune rags. They promised instant muscles if you used their miracle protein powders, gimmick exercise machines, and wonder workout courses. They were part of the dark stigma that has given bodybuilding a bad name over the years—suckering kids and young adults into thinking there is an easy way to achieve the body beautiful without the agonizing hours of work.

I was a bit surprised to have the investigation lead back to my own doorstep, but then again, Max Venables is a crafty bastard and probably knew the direction things would take when he recommended me to Harry Stein.

Even when Max was acting as my control—when we were *playing the game*—he often wouldn't tell everything he knew. It was his way of double-checking his own information. If I independently uncovered facts that coincided with intelligence already in Max's files, then chances were the information was reliable. It was also a system that allowed Max to pick the right agent for a job. If he believed Charity Ross's disappearance was somehow connected with the world of bodybuilding, even if it was the sleazy side of the game, it was no wonder he had steered things in my direction.

If I remembered correctly, Barbarians Inc. had recently been the subject of an investigation by a television news magazine. Claims were made that Barbarian exercise machines and equipment were worthless and could not possibly live up to the declarations made by the manufacturers. Even more damaging were the allegations that the protein powders sold by Barbarians were laced with illegal steroids—fat-soluble compounds used to increase muscle mass at a high risk to the user's health. Logic dictated a trip out to the home base of Barbarians to see what crawled out when I turned it over.

Westwood to Westlake is a thirty-minute trip across the San Fernando Valley and into the environs of Ventura County. Christmas tree lots were staked out along the route, but were not yet stocked. I pulled off the freeway at Hampshire road and stopped in the parking lot of a K-Mart to check my map. Another two minutes of driving through a tangle of side streets brought me to a small industrial complex where I found Barbarians Inc. sandwiched between an Adidas shoe warehouse and a clothing manufacturer's sweatshop.

When I tried Barbarians's front door, I found I should have saved myself the trip. The door was locked down tight and the interior of the office was as dark as the whale's belly after Jonah's candle went out. There were some deep gouges around the lock area of the doorframe. It looked as if someone had tried to break in. I walked around to the back of the building, but found the warehouse-type sliding metal door was also secured. There were no emergency numbers posted.

I was about to leave when a security guard came around the corner and approached me. "Can I help you sir?" Even though he was looking back at middle age, the guard was in fair shape, no potbelly or overflowing love handles. His uniform was crisply pressed and his leather gear was not only clean, but shiny.

"I'm looking for somebody connected with Barbarians Inc."

"You and half the rest of the world," he spoke with a smile. "Don't tell me they sucked somebody like you in with their ads," he said taking in my size. "If they did, you're probably their only success story."

I grinned a grin. "No I don't use their products. I'm just trying to get in touch with the owner or his representative."

"You're not a cop or a reporter," the guard said, giving me the eye. "What are you, private heat?"

I nodded confirmation.

"Thought so," he said. "I was an LA cop for thirty years,

and I can still spot a keyhole peeper a mile away. No offense intended."

"None taken. What did you mean when you said me and half the rest of the world?"

"Well, two days after that TV news magazine, *Contrast*, aired its story about Barbarians, investigators from the Federal Food and Drug Administration showed up here and started making noises about court cases and legal suits. As soon as they left, Barbarians closed their doors, and I haven't seen the staff since." The guard paused to adjust his leather gear slightly. "The following evening someone broke into the offices and threw the files all over the place. It was impossible to tell if anything was taken."

"Any idea who did it?"

"A few. The day before it happened, I caught a tall, skinny kid with dark, curly hair snooping around. He claimed he'd ordered some items from Barbarians, was dissatisfied with them, and wanted to get his money back. It's my guess he came back later to try and recoup his losses somehow."

I took one of Charity's publicity photos out of my jacket pocket and flashed it face-forward. "Have you ever seen this girl around?"

The guard's eyes flicked to the photo for an instant and then switched back to me. I wouldn't have wanted him hunting me while he was still on the force. I wouldn't want him hunting me now.

"I saw her go into Barbarians the day before they closed shop. She left a few hours later with the owner, Alex Rivers."

"You have a home address for Rivers?"

"Nope. And I wouldn't give you one if I did."

I spent a second wondering how far some long green might go. He seemed to read my mind.

"Don't bother reaching for your wallet. I wasn't on the

pad with the force, and I'm not about to jump on now."

I grinned another grin. Had I really found an honest man? "Okay, thanks for your help. If the girl or anybody else shows up, I'd appreciate a call." I handed him a card.

I drove back to the K-Mart and parked next to a pay phone. I was still burping Halloween candy, but the windows of the discount store were ready for Santa. I used the phone to call a television writer I knew from the gym. When I told him what I wanted, he quickly agreed to find out who wrote the Barbarians segment for *Contrast* and set up an interview for me along with a screening of the segment. It was exactly what I wanted to hear.

The following morning, a brisk wind had cleared the hills and I was on the road with the top down again by nine. I presented myself at the *Contrast* studio doors in Burbank. I was clean-shaven, and nattily dressed in brown slacks, a yellow Polo shirt, and a tweed jacket. My loafers were highly polished, but didn't sport any tassels.

I'd already put in ten miles of dawn roadwork. Exercise is my version of Holmes's cocaine habit. When the jagged edge of depression rears up, I turn to pumping iron and workout with a vengeance, to the point where nothing can penetrate my self-imposed wall of weight and pain. When I take on a case, though, my dormant instincts run rampant, keeping depression at bay, and for a while I feel like a live wire again. But I still had to do something physical every day.

Inside the lobby, I asked for Toby Wainwright, the writer of the Barbarians segment. I was told to wait and took a seat on a too-soft couch along one wall. Out of the corner of my eye, I watched the female receptionist struggle between being repulsed by my muscles or slipping me her phone number. Repulsion won.

After a couple of long minutes, a tall woman with long, well-shaped legs stepped out of the elevator and walked toward me on red high heels. Thick auburn hair tumbled down her back, and even across the lobby I could see light flashing off her jade green eyes. Her knee-length, cream-colored dress was made of a soft silk that flattered her curves and accentuated the upturned tilt of her breasts. The left side of the dress was slit high enough to catch my breath in my throat.

I remembered a friend who, when asked if he had ever slept with a redhead replied, "Not a wink." I knew what I was putting on my Christmas list. I certainly hoped I'd been good enough.

"Mr. MacKenzie?" she asked, extending the long fingers of her right hand towards me. "I'm Toby Wainwright."

I was caught off guard and almost stammered. I'd figured her for Wainwright's secretary and my pass to the inner sanctum.

"Your male chauvinism is showing, Mr. MacKenzie." The twinkle in her eye let me know she was used to my kind of response.

"Don't tell me, you have a brother whose name is Sue."

"His name is Leslie, actually. But he's learned to live with it." She smiled nicely, and I released her hand, which had been firm and cool.

She asked me if I wanted to screen the *Contrast* segment first and talk after. I agreed, and quickly found myself ensconced in a screening room with a cup of lukewarm coffee. The fifteen-minute piece of film which flashed across the screen was the standard type of TV journalism which leaves you feeling you know all the answers, but are a little foggy on what the questions were.

The main thrust of the segment seemed to focus on two

points—the unknown and shady background of Barbarians's owner Alex Rivers, and the allegations claiming Barbarians's protein powders were full of illegal drugs while their vitamin supplements were nothing more than gelatin based placebos. When the film ended, Toby brought me another cup of coffee and sat down in the seat next to mine. I could just sense the barest whiff of her perfume.

I asked the obvious question first. "What brought Barbarians to your attention?"

"*Contrast*'s producers were looking to do a series of segments on consumer rip-offs, it's the popular thing right now, and I was assigned to check into the chain health spas you see doing a lot of advertising. In the process, I came across numerous get-fit-quick schemes—the type of things designed to appeal to a person's initial enthusiasm in the hopes that, after paying their money, the consumer will stop following the program, diet, exercise or gimmick long before they realize it isn't working." She stopped talking for a moment to sip her coffee and rearrange her legs. The movements pulled her dress tight across her body.

She noticed me watching her and returned my gaze with a mischievous look. Bodybuilders thrive on being looked at, so I've never understood why some women get upset if you visually appreciate them. Toby's acceptance of my lecherousness made a nice change.

"I singled Barbarians out of the pack," she continued, "because their ads seemed designed to appeal more to the youth market. I was also able to come up with a few juicy horror stories, like the one in the film about the boy's liver failure which was blamed on the steroids in Barbarians protein powder." She looked a little sheepish. "I know it sounds callous, but you have to have something to use as a hook in this business."

I smiled reassuringly, and she continued.

"After the chemical analysis of Barbarians's products started coming back, I knew I was on to a good fraud story. I started a background check on Alex Rivers, but ran into a brick wall. Rivers didn't have a past, and it took my sources until the segment was written and taped before they could uncover any reliable info."

"They find anything interesting?"

"There's still not much, but apparently Rivers was a nickel-and-dime con-man kicking around the Midwest until he hooked up with a kindred spirit named John Vreeling. Together they went into a legitimate machinery rental/supply business in Texas.

"Surprisingly, the business boomed for about ten years before Rivers forced it to the verge of bankruptcy by fiddling the books. There was a big scandal and Rivers skipped town, leaving his family to the welfare rolls, and his partner, Vreeling, so desperate he committed suicide.

"Rivers moved around quite a bit after that, always one step ahead of the law and his creditors. He made some good money by running several medium-size mail-order scams, which gave him the backing to open Barbarians three years ago."

"Where does he get his supplies from?" I asked, mesmerized as she recrossed her legs.

"The body building gimmicks are made up and shipped from a warehouse in the Midwest, but the protein powders, diet supplements, and vitamins are all manufactured in Mexico. He has a small hideaway somewhere down there."

I drank some more of the tepid coffee. "How did Rivers react when you started snooping around?"

"To say the least, he was uncooperative. Byron Owens, who set up all of Barbarians's exercise programs, was more helpful until Rivers found out he was talking to us. I think Owens really believed everything was on the up-and-up."

I knew Owens. He was a second-rate bodybuilder with the physical potential to become a champion, but he didn't have what it takes between the ears or in the heart. Unfortunately, Owens was a walking stereotype of the muscle-bound oaf.

"You know, of course, what happened to Stella Constantine?" Toby asked me earnestly.

Bells jangled in the back of my head. "A couple of weeks ago, in the newspapers, they were reporting her murder. I remember the details as being pretty graphic, involving rape and torture. The police listed it as a S/M session gone bad when they recovered all the whips and chains from her house. Witnesses stated they'd seen her that night at a local club with a new man on her arm who nobody knew. Description was vague, tall, dark, slender, no further. What does she have to do with Barbarians?"

"She was Barbarians's nutritionist, and Rivers's on-again-off-again mistress. He didn't even show up for the funeral."

"I guess he was in one of the off-again stages." I paused. There was something nagging at me, but I couldn't quite capture it.

I pressed on. "What happened after the segment aired?"

"I gave all my information to the Food and Drug Administration. They started their own investigation and now want to bring Rivers up on charges. The police are also interested, having now linked Rivers to a warrant stemming from the embezzlement charges in Texas. That's all fine and dandy except Rivers is nowhere to be found."

"When did the Barbarians segment air?"

"A month ago. On the 28th to be precise."

I was definitely on a roll now. I could feel it. The 28th was the night Charity disappeared. I brought out the publicity photo of Charity. "Have you seen this girl since the segment was put on the air?"

"No, but I know who she is—Charity Ross. How is she involved?"

"She's missing, and I'm looking. The more I look, the more it seems like she's tied in with this Rivers character."

"Is she in trouble?" Toby's voice had taken on a note of urgency, and I looked at her sharply.

"Not that I know of, but she left her record company with a pile of it."

"I think I have a bomb for you, Blue. Alex Rivers's real name is Appleton Ross!"

The detective business is like swinging at a piñata—sooner or later, the bat is going to connect with the papier-mâché and the goodies are going to tumble out.

I spent another hour with Toby going over her research. As we did, a pattern of events rapidly emerged, with the *Contrast* segment as the catalyst. The TV ratings gave *Contrast* a 35% share of the viewing audience for Sunday the 28th, about 64 million people tuned in. Charity Ross had only been one of that 64 million, but she was also the only one that recognized Alex Rivers as the father who had abandoned her years before. I wondered if the reunion had gone anything like she anticipated.

After the *Contrast* segment aired, and the FDA began poking around, Rivers had responded like a true con-man—shutting down his scam, and dropping from view. My concern was that he had taken Charity with him.

There was also something else concerning me. The little feeling I hadn't been able to pin down had finally connected up the description of Stella Constantine's killer with the description of the suspect the security guard believed broke into the Barbarians office.

I asked Toby if she had a current address for Byron Owens. She dug it out of her files and scribbled it on a slip of paper for me. When we parted company, I looked at the note and saw she had added her home phone number in bold red letters. I grinned like a naughty schoolboy.

Returning to my car, I drove to Woodland Hills—a bedroom community at the west end of the San Fernando Valley. The address Toby had given me for Owens was in a large group of semi-detached townhouses on Topanga Canyon just below the Warner Center. Townhouses, like condominiums, have become all the rage as an alternative to the overpriced conventional housing in LA. Their huddled masses can be found all over the city like acne on a teenager's face.

The units I was interested in were all painted a uniform dull brown. With their identical wood and stucco fronts, I felt sorry for a drunk trying to find his way home in the middle of the night. After a couple of wrong turns, I located Owens's cubical and knocked on the front door. It was opened almost immediately by a tall effeminate looking youth with a shock of scraggly blond hair. He had a Christmas tree light earring and tinsel draped around his neck.

"My God! Are you a friend of Byron's?" he exclaimed as his eyes roamed all over my body. I suddenly understood about women and lecherous looks. I gave him a hard stare and he took a step backwards.

"Sorry," he said in a more normal voice.

"It's okay. I'd like to talk to Byron if he's in."

"He's down in the recreation room," said the youth pointing a long-nailed finger towards another brown building. "That's where he keeps his weights. Sometimes I think he cares more about his body than mine."

I looked at the kid's slight, willowish frame and wondered

what there was to care about. He took my look the wrong way.

"If you decide you'd rather talk to me, I'm at Whiskey Creek on Sepulveda most nights." The lisp had made a comeback.

"Thanks, but I don't go both ways."

"Shame," he said and closed the door.

As I passed the pool on the way to the recreation room, I could hear the familiar crashing of heavy metal weights which goes with weight training. I pushed open the recreation room's sliding glass door and stepped inside.

Owens was totally absorbed on a Nautilus bench press machine. He had 350 pounds held halfway up. His biceps bulged like small mountains, and his pectorals look like coils of heavy rope. I waited as he slowly pushed the weight up and then slowly brought it down again to finish his set. As he lay on the bench, sweat glistening on his skin, breathing returning to normal, I noticed a bottle of cheap vodka under the bench.

"Hi, Byron," I said with an over-accentuated lisp, which I couldn't resist.

He looked up violently, the initial anger in his eyes, however, changed to disinterest when he recognized me. We had never been close, but we had been on talking terms until now.

"I see you've met Larry," he said wearily.

"I just bet he prefers to be called Lawrence. I didn't know you were into boys."

"It isn't something I like to broadcast, and I'd appreciate it if you keep it to yourself."

That was fair enough.

With one hand he picked up the bottle from under the bench and took a long pull from its neck.

"What the hell are you doing?" I was amazed, wondering what kind of effect the alcohol was having on him during the workout let alone any bodybuilding diet.

"Don't even attempt to lecture me, MacKenzie. Especially if you want something. I'll work out my way, you work out yours."

"How did you know I want something?"

"You've got no other reason to come around here. You're just like everyone else. First that reporter bitch, then those pricks from the FDA, then some kid who I don't know from Adam, and now you. It's getting like I should open up shop and charge admission."

At the mention of the unknown kid, I felt the pot on my back burner start to boil over. I waited impatiently for Owens to finish another set on the bench.

"This kid? Was he tall, slender, curly black hair?"

"Yeah."

"What did he want?"

"Same as everyone else. He wanted to know where Alex was."

"Did you tell him?"

"Him, the police, and the FDA. That prick has brought me so much grief, it's only fair he should share some of it."

"When was the kid here? Did he tell you his name?"

Owens took another swig from his bottle. I noticed his eyes were becoming fuzzy around the edges. The pupils were beading up like a mean pig's.

"He was here about two weeks ago. If he told me his name I don't remember it."

That put the kid's visit after Stella Constantine's murder. For some reason I felt a chill run up my spine.

I tried a long shot. "Did Stella Constantine know where Alex was?"

Owens was quiet for a moment. "She loved him, you know —like I did. But when his daughter showed up after seeing that TV show, Stella became jealous. She didn't understand the girl was just a new toy for Alex—that as soon as he got tired of playing daddy, he'd dump the tyke and come back to us. But, because Stella was making such a scene, Alex didn't want her following him, so when he split, he didn't tell her anything."

Even though I didn't know her, I felt a little sick to my stomach at the thought of Stella Constantine in the hands of a torturer who was convinced she had information she didn't have. It can be a fine line between torture and murder, and the presence of the tall, curly headed kid, who was shadowing this entire case, had obviously stepped over that line.

"Where is Alex?" I asked.

"You too, huh? Well, the more the merrier, I guess. He's on his way to Mexico. He has a house there, hidden away on the south bank of Puerto Vallarta. 187 Calle de Pedregal."

"What do you mean on his way?"

"He's taking his time, sailing his boat down there. Said it would give him a chance to catch up with his daughter's life. He was really getting into the role of playing daddy, but my guess is he hoped some of her celebrity would rub off. He isn't due to dock there until tomorrow."

I sat for a few minutes watching Byron take several more slugs from the bottle. I should have been ready for it when it came, but my mind was miles away on a boat headed for Mexico with a con-man and his mixed up daughter, both being chased by an evil of which they were unaware.

I should have been ready for it, but I wasn't.

Byron shot up off the bench and tagged me on the right cheekbone with a clenched fist. I went down like a sack of bricks.

A lot of people equate a bodybuilder's large muscles with slow reflexes and no brains, but you don't ever find those people putting their money where their mouth is because deep down they know the muscle-bound cliché is crap.

Byron was fast, but the alcohol in his system was throwing his balance off. I rolled when I hit the floor, hoping to get to my feet before Byron could hit me again. I wasn't that lucky and received a kick to my ribs which lifted me over to fall flat on my back again.

When the next kick came, I didn't even try to get out of the way. I just took it hard on the flexed muscles of my ribcage, and then locked the foot against its point of impact by wrapping my arm around it and capturing it in the crook of my elbow. Then I rolled inward towards my attacker.

As off-balance as he was, with his foot trapped against me, Byron fell out of the sky like a giant sequoia. As he hit the hardwood floor of the recreation room with a dust-raising thud, I released his foot and continued to roll until I was out from under his legs.

I bounded to my feet, ready to tear his head off, adrenaline flowing like electricity through my body, but it was all over. Byron lay on the floor, curled into a fetal position trying to gain control of a crying jag.

"I didn't know about the steroids, man, or the kids he was ripping off." Tears rolled down his cheeks as he spoke. "I wasn't smart enough to be great like you. I was just happy to be working. I didn't ask any questions."

Neither did Hitler's henchmen, but if that was Byron's alibi I'd let him be happy with it. I rubbed the hot spot swelling on my cheek and left. On the way out of the complex, I knuckled the door of Byron's unit again. Lawrence answered.

"Oooh, look at you," he said observing my war wound.

"He needs you," I said, foregoing any smart replies.

Lawrence stared at me for a second and then took off

down the path to the recreation room without another word. He'd left the door to the unit open, so I pulled it shut with enough force to damn near tear it off its hinges. All that pent-up adrenaline had to go somewhere.

I checked in with Max and brought him up-to-date. He could pass word along to Stein. I could have talked directly to Stein, but it was easier dealing through Max. That way I didn't have to waste time being tactful with a client's feelings.

Max and I agreed that if we notified the police or the FDA of Rivers's whereabouts, they would just wait for him to come back stateside. A delay wouldn't affect their criminal case against Rivers, but it certainly wouldn't help my client get his singing star back.

There was also the specter of the tall, curly haired kid. If he killed Stella Constantine to get to Rivers, he wouldn't let something like a short trip to Mexico stop him. I didn't care a damn about what happened to Rivers, but if the con-man ran true to form, he wouldn't hesitate to put Charity in the line of fire if he found himself cornered.

Max immediately authorized additional expense funds and booked me a flight to Mexico via Areonaves Airlines. It was white knight time.

The next morning, I packed my passport and my armor, mounted a silver-winged stallion, and charged off in pursuit of a distressed damsel, a con-man, and a psychopathic windmill.

I rented a Jeep from the Hertz counter in Puerto Vallarta and headed down Airport Road towards town. After the movie studios had featured it as the background for the film *Night of the Iguana* with Liz Taylor, the once sleepy village had turned into a Mecca for the garish tourists who flocked to soak in the sun and wander down the twisting cobblestone streets.

The steep hillsides, covered with dense tropical foliage, provided precarious perches for homes and shops. From a distance the many red-tiled roofs looked like the beautiful blossoms of an ever-climbing bougainvillea. The natural charm and beauty of the area was helped along by the Christmas lights and decorations blooming like out of season flowers.

I drove across the Cuale River on the two-lane bridge which connects Puerto Vallarta's industrial north bank with the white beaches and tourist traps of the south side. The bedlam wasn't any less than that of a big-city rush hour. I dusted off my rusty Spanish, which was as passable as several other languages I'd picked up in my shady past, and received directions. I've found local residents are always surprised and flattered when you speak their language.

When the traffic eased, I picked up speed past the major shopping center along Lazaro Cardenes, refused to detour through the Zona Roja—Puerto Vallarta's red-light district —and followed the river along a narrow twisting trail with perilous drops down boulder strewn ravines at every switch-back.

I was beginning to think my directions were wrong when the houses clinging tenaciously to the ravine walls began to get more and more luxurious. I had entered the area the locals refer to derisively as *Gringo Gulch*, because of the large amount of rich Americans who maintain homes there.

If the residence at 187 Calle Pedregal was any indication, the con-game had been good to Appleton Ross, or Alex Rivers, or whatever he was calling himself in this part of the world. A more likely scenario, however, was that the house and the boat he sailed—which I had verified docked that morning by calling the harbor master's office from the airport —were all part of another elaborate scheme.

I drove past the 187 address, a rambling, ranch-style hacienda done in white stucco, and parked a hundred yards up the road. I got out of the Jeep, rescued my camera bag, and removed the lead-lined bag I use to get my film safely through the customs' x-ray machines. I also use it to get my derringer safely through the x-ray machines. I checked the load in the gun and tucked it safely away in its familiar holster under the lightweight windbreaker I was wearing. I locked up and headed toward the house.

The grounds were surrounded on three sides by six-foot high, white stucco walls. A wrought-iron arch spanned the gateless gap which formed the front entrance. The house was unapproachable from the rear, as it was nestled deeply into a natural cleft in the ravine wall. Across the street from the front of the house, the world fell away down a sheer drop to one of the many watery arteries which fed the Cuale.

A tiled red roof capped the one-story building in the traditional Mexican fashion, and white wrought iron had been used to form a trellis for the blue jacaranda which clung to the exterior walls. Large carved, hardwood doors defined the entrance to the house, and an old bell with a wooden clanger hung silently beneath a stucco arch above the doors.

Dusk had fallen, and I caught a trace of jasmine in the breeze. I tried to think of a fancy ploy to get inside the house, but I eventually decided there was nothing to be lost by trying a direct approach.

I kept one eye on the deepening shadows as I approached the entrance, but there appeared to be nothing more sinister than a large crow who startled at my approach. I found no reassurance in finding no trace of the presence of the tall, dark, curly haired shadow who had been ahead of me the whole case.

My knock on the door was answered by a stocky Mexican woman in a flowing black gauze dress which had been enlivened with red and blue embroidery. She had a ready smile, but her carriage marked her as the housekeeper.

"Buenas noches, senora. Podria hablar con el Senor que vive en la casa, por favor?" I inquired.

"Your Spanish is very good, Senor, but my English is better."

"Si, senora, es muy bueno." I smiled at her.

"Who shall I tell Senor Raven is calling?" she asked, smiling back.

"My name is Blue MacKenzie." If we kept on smiling at each other someone was going to mistake us for a couple of happy face pins.

The woman stepped back to allow me to enter the hacienda's lobby and asked me to wait while she spoke with Senor Raven. Ross, Rivers, Raven. Maybe he took a perverse pleasure in retaining his initials, some kind of private joke on the world.

I watched the maid walk down the hall and turn into a den-type room on the left. I decided to forget my manners and followed her without waiting to be announced.

I didn't know what to expect, but what I found was evidence the father and daughter reunion was not all smooth sailing. Charity was there, sitting on a lumpy floral couch pushed up against the left wall where it had caused a small wear mark in the grass cloth wallpaper. Her punkish hair had grown out some. It now laid flat and lifeless across her skull. Her eyes were red and puffy from crying, and she was systematically shredding a tissue in her hands.

Raven, or Ross as I had come to think of him, was standing

by a large picture window with a drink in his hand. His bulky frame was slightly stooped, his hound dog features softened by the room's dim lights.

"Who the hell are you?" he snapped when I walked in. The housekeeper turned around sharply, anger flaring across her features because I hadn't waited. I put on my best smile.

"Hello, Charity. I've been looking for you," I said gently. She looked up at me from the couch like a scared rabbit.

"I asked you a question, Mister, and I want an answer!" Ross's voice had a slightly drunken blur to it. I turned towards him.

"I've been looking for you too, Ross," I said, still ignoring his question. The use of his real name, however, put a befuddled look on his face.

"He said his name was Blue MacKenzie when he came to the door." The housekeeper's voice was full of scorn, almost as if she expected me to be a liar as well as bad mannered.

"Muchas gracias, Senora," I said without turning to face her, my eyes locked onto Ross. "Would you please leave us. Senor Raven and I have business to discuss."

She didn't like being told what to do in what she obviously considered her own house. I continued to stare down Ross until he waved the woman away.

"Yes, yes. Go on, Carmella. Everything is okay. Thank you." I felt the daggers of her eyes piercing my back as I listened to her withdraw from the room with a swirl of her skirt.

I reached into my windbreaker and pulled out the subpoena Stein had given me. "Nightsong Records want you to come home, Charity," I said handing her the paper. When she didn't take it I dropped it in her lap. "In fact they want you bad enough to subpoena you to court." She didn't say anything, but I sensed I had just kicked out the foundation from an already shaky house of cards.

"That subpoena is no good down here, MacKenzie, or whatever your name is!" Ross said gruffly, his voice rising to form the exclamation point.

"It is if she ever wants to go back to the States without a contempt of court warrant waiting for her," I said. "And as far as you're concerned, Ross, I think I'll take you back with me as well. There are a couple of organizations who want a crack at you, and I dislike your methods enough to enable them to take one."

"You're crazy! What makes you think you can walk in here and take over?"

"I guess I'm just that kind of guy. A real A-type personality. If you're thinking of giving me a bad time, I'll contact the local federales and let them know about the warrants for your arrest. You can spend Christmas in the rat pit they call a jail waiting for extradition." I was reaching, but it's easy to con a con-man because they believe it can't be done.

Ross looked like he was going to explode. I thought for a moment he was going to do something stupid like rush me, but the tension was broken by the sound of the housekeeper's scream, which was suddenly cut short.

We all turned to look at the doorway to the den we were in and I felt like I was waiting for the other shoe to drop. Framed in the doorjamb was the curly headed enigma I had known in my bones would turn up like a bad penny.

He was holding Carmella in front of him, one arm around her throat. Ugly red finger marks were beginning to glow on her right cheek. He suddenly pushed her forward into the room, revealing a .357 Magnum clutched in his other hand. It looked like a sleeping giant. I spared a glance at Ross who just looked confused.

"Don't you recognize me, Appleton?"
"Who?"

"Tommy Vreeling, you bastard! I'm not surprised you don't remember me. It's been a long time, but here I am." Vreeling's voice was filled with a lunatic tremor, which was reflected in his eyes but not in his steady gun hand. In the flesh, Vreeling was as wiry and tall as my imagination had made him. He was wearing a white tee-shirt tucked into stove-pipe Levis, and a brown bomber jacket which was as scarred as a gnarled oak.

"What are you doing here, Tommy?" Ross seemed to have sobered instantly.

"Isn't it obvious? I've come to kill you." This was delivered in a soft monotone, like an epitaph.

"What are you talking about?" Ross was frantic. "Back in Texas, I used to bounce you on my knee when you were small. What reason could you possibly have to kill me?"

"Reasons!" Vreeling yelled and we all jumped. "My father used to bounce me on his knee too until you killed him. He thought you were a big man—as big as all Texas—and then you turned on him and killed him. So I'm going to finally kill you."

"Don't be ridiculous, Tommy," Ross's voice was beginning to crack. "Your father committed suicide."

The gun in Vreeling's hand started to jerk around like it had a life of its own. "Don't you dare call me ridiculous, Ross. My father killed himself because you milked him dry and ran out on him. You may as well have pulled the trigger yourself for all the difference it made. I've waited a long time to track you down, and then I saw you on TV in your swanky suits and executive offices—ripping other people off just like you ripped my father off when you stole the business blind and left him to hold the bag."

I could see his finger begin to whiten. "Don't do it, Tommy." Even though I spoke quietly my voice startled him, as if he had been unaware there was anyone else in the room. "He's not worth it. Let the police handle it. I know you think you've got nothing to lose after killing Stella Constantine, but I know someone who can help." I hoped Max would forgive me.

Vreeling's gun swung towards me, which wasn't what I considered an improvement.

"What are you talking about?" Tommy asked. "I didn't kill that broad. She couldn't tell me where Ross was so I dumped her. Who said I killed her?"

So much for my deductive reasoning and gut feelings.

Ross chuckled. "You're a fool, MacKenzie. Look Tommy, I'll make everything up to you somehow. Kill this ape and we can talk about it. I loved you, Tommy, you were like a son to me. You've got your facts confused is all. Give me time to explain things."

Warrants pending stateside weren't enough for Ross to want me dead. There was another reason which had become abundantly clear.

"Maybe I'm the one with my facts confused," I said. The gun was still pointing at me, the entrance to the barrel looking like the Holland Tunnel. I tore my eyes away from it and concentrated on Tommy. Neutralize him, and the gun was useless. "If Tommy didn't kill Stella then you must have done it, Ross. What happened? Did one of your sicko sex sessions get a little out of hand? Didn't she want you to go sailing with Charity—your new toy as you called her?" Out of the corner of my eye I finally saw a reaction from Charity. She jumped as if she'd been pinched.

"Shut up, MacKenzie!" Ross yelled. "It was a mistake. She liked being beat up. She called me before I left with Charity and said she needed to talk. When I got to her apartment she threatened to call the police and turn me in unless I left Charity and brought her here instead. I hit her and she laughed at me. I hit her again and again, but she just kept laughing until she was dead. Killing Stella was a mistake, but killing you won't be. Do it, Tommy—shoot him now. I'll make everything up to you."

Tommy wavered in a state of mental confusion. I was getting ready to do something, anything. Anything but stand there and die. But Tommy had been living with his obsession too long and he finally swung his gun back towards Ross.

"How can you make up for a lifetime of being without a father? You weren't even one to your own daughter." The gun came up into a two-handed grip and Tommy spread his feet into a secure stance.

A professional does all his talking with his weapons, never giving a victim a chance. A psychotic bent on revenge like Tommy Vreeling, however, needs to verbalize the deed. His pleasure comes not in the killing but in watching the victim squirm.

While Tommy talked, I had moved slightly, putting a low coffee table between us. With my right foot, I viciously shoved it across the tile floor into Tommy's shins. I followed behind the table, my entire two-hundred-and-seventy-five pound frame slamming into the potential killer like a defensive cornerback trying to destroy an offensive receiver.

Air whooshed out of Tommy's lungs and the gun flew across the room on wings. He went like a rag doll in my grasp. As we fell to the floor, I smacked my head against the doorjamb. I hung onto Tommy, pinning his arms, while my head spun and I fought to remain conscious.

The sound of a shot penetrated the fog behind my eyes, and self-preservation kicked in. I propelled off the floor and into the hallway, snatching my derringer from its holster. I peered around the bottom of the doorframe.

Vreeling was out cold, but it was Charity who drew my attention. She was holding the ugly Magnum out in both hands at arm's length. Smoke drifted almost nonchalantly from the barrel. I looked to where she had the gun aimed and saw her father sprawled across a wicker chair, his right shoulder a red pulsing mess.

I thought for a second, she was going to shoot again. Instead she started to cry, hysterical sobs wracking her body. The gun dropped to the floor. I crossed the room and put my arms around her.

"It's okay. It's over."

"When I was a child," she spoke through her tears, almost inaudibly because her face was pressed into my chest, "I never knew why he left. I thought it was because he didn't love me anymore because of the glass I broke the day he didn't come home. After all these years I still wanted to be forgiven. When I found him again, I was happy just to be around him. He talked of all the things we would do together to make up for the lost years.

"When he asked me to sail to Mexico with him, I couldn't believe it. It was better than I had ever imagined. I couldn't tell Harry where I was going because Daddy was in so much trouble. He convinced me that if I told anyone I was with him, they would tell the police and I would lose him again. I didn't care what he'd done. I had a father again."

"But then he ruined it. He got drunk on the boat and started to slap me around. He said all his problems were my fault because I had so much money and had never helped him. He started to scream at me and then—he—then he ripped my clothes off and—and—My own father!" She started to pummel my chest with her tiny fists. "I hate him! I hate him!" She stopped struggling and began to cry steadily. "All I wanted was to be forgiven."

Carmella came over and took Charity from my arms. I checked Ross. He was losing blood, but still alive. I made like Florence Nightingale and then called for an ambulance from the phone in the hall. I also called the police, but only after I had called Max who promised to contact an efficient local lawyer with enough *mordida* money to get Charity and me back on American soil in a hurry.

Finally, I walked back to the den and settled down to wait.

Life was not pleasant. Somehow, I doubted Harry Stein was going to get his CD on the racks in time for the Christmas rush, but that was a problem I could do nothing about.

I had done what I'd been hired to do.

I tried thinking happy thoughts.

I wasn't the one who'd been naughty.

I'd been nice.

Toby Wainwright was still at the top of my Christmas list. As I waited, I wondered if she had plans for Christmas Eve.

THE FUNNY STUFF

Most police personnel are aware that motorcycle
cops are a breed apart. They have a screw loose.
Their elevator doesn't go all the way to the top. They are two fries
short of a Happy Meal.
Officer Charlie McQuarkle is no exception to the
stereotype. The following short-shorts, contained in
***The Legend of Charlie McQuarkle**, were*
designed as one-off laughs to be used as fillers.
They are collected here for the first time.

THE LEGEND OF CHARLIE MCQUARKLE
Wish Fulfillment

Officer Charlie McQuarkle sat astride his Harley-Davidson police motorcycle. He was well hidden by a stand of trees near the intersection of Woodley Avenue and Burbank Boulevard when a red Trans-Am blasted by. The Trans-Am was speeding at least twenty miles over the posted limit. McQuarkle grunted in pleasure, activated his red lights, and took off in pursuit.

The Trans-Am was driven by a muscular young man wearing a sleeveless sweatshirt bearing the logo of a local university. As the car pulled to the curb, McQuarkle could see another university-jock-type in the passenger seat.

Dismounting from his motorcycle, McQuarkle took his nightstick from the ring on his Sam Browne and used it to tap on the Trans-Am driver's window. The young man inside

213

began to roll down the window. When it was open far enough, McQuarkle used his nightstick to whack the driver in the head.

"Hey!" the driver yelled in pain and surprise. "What did you do that for?"

McQuarkle turned his mirrored sunglasses on his victim and spoke in a gravel-pitted voice. "Son, when you get pulled over by a police officer, you have your window down and your driver's license and registration ready to go. You hear me?"

"Yes, sir. I'm sorry, sir," stammered the driver, hastily removing his license from his wallet.

When McQuarkle finished writing the ticket and getting the driver to sign it, he walked around to the passenger side of the Trans-Am. Using his nightstick again, he tapped on the passenger window. When it opened far enough, McQuarkle whacked the passenger in the head.

"Hey!" the passenger yelped in surprise. "What was that for?"

"I was just making your wish come true," McQuarkle told him.

"What are you talking about?" asked the passenger.

McQuarkle almost smiled. "I just don't want you to get two miles down the street, and say, 'I wish that jerk cop had tried that crap with me.' "

The California Stop

One bright California morning found Officer Charlie McQuarkle, astride his Harley-Davidson police motorcycle, happily pulling over a young man for failing to stop for a posted stop sign. As McQuarkle approached his victim, the young driver stuck his head out the window.

"Why did you pull me over, officer?"

"You didn't stop for the stop sign at the last intersection," Charlie growled.

"Yes, I did," said the young man.

"Save it for the judge," McQuarkle said, taking out his ticket book.

"But I stopped."

"No you didn't."

"Come on," the young man pleaded. "I slowed down."

"You didn't stop."

"Yes, I did. It's called a California rolling stop. Everybody does it."

"You didn't stop," insisted McQuarkle.

"I slowed down."

"You didn't stop."

"I slowed down."

In frustration, McQuarkle put down his ticket book, whipped out his nightstick, grabbed the young man by the shirtfront, and hauled him out through the car window. McQuarkle began hitting the young man with the nightstick.

"Now," McQuarkle asked. "Do you want me to stop or slow down?"

The Bridge

Officer Charlie McQuarkle was sitting astride his Harley-Davidson police motorcycle clocking vehicles crossing the Vincent Thomas Bridge on radar. Not seeing the concealed officer, Bob flew past at eighty miles per hour. Like a good citizen, Bob pulled over when McQuarkle caught up with him and hit him with the reds.

McQuarkle swaggered up to Bob's window and asked,

"You know how fast you were going, son?"

Bob thought for a second and asked, "Uhhh, over 55?"

"83mph, son! 83mph in a 55 zone!"

"But if you already knew," replied Bob, "why did you ask me?"

Ignoring Bob, McQuarkle continued in his normal charming fashion. "That's speeding, boy! You're getting a ticket."

Returning with his citation book, McQuarkle turned his mirrored sunglasses on Bob to take a closer look. "I don't know how you're going to pay this fine, son," he said. "I've never seen anyone so scruffy in my entire life. You don't even look like you have a job."

"I've got a job," Bob said, offended. "I have a good, well-paying job!"

Smelling of day old donuts, McQuarkle leaned in the window and asked, "What kind of a job would a bum like you have?"

"I'm a rectum stretcher," Bob replied.

"A what?" asked McQuarkle.

"A rectum stretcher."

"What does a rectum stretcher do?" McQuarkle asked.

"I work for a proctologist," Bob explained. "I assist him when people come to get their rectums stretched."

"How do you do stretch a rectum?" McQuarkle asked.

"Well, I start with a couple of fingers, then a couple more, and then a whole hand, then two. Finally, I pull their rectum farther and farther apart until it's six feet across."

Absorbed in this grotesque image, McQuarkle asked, "What the hell do you do with a six-foot rectum?"

Bob smiled. "You give it a radar detector and stick it at the end of a bridge!"

Fishing

Norm was speeding down the highway, feeling secure in a gaggle of cars all traveling at the same speed. However, as they passed a speed trap, he got nailed with an infrared speed detector and was pulled over by Officer Charlie McQuarkle. McQuarkle dismounted from his Harley-Davidson police motorcycle and retrieved Norm's license and registration. When he finished filling out the ticket, McQuarkle handed it to Norm, received his signature, and was about to walk away when Norm said, "Officer, I know I was speeding, but I don't think it's fair. There were plenty of other cars around me who were going just as fast, so why did *I* get the ticket?"

"Ever go fishing?" McQuarkle suddenly asked the man in his gravelly voice.

"Ummm, yeah," the startled man replied.

McQuarkle almost grinned, adding, "Ever catch *all* the fish?"

Every once in a while, you have to break loose from commercial constraints and write something just for the hell of it, or because you are moved to use your writing gifts to create something special. Over the years I've created several special pieces of writing for extremely limited audiences, my wife, my son, and a few close friends.
The following story, **Night of the Frankengolfer,** *is one such piece. It was written to celebrate a friend's forty-fifth birthday. It is included here, first because it's funny (hopefully), secondly because you don't have to know the real-life players involved, thirdly because I swore one day I'd reveal my friend's obsession to the world, and finally because I started the story blind—having no idea of the ending, or even if there was going to be an ending—only to have the final line turn up out of the blue and amaze me. More writing days should happen that way.*

NIGHT OF THE FRANKENGOLFER

Chapter One

Go Go Gadget

The evil genius, Professor Kevin Staker, stared down at the *Uraniamic®* golf ball (guaranteed to add twenty yards to your drive and remove the hair from your legs and nostrils—$75.00 for three from *Sharper Image*) perched on the parapet of his Spanish Hills castle. Behind him, acting as caddy, Professor Staker's evil (but beautiful) assistant, Marisa, handed him an *Extra Big Bertha® driver (guaranteed to add 25 yards to your drive—$450.00* from *Wyoming Ralph's Discount Golf Catalogue*). This time the evil professor was determined to clear the castle moat.

Adjusting the *Lee Travino Knee Master®* (a blue plastic form that runs down the left leg to keep the knee from bending, guaranteed to add ten yards to your drive—$29.95 from the *Shopping Channel*), Professor Staker attempted to mentally *center his chi* (advice from *Chi Chi Rodriguez's Golf for Dummies* guaranteed to add fourteen inches to your drive—$17.95 from *Amazon Books*). To the tip of his club, he attached the swing line of his *John Daly Swing Master®* (a wide belt that fits around your arms, with a bent rod running up your back to a point three feet above the center of your head and a swing line dropping down to attach to the tip of your club, all to help keep your elbow from flying out on your back swing while adding fifteen yards to your drive—$150.00 with a free subscription to *Golf Digest Magazine*). He pushed his glasses with the *Tom Clancy Depth Perception/Golf Distance Lenses®* (they don't do anything, but they sound cool— $1750.00 *Pentagon Surplus Catalogue*) up his nose and prepared to swing.

"Masther?" Marisa always lisped the word "master" due to the stainless steel controlling electrode the evil Professor had surgically placed through her tongue.

Professor Staker checked his backswing, aggravating his groin pull. The mysterious malady was the result of a curse put on the professor by his arch enemy, the sinister Doktor Boob MacDonald, and had so far defied all medical treatments.

"Wha . . . wha . . . what is it now, Marisa? If you don't stop interrupting me I will place you in the dun . . . dun . . . dungeon for a week with only your brother Sean, the evil but extremely smart Ninja warrior, for company."

"No, masther. Please! Anything but that! I was only trying to help. You forgot your new Japanese cup tee, guaranteed to add thirty yards to your drive."

The evil professor narrowed his already narrow eyes before snatching the offered item from the evil (but beautiful) Marisa's extended hand.

"Thank you, my dear. I may let you live another day. Now, zip it."

"You are too kind, masther."

"Zip it!"

"Yes, masther."

"ZIP!"

Professor Staker removed his *Uraniamic®* golf ball from its perch on the castle parapet and shoved it into the *Toshioma Power Tee®* (a plastic half-cup on a peg—$4.50 at *K-Mart*) and set the ball and contraption back on the parapet.

Everything was finally set. Combining the extra yardage on all his contraptions, the evil professor should drive the ball at least 450 yards 14 inches—meaning he would have to chip back on par-four holes.

The evil professor smoothly and slowly drew back the head of his *Extra Big Bertha®*, *chi* centered, shoulders even, elbows in, knee straight, depth perception perfect. The *Extra Big Bertha®* reached the perfect extent of the torque allowed by the *John Daly Swing Master®* and the evil professor began his downswing toward his *Uraniamic®* golf ball nestled in the *Toshioma Power Tee®*. This was going to be one *Shagadellic®* (Austin Powers nonsense thrown in for no reason) drive, baby.

"Oh, Professor! Yoo-hoo, Professor!" The beautiful, but cruel Princess Marilou was waving her scarf out the window of the castle turret next door.

Distracted, the evil professor jerked the string of his *John Daly Swing Master*®, twisted his knee inside of his *Lee Travino Knee Master*®, which destroyed *Chi Chi's Chi* and bounced the head of his *Extra Big Bertha*® so it topped his *Uraniamic*® golf ball and splintered the *Toshioma Power Tee*®. The ball dribbled fourteen inches and dropped sadly over the parapet, falling twelve yards into the moat below.

"Doh!!!!" the Professor ranted. There had to be a better way. There had to be!!! And suddenly a cunning plan sprang full-blown into his evil mind.

The first professional golfer disappeared at midnight.

TO BE CONTINUED . . .

Chapter Two
Watching the Detectives

So far in our story, the evil Professor Staker and his evil (but beautiful) assistant, Marisa, have hatched a cunning plan to turn the evil professor into the greatest golfer in the world! Their earlier plan was foiled when distractions by the beautiful (but cruel) Princess Marilou caused the evil Professor Staker to discombobulate all of his golfing gadgets and drive his golf ball fourteen inches out and twelve yards down into the moat of his Spanish Hills castle. This disaster has only made the evil professor more determined to become the greatest golfer in the world by even more nefarious means.

"What do you mean exactly when you say the golfers disappeared?" Sheerluck Bishop, the world's most sort-of-adequate consulting detective asked the assembled chiefs of police.

"They vanished, vamoosed, went up in a puff of smoke, weren't around anymore." Chief Barks the spokesperson for the desperate group replied.

"All of them?"

"All the best—Arnold Knuckler, Tiger Irons, Lee Bambino, Cha Cha Hernandez, Fuzzy Cellar, and John Weekly."

"What about the sinister Doktor Boob MacDonald? I understand he's been tearing up the senior circuit lately."

"The sinister doktor is in Arabia at the moment building a merry-go-round for Sultan of Quish."

"Hmmm," Sheerluck said, rumpling his brow in a thoughtful and manly kind of way. "And you're telling me that after disappearing one at a time, the golfers reappeared suddenly in a group last night on the ninth hole of the Spanish Hills Golf Course? No ransom demands? Nothing?"

"That's right," Chief Barks confirmed. "You must help us Sheerluck. The fate of the free world could hang in the balance if these great golfers were to disappear again—perhaps forever! What would people watch on TV Sunday afternoon? It doesn't bear thinking about!"

"Is there anything else you can tell me?"

"There is one small thing. When they were returned, none of the golfers had any memory of what had happened to them, yet each had a small wound on a different part of their anatomy as if a biopsy had been taken."

"Hmmm," Sheerluck replied rubbing his chin in a manly kind of way.

"Do you think it could have been alien abductions?" Chief Barks asked. "Should we call NASA security?"

"I don't think that will be necessary. I do not believe this to be the work of aliens, but it does have the dastardly ring of a cunning plan being executed by my arch nemesis the evil Professor Staker."

"No!" Chief Barks gasped. "This is worse than we thought."

"Have no fear, chief. I'll handle this."

"Thank you, Sheerluck. We will be forever in your debt."

As the assembled chiefs exited Sheerluck's Camarillo mansion, Sheerluck turned to his assistant.

"Quick, Watson, to the Bish Cave. The game is a spleen."

The young assistant rolled his eyes. "My name is Greg, not Watson. We don't have a Bish Cave, and the game is afoot, not a spleen."

"Whatever," the world's most sort-of-adequate consulting detective said, already preoccupied with his cunning counter plan.

Sheerluck's disguise was a stroke of genius.

TO BE CONTINUED . . .

Chapter Three
Terror on the Course

So far in our story, the evil Professor Staker has carried out a cunning plan to abduct all of the world's greatest golfers, returning them en masse to the ninth hole of the Spanish Hills Golf Course unharmed except for a biospy taken from a different part of each golfer's anatomy. Sheerluck Bishop, the world's most sort-of-adequate consulting detective has been brought into the case by a baffled assembly of chiefs of police. Disguising himself as the sinister Doktor Boob MacDonald, the one great golfer who has yet to be kidnapped because he is in Arabia building a merry-go-round, Sheerluck and his faithful assistant are poised to challenge the evil professor at his own game.

"You don't look like the sinister Doktor Boob Mac-Donald," Greg told Sheerluck, the world's most sort-of-adequate consulting detective.

"Yes I do."

"No you don't."

"Listen here, Watson—"

"Greg."

"Whatever. The game is a pancreas—"

"Afoot!"

"Whatever. I have disguised myself as the sinister Doktor Boob MacDonald, the only one of the world's greatest golfers not to be kidnapped yet by the evil Professor Staker."

"All you've done is cross your eyes and shave your head except for two strands of hair that you've combed over the top."

"Exactly. So I am now a perfect double for the sinister Doktor Boob MacDonald."

"No you're not."

"Yes I am."

"No you're not. You're too fat."

"I'm not fat, Watson. I'm svelte."

"I'm Greg, not Watson. And you're fat, not svelte."

"Well, thank you very much, freckle boy. Remember, I can always change you back to when you wore glasses, your teeth stuck out in all directions, and your hair was the color of a baboon's rear end."

Greg scratched his head in a manly, but boyish, kind of way. "Funny, but in this light, I could swear you look exactly like the sinister Doktor Boob MacDonald."

"Right then, Watson. Let's get out to the golf course so I can get kidnapped. The game is a kidney."

"The game is afoot! And how do you know the evil Professor Staker will kidnap you?"

"Easy. All of the kidnapped golfers had a biopsy taken from a different part of their anatomy. From Arnold Knuckler it was his right arm. From Tiger Irons it was his left arm. From Lee Bambino it was his left leg. From Cha Cha Hernandez it was his right leg. From Fuzzy Cellar it was his front tooth. And from John Weekly it was his massive, manly torso."

"Yeah, so?"

"My dear, Watson, use your powers of ratiocination. This is why I am the world's most sort-of-adequate consulting detective holding the fate of the free world and Sunday afternoon televised golf in my hands. There is only one part of the body missing from the evil Professor's collection."

"And that would be?"

"The perfect golfer's butt, as possessed by the sinister Boob MacDonald! Without it, the evil Professor Staker will never be able to complete his evil golf clone and turn himself into the world's greatest golfer."

"A golf clone?"

"Yes, but not just any golf clone. The evil professor's golf clone will be made up of body parts cloned from the greatest golfers in the world."

"Won't the clone then be the world's greatest golfer, not the evil professor?"

"Whatever! The clone will be an extension of the evil professor's ego, made to do his bidding and take over the world of golf."

"Yeah, right."

"Come, Watson. We must get moving before it's too late. The game is a lower intestine."

Sheerluck Bishop had no idea of the tortures awaiting him.

TO BE CONTINUED . . .

Chapter Four
Send in the Clones

So far in our story, Sheerluck Bishop has disguised himself as the sinister Boob MacDonald, one of the world's greatest senior golfers and possessor of the perfect golfer's butt. This bold strategy has been initiated in order for Sheerluck to be kidnapped by the evil Professor Staker who is looking to complete his perfect golfing clone and take over the world of golf.

Strapped facedown to the operating table in the evil Professor Staker's castle laboratory, Sheerluck Bishop, the world's most sort-of-adequate consulting detective was in a bind. His naked posterior was raised ready to be biopsied by the evil professor.

Marisa, the evil professor's evil (but beautiful) assistant surveyed the patient. "Are you sure this is the great senior golfer, the sinister Doktor Boob MacDonald, masther? His butt looks too fat."

"Of course, I'm sure. Look at the bald head with the two strands of hair combed over it and the crossed eyes."

"Still looks too fat to me."

"That's svelte, not fat," Sheerluck suddenly spoke from his precarious position on the operating table.

"You're awake," the evil professor was startled. "How can it be?"

"Easy, Professor, for I am not the sinister Doktor Boob MacDonald."

"You're not?"

"No. It is I, Sheerluck Bishop, the world's most sort-of-adequate consulting detective, here to foil your evil plan."

"Curses. I was fooled by the hair. I should have known—you're too fat."

"Svelte."

"Whatever. How is it you were not knocked unconscious by my patented knock unconscious drops?"

"Because I prepared myself by taking a little known and very expensive antidote of Amazonian parrot spit prior to allowing you to kidnap me."

"Curses. But you have still allowed me to strap you to this operating table from which you will never escape."

"There is that," Sheerluck said, feeling the cold air of the castle laboratory on his exposed and precariously poised posterior.

"Since you are going to die," the evil Professor Staker continued to gloat, "I have no qualms about exposing my extremely evil plan to you. Look to the right, Sheerluck. What do you see?"

Sheerluck painfully moved his head to glance in the direction the evil professor had indicated.

"Oh, my saints. It's heinous," Sheerluck said, appalled.

"Yes, but it can play golf like the devil himself. All he needs is the perfect golfer's butt to provide his center of gravity, and he will be ready to take over the golf world under my command."

The creation standing in the corner of the evil professor's laboratory had the right arm of Arnold Knuckler, the left arm of Tiger Irons, the left leg of Lee Bambino, the right leg of Cha Cha Hernandez, the front tooth of Fuzzy Cellar, and the massive, manly torso of John Weekly.

"It's horrible. That's the most obscene clone I've ever seen," Sheerluck said. "It looks like Roger Lund on steroids."

"Why thank you," the evil Professor Staker chuckled. "I am rather proud of him."

"You'll never get away with this."

"And why not?"

"Because my assistant Watson has followed us here to the castle and at this very moment he is summoning help."

"My name is Greg, not Watson," Greg said as he entered the laboratory. "And I called the cavalry five minutes ago." He looked over at the evil professor's evil (but beautiful) assistant. "Hey, sweetcakes. How are you?"

"Fine, Greg," Marisa simpered.

"How about we get together Saturday night? I could remove that electrode from your tongue that the evil professor placed there and then you wouldn't spin around and have your eyes light up every time somebody changed the TV channel with the remote control."

"Sounds divine."

"Do you two mind?" the evil professor interjected. "You can canoodle on your own time. Right now, Marisa, you must help me get rid of the evidence before Sheerluck's reinforcements arrive."

"Yes, masther," Marisa said, batting her eyes in Greg's direction and exposing the electrode through her tongue. Was there no end to the evil professor's wickedness?

"Stop them, Watson!" Sheerluck implored as Marisa and the evil Professor Staker hustled the obscene golfing clone out of the laboratory and upward toward the castle ramparts.

"The name is Greg."

"Whatever," Sheerluck said. "Help me get these straps off."

Greg observed Sheerluck's bottoms-up position. "Another fine mess you've gotten yourself into."

Sheerluck struggled within the straps. "They're getting away. The game is a hernia. Hurry, Watson!"

"It's Greg. And I keep telling you, the game is afoot!"

"Whatever. Just get me free."

"Hmmm," Greg said in a manly, yet boyish, way. "How about a raise in my allowance?"

"What?"

"And two tanks of gas per month on mom's credit card?"

"That's blackmail!"

"And your point is?"

"Okay, okay. Ten dollars more a week in your allowance and two tanks of gas a month on mom's credit card."

Greg put his hand on one of the strap buckles restraining Sheerluck. "And I get to drive your car to school every day for a month."

"Don't press your luck, Watson, or I'll use an indelible laundry marker to play connect the dots with your freckles."

Once released from the evil professor's chamber of horrors, Sheerluck bravely raced up the castle stairs to the ramparts only to see the evil Professor Staker push his evil creation over the edge. The obscene clone splashed into the moat below. As it was a non-fat clone, tasted like cardboard, and contained 90% of the daily requirements of vitamins and calcium, the clone was immediately eaten by the voracious Dell fish living in the moat.

"You have failed, Sheerluck," the evil Professor Staker gloated. "I have destroyed the evidence of my nefarious plan."

"Not so," Sheerluck informed him. "Camera men from America's Most Heinous Crimes and This Week In Golf have filmed your actions from the windows of the beautiful (but cruel) Princess Marilou's castle."

"That will prove nothing. The clone is destroyed. You can't prove I kidnapped the golfers, or that I cloned their body parts. I've beaten you."

"On the contrary, Professor. By the power invested in me

by the Boy Scouts of America and in the name of the Queen of England, I—Sheerluck Bishop, the world's most sort-of-adequate consulting detective—am placing you under arrest."

"Whatever for?"

Sheerluck smiled. "Why for making an obscene clone fall, of course."

THE OTHER STUFF

*The Framing Game was originally written for **Bad Blood**, a young adult mystery anthology edited by Mary Higgins Clark. The idea for the story was generated by a hot shoplifting trend. Until store procedures were changed, there was a rash of incidents of kids entering sporting goods stores, taking expensive athletic shoes off the racks, trying them on, and then running out of the store (wearing the shoes) without paying.*
***The Framing Game** points out there are other ways of paying besides check, cash, or charge.*

THE FRAMING GAME

"Go on, Tommy. Take 'em!"

"No way, man. We're gonna get caught."

"How? Nobody's looking. Just put 'em on and take 'em."

"If it's that easy, you do it."

"Hey, I'm ready," Spider said, pointing at the new pair of Air Jordans that he had just taken off the store shelf and put on his feet. "But you need the new *vrooooms* more than me. Look at those things you're wearing."

Tommy Norman looked down at his worn-out canvas high-tops.

Spider nudged him with his elbow. "The only way you're gonna score any hoops against Mansfield in those things is because everyone'll be laughing so hard."

"I don't know," Tommy shook his head. "It ain't right."

"Man, don't be such a wuss," Spider said. "You think the store's gonna miss a couple pairs of shoes? Just put 'em on your feet and run."

Tommy examined the flashy pair of high-top basketball shoes in his hands. It was as if they had *high-scorer* written all over them. A tiny orange basketball on the side of each shoe acted as a pump to tighten the leather around the foot. Tommy figured that feature alone was worth an extra ten points a game.

The shoes would be like magic. They would make him fly down the court, slash through defenses, and slam-dunk with ease. He was already the top scorer in the toughest high school league in the Los Angeles area, but these babies would make him an even bigger star. College scouts from all over were going to be in the stands for Friday's league championship game, and Tommy wanted to be sure he made an impression. The game was going to be a monster bash. Tommy and his Franklin High teammates against their cross-town rival Mansfield. The game was considered so big it was going to be played in the Staples Center, which was the home court of the Los Angeles Lakers.

The game was still two days away, but the two boys were already feeling the jitters.

Tommy fingered the pricetag. One-hundred-and-twenty-eight bucks. No way did he have that kind of money, and his mom certainly wasn't going to cough up that many dead presidents just so he could score more points on the basketball court. She had too many other things to worry about —like paying the rent.

Spider Thompson was grinning at him, wriggling in anticipation. "You gonna be one awesome dude with them wings on your feet. Even Dolbert won't be able to slow you down."

Tommy's heart jumped. Eddie Dolbert was Mansfield's starting center and had been all-conference for the past three years. He was big, tough, and aggressive, and controlled the key like King Kong.

"You really think these will help me against Dolbert?"

"Man, I know so. You gonna be like a hot wind. And all you gotta do to own 'em is put 'em on, blast past the cash registers, and keep running."

Tommy looked around again. Anything you could possibly want for any sport was somewhere on the Sports Depot store's shelves. The shoe section stocked every brand and style you could imagine in help-yourself racks. Under each style were boxes in different sizes. You tried the shoes on and, if they fit, took them up to a register to pay for them—unless you were planning to steal them.

A Sports Depot employee suddenly appeared out of nowhere. "You guys need help?" he asked.

Tommy's heart jumped. "Nnnnn . . . no thanks," he stammered.

The employee took a hard look at both boys before moving away.

"Oh, man," whined Tommy. "That guy figures we're up to something."

"Be cool," Spider said, urgently. "He don't know squat."

"Man, his eyes were all over us," Tommy said, watching the corner where the employee had disappeared. "It was like he knew us or something."

"That's 'cause everybody knows us," Spider said. "We be stylin' on the basketball court and everybody knows we gonna blow the Mansfield team off the court."

"No, man. I know that guy from somewhere, and he spells trouble."

"You crazy, dude. The only thing that guy can spell is words of three letters or less. If he's such big-time trouble, how come he's working in a square joint like this?"

"I don't know, but I still have a feeling he's bad news."

"Man, you are such a chicken. Are you gonna pick yourself up a new pair of scoots or not? Make up your mind 'cause I'm outta here."

"Wait!" Tommy said, but it was too late. Spider was off and running toward the registers.

With the shoes still in his hands, Tommy followed his teammate out of the shoe section.

The next morning on the school bus, Tommy did not sit beside Spider like normal. Spider was at the front of the bus being cool and showing off his new shoes. Tommy sat in the back still upset about what Spider had done.

As the bus turned the corner, Tommy could see a huge crowd of kids gathered in front of Franklin High's main entrance. They looked upset and it was easy to see why.

During the night somebody had used green and white spray paint on the front doors, walls, and windows. Green and white—the colors of Mansfield High. In several spots there were the letters MJAM in green spray paint. Tommy knew the letters were the signature of a tagging crew known as the Mansfield Jammers.

When Tommy stepped off the bus there was even bigger trouble waiting for him personally. Coach Jackson and Mr. Smithson, Franklin High School's Dean of Discipline, were waiting on the sidewalk a short way from the bus. Coach Jackson was holding on to the arm of a scared looking Spider and called Tommy over as soon as he spotted him.

"What's going on?" Tommy asked as he reached Spider's side.

Coach Jackson sighed. "Tommy, I'm very disappointed in you."

"What are you talking about, Coach? Everybody on the team has been real low-key about the rivalry, just like you asked us. This isn't our fault."

"I'm not talking about the graffiti," Coach Jackson said. "I want you in Smithson's office, right now."

As the two boys were escorted through the school's entrance in front of almost the entire student body, Tommy's mind was in a whirl. He hadn't done anything wrong. He couldn't believe he was in trouble.

Once in Mr. Smithson's office with the door shut, the two boys sat in chairs in front of a large metal desk. Mr. Smithson sat on the other side of the desk. Coach Jackson leaned against the closed door of the office as if he expected the boys to make a sudden break for freedom.

Mr. Smithson leaned forward. "Those are pretty fancy shoes you're wearing, Spider. Where did you get them?"

Tommy felt the blood drain out of his face. How could Mr. Smithson know about the shoes Spider snatched?

"I bought them," Spider said. His voice cracked with the lie.

"No, you stole them," Mr. Smithson said calmly. "From the Sports Depot."

Spider looked at Tommy angrily.

"Hey, I didn't say anything," Tommy said defensively.

"No, you certainly didn't," Mr. Smithson said. "Because then you would have to explain these—" From under his desk, he brought out the Air Jordans Tommy had been holding while in the Sports Depot.

Tommy looked confused. "Where did those come from?"

"Don't play stupid, Tommy," Coach Jackson said. "We found them in your gym locker."

"But—" Tommy started to defend himself. Mr. Smithson cut him off with a raised hand.

"Don't dig yourself in deeper by lying. The evidence is clear." Mr. Smithson swiveled around in his chair and turned on a television set and a VCR that sat on the shelf behind the desk. He pressed the play button on the VCR's remote control.

A grainy, black-and-white tape began to play on the television screen.

"This is the security tape that was made at the Sports Depot yesterday. Every ten seconds it changes to a camera in a different part of the store."

Tommy and Spider watched the tape in silence. After a few seconds they could see themselves standing in the shoe section of the store. Spider was putting a pair of shoes on his feet and Tommy was holding a pair in his hands. The tape moved off to show ten-second snippets of the camping section, the cash registers, and other parts of the store. After about a minute, it again showed Tommy and Spider in the shoe section. Tommy still had the shoes in his hands, and Spider was waving his arms around talking to him.

The next time the tape showed the shoe section, the Sports Depot employee who had surprised them was standing with the two boys. The tape moved away to the camping section. When the tape moved on the cash registers, it showed Spider running through and out the front door. Just before the tape moved on again, it showed Tommy's head and shoulders as he followed Spider.

"This tape and the shoes on Spider's feet," Mr. Smithson said, "are all we need to prove that the shoes found in Tommy's locker are stolen property." He pointed at the pair of beautiful, new Air Jordans that sat on his desk like prisoners before a judge.

"But—" Tommy tried again.

"I don't want to hear it," Mr. Smithson said, interrupting.

"Tommy didn't steal—" Spider started, but he too was cut off.

"Spider, unless you can show me a receipt for those shoes, I don't want to hear any more out of you. Take them off now and put them on my desk."

Spider hesitated only for a moment.

"I think both of you boys should consider yourselves lucky. Sports Depot has said that they will not press charges with the police as long as the shoes are returned. But, I don't believe we can let things go without some form of punishment."

Tommy and Spider looked at each other.

"As of this moment," Mr. Smithson continued, "you are both suspended from the basketball team."

"Hey! Wait a minute," Tommy stood up as if someone had lighted a fire under his seat. "That's not fair. I didn't steal those shoes."

"Are you denying you were in the Sports Depot?"

"No, but—"

"Are you denying these are the shoes you had in your hands on the tape?"

"No, but—"

"Are you calling Coach Jackson and myself liars when we say we found these shoes in your gym locker?"

"No, but—"

"Then I don't think there's anything further to talk about."

"Coach?" Tommy pleaded. He was on the verge of tears. This could ruin everything, the championship, his scholarship chances, everything.

"I'm sorry, Tommy. There's nothing I can do. You made

your choices. Now you have to live with them." Coach Jackson's eyes were as cold as two dead fish. "And so do the rest of us. You not only let yourself down, you let the team down."

"But I didn't, Coach. I didn't steal those shoes."

"Then how did they get in your gym locker?"

"I don't know." Tommy couldn't think, and he couldn't trust himself to say anything more.

"It's not fair," Spider said. He and Tommy were sitting alone at a lunch table.

"Shut up," said Tommy. He couldn't remember anything that had happened in class all morning. All he could think about was being suspended from the basketball team for something he didn't do.

"Man, I couldn't believe Coach Jackson. And that jerk Smithson wouldn't listen to nothing."

"Just shut up," Tommy repeated. "Would you have listened to us? Anyway, you stole the shoes, so you don't have anything to cry about."

"It's not like you weren't thinking about it."

"Right. But, the fact is, I didn't steal 'em. So, somebody else put 'em in my locker."

"What are you gonna do about it?"

"I'm gonna find out who did."

Tommy looked around the lunch area. Even here, the vandals had managed to spray paint on several walls. Tommy even saw the MJAM tag signed across one of the lunch tables. He looked away, and then back again.

"Wait a minute," he said to Spider. "The Jammers."

"Yeah? So what?" asked Spider.

"The Jammers, man. The Jammers," Tommy said, sounding excited.

Spider looked confused. "Like I said, so what? Everybody

knows they're the only ones who would do something like this. I bet the cops are all over them already."

"Yeah, but you can bet they're clean by now—dumped all the paint cans. And the crew ain't gonna split on each other. They'll walk like they always do."

Spider shrugged. "So what are you getting so excited about?"

"Think, man. Who runs the Jammers?"

"Jammer Dolbert," Spider said without hesitation. "Eddie Dolbert's older brother.

"Now think about yesterday at the Sports Depot."

Spider looked confused again.

"The guy," Tommy insisted.

"What guy?"

"The guy who almost caught us stealing the shoes."

"Too cool," Spider said as he suddenly understood. "That was Jammer Dolbert!"

"Yeah, yeah!" said Tommy. "I've only seen him around a couple of times before with his tagging crew buds. I almost didn't recognize him with his hair mowed down and wearing straight clothes, but that was him."

Jammer was a year older than his basketball-playing brother, and as different from him as night was from day. Eddie Dolbert was a tough guy on the basketball court, but he had worked hard to hone his skills and deserved his reputation. Jammer, however, was a different story. Tommy was surprised that Jammer was even working a legitimate job.

"You think he's behind all this?" Spider asked, waving a hand around at the vandalism.

"Not just this," Tommy said. "But maybe something else as well."

Later that afternoon, Tommy knocked on the door to

Coach Jackson's office.

"Come in."

Tommy opened the door and stuck his head around. "I'm sorry to bother you, Coach," he said, gathering up his courage. "But could I please ask you a question?"

Coach Jackson looked at his star center. "What is it?" The coach's voice was flat and calm.

"I wanted to know how you got into my locker today?"

Coach Jackson gave Tommy a hard look before answering. "We cut the lock off."

"Do you still have it?"

Coach Jackson pointed to the lump of metal on his desk. The hasp had been cut through on one side.

Tommy took a key out of his pocket. He picked up the lock and examined it. "This isn't my lock, Coach. Mine was a Master Lock." Tommy held up his key. "This one is a Weskey." He inserted the key into the lock, but it didn't turn.

Coach Jackson raised his eyebrows. "You could have simply brought in a different key."

"I could have, but I didn't," Tommy said defiantly. "I'm telling you I didn't steal those shoes. I thought about it, but I didn't steal 'em."

Coach Jackson shrugged. "You're going to have to do better than that if you expect to convince Mr. Smithson."

"Oh, I'll do better," Tommy said. "But can you please tell me why you checked my locker for the shoes?" Tommy was trying hard to talk polite like his mother had taught him. He needed to get Coach Jackson on his side.

The coach hesitated, then answered. "The security tape was brought to the school this morning by one of the Sports Depot employees. He told us the manager of the store asked that we look at the tape and then check your locker to see if you had hidden the shoes there."

242

"Did he ask you to check Spider's locker?"

"No," Coach Jackson said thoughtfully. "But when we viewed the tape, of course, we recognized Spider. But, after finding the shoes in your locker, we didn't have time before the busses arrived to check any further. We waited for you and Spider and it was real obvious that Spider was wearing the stolen shoes when he came off the bus."

Tommy nodded. "Well," he said, still trying to talk polite. "I called the Sports Depot manager and asked him what they do about guys they catch ripping them off. He said the store always calls the cops."

Coach Jackson continued to look unimpressed, but Tommy was sure his argument was working.

"Spider stole the pair of shoes he was wearing when he ran out of the store," Tommy said. "But that tape just shows my back. You don't get a look at my feet. I was wearing my regular gym shoes, not those Air Jordans you found in my locker. I tossed 'em before I left the store. I didn't want to steal 'em. I knew it was wrong."

Coach Jackson shook his head. "Well, if you didn't steal them, then who did? And how did they get in your locker?"

"I think I know. All I have to do now is prove it."

Despite Spider's taunting words when they had been in the Sports Depot, Tommy didn't think of himself as a chicken. Still, as he waited in the parking lot of Mansfield High for school to let out, his stomach hurt with tension. He felt as if he were in enemy territory, and he knew if he didn't play things right he could end up getting thumped on.

The school bell rang and students started to empty out of buildings. Several people spotted Tommy in his Franklin High letterman's jacket as he leaned against the bumper of Eddie Dolbert's wicked looking Toyota truck, but they left him alone. Tommy felt their eyes on him and he felt like dead meat.

Maybe he shouldn't have come. Maybe this whole thing was a real bad idea. He felt himself start to sweat.

He was about to change his mind about sticking around when Eddie Dolbert and two of his buddies saw him by the truck and walked deliberately toward him.

"Are you crazy coming here?" Dolbert asked Tommy when he was close enough. "Get off of my truck."

Tommy stood up. He hoped Eddie and his buddies couldn't see his knees shaking inside his jeans.

"We heard you got yourself bounced off the team," Eddie said.

"Bad news travels fast," Tommy replied.

"Good news for us," said one of Dolbert's buddies.

"We don't like thieves at Mansfield," Eddie said.

"I'm not a thief."

"Oh, yeah. So how come you got bounced?"

"Because your brother, Jammer, set me up," Tommy said defiantly. "At the same time he and his crew vandalized Franklin last night."

Eddie's buddies started to move threateningly toward Tommy. Here it comes, Tommy thought.

"Wait a minute," Eddie said. Everyone stopped, and Tommy started to breathe again. "What makes you think my brother is behind this?"

"Come on," Tommy said. "If you didn't know he was behind half the petty trouble in this town you wouldn't be asking me that question."

When Eddie didn't say anything, Tommy continued. "Jammer works at Sports Depot, right?"

Eddie nodded.

"He saw me with Spider when Spider took the shoes. He

also probably saw me dump the pair I was carrying. He knew I didn't steal 'em, but when he looked at the security video-tape, it showed me running out after Spider, but the tape changed to another part of the store before my feet came into the picture. Jammer saw that as a chance to frame me and get me out of Friday's game."

Eddie still didn't look totally convinced. "How do you figure he framed you?"

"He must have snuck that pair of shoes out of the store when he got off work. Then, when he and his crew hit the school last night, I figure he broke into the locker room, cut the lock off of my locker, put the shoes inside and then put his own lock back on. Then he sent the security tape to Mr. Smithson this morning and asked him to check my gym locker for the shoes as if he was representing the Sports Depot."

"How did he know which locker was yours?"

"Our names are on them, just like they are here."

Eddie nodded.

Tommy stood looking at Dolbert. "So," he said eventually. "Do you want to play this game tomorrow on even terms and let the best team win? Or do you want your brother to have handed you the game on a platter?"

"I ain't afraid of taking you on," Dolbert said. "But what do you expect me to do about it?"

Tommy told him.

It was Friday night and the Forum was packed. Tommy was tying the frayed laces on his canvas high-tops and trying to stay calm. Spider was not dressed to play.

Spider hadn't been allowed to participate in any of the team activities that had taken up most of the day. He wasn't even supposed to be in the locker room now, but he had snuck in to talk to Tommy.

"Man, I wish I was going out there with you," Spider said.

"Me too," Tommy told him. "But—"

"I know. I know," Spider interrupted. "I screwed up. But at least the cops nailed Jammer for framing you. How did they know?"

"They found green and white spray paint cans when they searched his car and then took it from there."

"I can't believe Jammer was stupid enough to keep the paint cans he used," Spider said.

"He wasn't," Tommy told him with a sly smile.

"What do you mean?"

"Well, two can play at the framing game. Eddie Dolbert didn't want to walk off with this game and have everyone say Mansfield was just lucky because you and I weren't playing. So, he gave me the spare key to his brother's car. I put the cans in the car while Jammer was at work. Then I called the cops and tipped 'em off."

"Oh, man," said Spider. "That was really sly."

"After they got the spray cans and started questioning Jammer, he rolled over and told them the whole story. Of course it helped that Eddie talked to his brother and made him come clean about the shoes."

"And Smithson bought off on it?"

"He didn't have much choice," Tommy said. "He talked to the Sports Depot's manager and confirmed they didn't send the tape over here. It was Jammer himself who brought the tape over and gave it to Mr. Smithson. The Sports Depot manager also said that Jammer had been suspected of stealing from the store for a while now, but just hadn't been caught."

"Now that's what I call fighting fire with fire," Spider said.

Coach Jackson gave the team the word to head out to the

court for warm-ups. He slapped Tommy on the shoulders as he moved by.

"You're going to smoke 'em tonight, kid," he said.

Tommy stopped on the court and looked over at Dolbert. The tall, heavily muscled Mansfield center ignored him.

Yeah, he was going to smoke 'em tonight all right. And he wasn't going to need a pair of fancy basketball shoes to do it.

The Samaritan was my first published work of fiction.
It appeared in an issue of Mike Shayne's Mystery Magazine
(1982) during the last years of
that lamented publication's existence. We won't discuss how many
mystery magazines have died shortly
after carrying one of my stories.
The idea for the story was born while I was working an
undercover narcotics assignment as a student
on a high school campus. Driving home, looking suitably grungy, I
observed a hitchhiker with an oversized
backpack. While I knew better than to stop and
offer a ride, my mind immediately began to play with the idea of
what might have happened if I had
picked up the hitchhiker. The Samaritan is the result of that
game of "What if?"

THE SAMARITAN

I don't usually make a habit of picking up hitchhikers, so I don't really know what made me stop and pick up this one. Maybe it was intuition, or maybe it just seemed like a good idea at the time.

I was in the middle of three days off and was just going over the hill to visit my sister and her kid. The sky was threatening rain, and a biting wind was swirling the roadside debris into a symphony of confusion. I turned my battered VW down the on ramp to the LA bound Ventura Freeway and started to pick up merging speed.

I saw him standing close to the end of the ramp with his thumb sticking out beckoningly. He was dressed much the same as I was in tatty blue jeans and a green army jacket. His long hair was being whipped back by the wind, and a hand-lettered sign, proclaiming his destination as LA, rested on top of the knapsack leaning against his left leg.

As I approached, he stared directly into my windshield, trying to make eye contact. With my dirty blond hair tied back in a ponytail and my scraggly beard, I figured he recognized a kindred spirit. His face broke into an infectious grin, and he waggled his thumb at me a couple of times until he realized I was going to pass him by.

In a last bid to get my attention, he brought his hands together in front of his chest, prayer-like, and dropped down to his knees in a comical fashion.

I had driven past him at this point, but something made me brake to a stop and reverse back to where he stood. I popped the lock on the passenger door, and my new companion clamored inside after stowing his knapsack on the back seat. I said hello and picked up speed down the ramp again.

"Jeez! Am I glad you stopped man. I've been waiting there for friggin' ever. How far are you going?"

"Not far really, about four exits is all."

"That's okay man. It's cool. Anything to get off that ramp. Everybody is so paranoid about giving rides these days, think you're a killer or somethin'."

"Yeah, I know what you mean. I even almost blew past you. If I was a straight, you'd be history now. It's not like it was back in the 70's."

"Hey, were you kicking around then? You don't look that old. Jeez, those were the days, man."

"Sure were. I spent time crashed out up by Berkeley, everybody giving you stuff, all the dope you could smoke, all the girls coming across with free love."

"Yeah man, never had no trouble getting rides then. Heck, I started down from Frisco two days ago and I still ain't made LA. That wouldn't of happened back then."

Out of the corner of my eye I saw my passenger dig into his jacket pocket and come out with a marijuana joint.

"You want some of this, man?" he asked.

"Yeah but I better not. I get too mellowed out and my driving goes to hell. I got a couple of outstanding traffic warrants. If the cops stop us, I'm bought and paid for."

"That's tough man. You don't mind if I light up do you? I gotta relax, man."

"Go ahead, just be cool, and keep an eye out for cherry tops."

My passenger took out a battered matchbook and toked up. The car filled with the sweet pungent smell of burning marijuana.

"What's your name man?" he asked, holding the smoke in his lungs. "Mine's Danny."

"How you doing, Danny?" I said. "I'm Reed."

"You live around here?"

"Yeah, back there where I picked you up. I'm just on my way over to my sister's for dinner."

"Nice area. What do you do for work?"

"Construction. Bad time of year though. No work and no bread."

"That's too bad, man." Danny paused for a second, took another hit off his joint, and turned to look at me.

"Look man, I'm kind of in a jam," he said tenuously, "I got to get to LA as soon as possible. I'm already late for an appointment that means a lot of bread in my pocket, and my head on a platter if I'm much later."

"Yeah, so?" I prompted.

"Well look, if you can give me a ride all the way to where I'm going, I can score you off some really clean cocaine."

"What do you mean, man? Where you going to get the nose candy from?"

Danny was silent for a second. I could feel him looking at me, judging me.

"Can I trust you, man?" he asked finally.

"If your appointment is that important, I don't see as you have much choice. The off-ramp where I'm gonna drop you isn't much busier than where I picked you up."

Danny chewed his lip as he thought that over. He took the last toke off his joint and flipped the roach out the window. I was starting to get a contact high from the smoke in the close quarters of the car and rolled down my window.

"Look, man," Danny started again, "I'm muling two pounds of righteous snow in my knapsack for a buyer in *The Valley*. It's worth two grams to you if you get me to him."

My heart skipped a beat. "What are you saying man? At sixty dollars a gram that's almost half-a-million bucks of cocaine you're hauling. What happens if the cops stop you?!"

Danny laughed. "Hasn't happened yet, man. As long as you play the game, watch where you hitchhike, and look like you smell bad, the pigs don't want to mess with you. Anyway, if it gets hairy I'm ready." Danny hauled a .25 caliber automatic out from his groin area. "If the cops shake you down it's a good place to keep your heat. Most pigs don't like to get too friendly."

"Hey, man! Put that thing away."

"It's cool, it's cool." Danny laughed, putting the palm-sized gun back in its hiding spot. "What's it gonna be? You gonna take me all the way?"

"Where we going?"

"Well, all right! Take the Desoto Avenue off-ramp north, and I'll direct you from there."

"Okay, man but I still got one small problem. I need gas, and I don't got no cash. I was going to hit my sister up for a loan to tide me over to payday. I'll have to stop there first."

"It's cool. I'll pop for the gas and throw you a ten spot to cover you."

"Great. Thanks. I'll pull off here and fill up." I smiled at my newfound friend and pulled off the freeway at Kanan Road. A hundred yards later, I turned into a gas station. A young attendant with punk rock hair took my money.

"I'm gonna have to call my sister so she doesn't worry where I am. That okay with you?" I asked Danny, while the gas was pumping.

Danny's eyes filled with suspicion. "I don't know, man. How do I know you're not gonna try and set something up to rip me off?"

"You can listen in if you want."

"That sounds okay."

Danny followed me over to the phone booth on the corner of the lot and stepped inside. I dropped in some coins and dialed the number from memory.

"Hi Sis," I said when I got a feminine answer on the other end. "It's me, Reed." Danny crowded his ear over the receiver. "My car's broken down out here at Pierce. I'm not going to be able to make dinner." Danny pulled the phone away from me and covered the mouthpiece.

"What's Pierce?"

"Take it easy. It's where I go to night school, I'm supposed to be there now. I don't want her to know I didn't go."

Danny shoved the phone back to me.

"Yeah, Sis, I'm still here. No, I don't need you to come get me. I can fix it myself, but it'll take a little while. Tell Kenny I'll be by tomorrow. I'll play ball with him then."

Danny and I listened for a minute to a lecture from the other end of the phone about keeping my car in better shape, and then I hung up after saying goodbye.

I grinned sheepishly at Danny. "She's the oldest of the family. Ever since our folks passed away, she has this need to play mom. She's not satisfied with just raising her own kid."

Danny shrugged, "No sweat. Let's get going."

When we hit the freeway again another joint appeared in Danny's hand. He lit up and settled back in his seat.

"Where does the dope come from?" I asked.

"Oh, man, it's a sweet little deal I got goin'." The smoking dope was making him talkative. "I pick up the cocaine from a lab in Mexico every other month and bring it up to the border. I then wait for a load of wetbacks to try and make a crossing to the land of milk and honey, setting off the border ground sensors as they go. While the border patrol is busy rounding up the illegals, I slip across on their blind side and just keep walking until I get past the check point above San Diego. Then I start hitchhiking.

"I have two delivery points, one in LA and the other in San Francisco. I usually hit LA first, but this trip I got a ride straight through from San Diego to San Francisco. I couldn't turn that down, but it kind of made me late getting to LA cause I didn't have the same kind of luck coming back down. The kind of bucks I make doing this, I'll be able to retire by the time I'm thirty-five."

"Sounds like you got it licked, man," I said. "You think these people you deliver to need any more help? It would sure beat nailing studs and laying shingles."

"Hell, I don't know man. I'm taken care of, and that's all I'm worried about. I got a partner who meets me at the delivery points and handles the money. He's kind of like my banker. I split some of the cash with him, but I don't need nobody else trying to muscle in and steal my thunder, so don't get no fancy ideas. You ain't got my kind of contacts."

"Take it easy. I was just asking, you know? I'd be a fool not to want to see if there was anything in it for me."

"Well, there ain't, okay?"

"Okay, man. Just askin' is all."

I pulled off at the Desoto exit and headed north across the valley. We passed the large Data Products building on the left and the agricultural fields of the local junior college on the right. As we crossed through the yellow tri-light at Erwin Street, I glanced nervously at the black-and-white police car parked at the curb, but it made no move to come after me and argue about whether the light had been red or yellow.

We kept going straight until Danny told me to turn left on Sherman Way. It was an area dominated by rundown businesses and deteriorating apartment complexes covered with barrio graffiti. We crossed Canoga Avenue and turned left down a small side street. Danny pointed to a driveway, and I pulled the car through a gap in a corrugated metal fence surrounding a medium-size rock quarry. Above the fence, the tall necks of cranes and other heavy machinery looked like so many obsolete dinosaurs.

Inside the quarry, activity appeared to be at a minimum. Danny directed me around several large mountains of gravel. Eventually, Danny pointed at a dented trailer with an office sign on its front door and told me to pull up next to it. A cloud of following dust caught up with us as I stopped the car. It settled lightly over a Toyota pickup, an already dirty Porsche, and a year-old Cadillac that were parked nearby.

I asked Danny if he wanted me to wait outside for him, but he signaled for me to follow him. As we walked toward the trailer, I notice a gnarled workman-like face peering at us from the lone window. After a moment, it disappeared only to emerge a second later atop the barrel-shaped body that opened the front door.

We entered the trailer and the barrel closed the door behind us, leaving himself on the outside. Three business types were gathered around a paper-littered desk. As we moved in to the room, one of them stood up and moved over by an empty water cooler up in a corner. He had a bulge under his right arm, which had nothing to do with any sort of glandular problem.

The man sitting at the desk had the face of a bulldog and the body to match. Instead of dog hair, though, he wore a three-hundred-dollar gray pinstripe suit. An unlit, but well-chewed Corona cigar stuck out of his left fist like an extension of his index finger, which had been chopped off at the first knuckle.

Behind the bulldog stood the man I took to be Danny's banker. It was a fairly safe assumption, as the man had taken obvious pains to resemble a member of that profession. Cool and lean, he stood casually relaxed, one hand on the back of the bulldog's chair.

Nobody spoke for a couple of beats, and the hackles on the back of my neck started to rise. Finally, the bulldog shifted in his seat and his voice growled out calmly but filled with menace.

"I'm major pissed, Danny." Danny made an attempt to interrupt but the bulldog cut him off with a point of his corona. "I've been in this stink-hole for two hours at a time for the last three days waiting for you to show up. I've lost customers, money and, more importantly, time. And now, when you finally do show up, you bring a stranger with you. You're real stupid making me unhappy, Danny. Who else are you going to find to deal with, if I cut you off and put out the word that you're unreliable?"

"Hey, be cool, Mr. Manicotti, I'm sorry—" Danny started.

"Don't tell me to be cool, you little scrote! I oughta just kill you and walk away—cut my losses!" Manicotti came snarling out of his chair. When he stood up, his beefy shoulders hunched back making the impression of a bulldog even stronger.

"I'm sorry! I'm sorry! I won't let it happen again, okay man?" Danny threw his hands out in front of him, palms up as if trying to ward off an unseen blow. "I've got the goods. We can do business right now, and then we can get out of here."

Manicotti looked at me. "Who's this dirt-bag you brought with you?"

"This is Reed. He's cool. He's an old friend. Came out to give me a ride when I got stuck." Danny's eyes flicked over at me to see how I was taking the old friend schtick. My knees were shaking a bit with all the talk about cutting losses. I felt like a turkey with his neck on the chopping block, but I put on a smile for Manicotti—trying not to look like I was wearing a sign stuck to my forehead saying, *kill me.*

"Search him, Tony," Manicotti growled.

Tony pushed himself away from the water cooler. He spun me around, so I was leaning with my palms pressed against the far wall. Roughly, I felt Tony's hands moving over my body. He had no qualms about getting friendly.

When he was satisfied, he moved back to the water cooler. I turned around to face the crowd again.

"Okay, let me see the snow," Manicotti said to Danny. He was still giving me the evil eye.

"Sure, man, sure. I got it right here," Danny said, seeming relieved to have something to do. He reached inside his knapsack and brought out two clear plastic bags containing the cocaine. He set them on the desk.

Manicotti picked up a briefcase from beside the desk chair and handed it to Danny's banker. Danny moved over next to his partner and started to help him count the money.

"Hey, Mr. O, it looks like we're in the chips again," Danny said, patting his partner on the back with one hand and riffling bills with the other.

When the counting was done, the briefcase was closed and the banker took it out of the trailer after handing Danny a banded bundle of twenties. The whole time he was there, the banker hadn't said a word.

"Hey, Danny, what about the blow you promised me?" I asked, as I watched Manicotti snort up a sample of his newly acquired goods.

Danny came over all smiles and put his arm around me.

"Yeah, yeah. Okay, man. It's right here," he said, reaching into his knapsack again. He brought out two small amber vials filled with the stuff that dreams are made of. He handed them to me. "I'll give you a couple more after we split. Okay?"

That was okay by me. I just wanted to get out of there and get back into the open.

Manicotti put his cocaine in another briefcase and handed it to Tony.

"I'll see you again in a couple of months creep. Don't be late again."

"Yes, sir, Mr. Manicotti. I'll be there I promise, man. On time and everything." Danny appeared to be real good at groveling.

Manicotti started for the door followed by Tony. Danny and I brought up the rear. As Manicotti stepped away from the trailer, however, an ominous, feminine voice

---

boomed out from behind my VW.

"Freeze! Police! Move and die, turkeys!"

There was a bristling of revolvers and shotguns as the narcs surrounding the trailer came out into the open, but Tony and Danny still changed directions and started back towards the trailer's interior.

As Danny started to grope for his hidden gun, I dropped my shoulder into his side and drove him backward into Tony. We all went down in a heap. I drove my fist into Danny's groin again and again until he curled up in a ball of pain. He put up no resistance when I tore his gun out of its hiding place and stuck it in his ear.

When the dust settled, I could see Tony proned out, face down, in the dirt, and Manicotti sprawled over the hood of my VW with his tail between his legs. Sybil Lyman, my narcotics partner, the *sister* I had called from the gas station, was walking towards me all smiles and dimples.

"You okay, Reed?" she asked, helping me haul a dazed Danny up from the ground and into the arms of another narc.

"Am I glad you remembered that silly telephone code we worked out," I said. It was something most partners did when they started working together, just in case one of them got into some kind of unplanned caper. "I thought I was all alone here until the first guy left and I didn't hear his car start up." I looked over to where Mr. O, Danny's banker, sat in the back of a plain detective sedan.

Sybil smiled "I have to admit it took me a couple of seconds after you called me Sis to figure out what was going on. I thought you were some crank with a wrong number. Even after I caught on, it was a panic to get enough plain cars to cover all four sides of Pierce College. In fact, it was a black-and-white unit who picked you up on Desoto when you passed by the school. How in the world did you get into this in the first place?"

"You wouldn't believe me if I told you. I was just being a good Samaritan by giving a guy a ride."

Sybil shook her head. "Let's head for the station. You can get started writing this caper up."

I nodded. "When we get there, remind me to call my sister and tell her I'm going to be late."

*Dead Easy also made it into the pages of **Mike
Shayne's Mystery Magazine** (1983) before it
disappeared from the newsstands. The power of
intimidation, subtle and otherwise, has always fascinated me.
Dead Easy came to me when I began thinking
about the result of taking intimidation to extended lengths.*

DEAD EASY

Grantly's obscene form thudded into the deep armchair and
slumped into a disoriented mass. When he looked up at the
black-garbed figure in front of him, he was rewarded by the
jarring impact of a gun barrel being slammed into his forehead. The tip of the barrel was twisted into the expanse of
wrinkled fat.

The time span between the trigger releasing the cocked
hammer, and the firing pin striking home was infinitesimal.
Still, it was long enough for the events of the past evening to
flash through Grantly's brain. The flashback was just a little
pffft, and then it was gone. Mercifully, he was saved from
reviewing his wasted life in its entirety.

The noise of glasses tinkling and soft music made an
almost indefinable background to the ever-increasing roar of
conversation. The cocktail party was being thrown by the
new owners of the Cosmopolitan Syndicate of Broadcasting,
station KCSB, a new cable channel due to start broadcasting

in Los Angeles. It was being given to celebrate the end of the weeklong broadcast format presentations. One of the formats would provide the direction for the new station's programming.

Today was Friday. The last of the three main presentations had ended that afternoon. Voting by the KCSB board would be held the following Monday. All the board members would have a chance to think over their decisions during the weekend ahead.

Phillip Grantly was a grotesque lump of a human being. He had just passed his fifty-fifth birthday and weighed more than two normal-size men. Even his 6'5" height could not compensate for his great amount of excess weight. His head was totally bald. Large brown spots competed for space on this ample pate. As he sipped his drink, his triple chin quivered, dribbling beads of sweat down the front of his ill-cut tux. Grantly was sweating profusely, he always sweated profusely. There was always a lingering odor around him, making people stand far back or upwind.

That was one reason why he was standing by himself in one corner of the room while the party crashed on around him. The other reason was that Grantly was a rude, son-of-a-bitch to anyone who talked to him. He had money, which had bought him position, and believed he needed nothing else.

His isolation aside, Grantly was feeling very pleased with himself. After all, wasn't his going to be the deciding vote on Monday? Wasn't he the only board member who hadn't committed himself to one or the other of the format presentations? Didn't he hold the power of success or failure over all the hopefuls involved? *Damn right on all counts,* thought Grantly. He finally was in a position to squeeze out all the respect he was due. The feelings of power he conjured up made him feel slightly giddy.

Grantly swirled the ice in his drink and glanced about him at the other partygoers. His wife had not come with him tonight, begging off at the last minute by claiming a headache. It was probably just as well he thought. Now at least, he wouldn't have to put up with her insistent nagging.

Standing by the open French doors, Grantly spotted David Thomas and Mark Richards who headed the first of the format presentations. They were dressed as always in identically cut suits of complementing colors, a habit earning them the nicknames of *Ping* and *Pong*. Both were in their late forties. They had been in *The Business* for a long time, still looking for the break which would shoot them to the top.

Ping and Pong's format was based on the standard educational approach. Nothing really new or flashy, but a solidly thought-out presentation with the facts on viewer needs and interests to back it up. After a week of striving for the spotlight, they seemed content to blend in with the gracefully flowing draperies billowing gently in the evening breeze.

"I hope you're sweating, you little creeps," Grantly said under his breath. "I'm going to make all of you wait till Monday to see which way I'm going to jump." He knocked back the rest of his drink before having his attention drawn to a commotion by the exit.

Kurt Desmond, the head of the second presentation—a commercial format that had some rather lucrative benefits to its credit, had been helping his young wife into her coat when she had dropped her purse. The contents had spilled onto the polished hardwood floor. As Desmond bent over to help retrieve the items, his clothing clung to his body in strange folds, making his thin angular body look more awkward than normal.

Grantly's sense of power grew by knowing if he voted

against Desmond's presentation, the man would begin a rapid decent to the bottom of the executive ladder. The week of lobbying and showmanship had taken its toll on Desmond. The strain could clearly be seen etched into his face.

"I can break you, you simpleton." Grantly swelled visibly with the thought. This power felt good! Maybe when he got home, he would find enough *oomph* to give his wife a quick tumble. To hell with her headache. She'd love it.

Grantly was still standing alone when he felt, rather than saw, somebody staring at him. He looked behind him and searched the crowded bar until his eyes locked onto those of the dynamic young executive who represented the third and final faction of the format presentations. Adam Twill.

Twill was staring intently at Grantly over the rim of the tall glass he held in his long tapering fingers. It made Grantly feel uncomfortable. The feelings of power he'd experienced all evening started to dissolve under the scrutiny.

Twill was an imposing figure by any standards. His 6'2", 180-pound frame was graced with long flowing lines. Muscles stood out under his evening dress as if they had been slapped on with a towel. A shock of close-cropped blond hair topped off his razor-sharp facial features. Like Twill, his broadcasting format was innovative and unique. His approach ran the gamut of experimental television—everything from advanced educational programs for children and adults to the latest in laser and heliograph techniques in programming.

Grantly started to sweat more profusely than normal. Twill's stare had unsettled his feeling of well-being. He did not like Twill. He felt Twill to be the kind of man who does not let anything shake him, a man able to take all things in his stride. Grantly disliked Twill because he could not control him, he had no power over him. He knew if he voted against

263

him, Twill would just take his effort elsewhere until he finally clicked. He was not the type of man you could hold back. You could delay him for a time yes, but you couldn't stop him completely.

But here Grantly was wrong in a way. Twill had had enough of delays and hold ups. For him, this project was the culmination of too much effort and time to be dropped because some obese manifestation of an armpit held the deciding vote. Twill already knew Grantly would vote against him. His programming ideas were too avant-garde for a man in Grantly's position to take a chance on—unless the right encouragement, the right pressure was applied with just the right amount of flair and evil.

Twill diverted his eyes away from Grantly and sipped his drink. His sharp features assembled into a wiry grin. Yes, it was going to be dead easy really. All that you needed was the right pressure.

Miguel, a white-jacketed waiter, moved through the bobbing crowd with a long cool glass balanced on a silver tray extended above his shoulders. Other party revelers beckoned to Miguel who studiously ignored them and continued his beeline towards Phillip Grantly. As he approached, he slowed and wrinkled his nose in disgust at the smell emanating from this mountain of a man. However, he had been well paid by the fair-haired gentleman at the bar to deliver the drink with the funny coaster he had not been allowed to see. It was all part of what the man at the bar had deemed a practical joke.

Miguel didn't care. His shift was over in five minutes. All he was thinking about was seeing Maria, who would be waiting for him, her proud body so vibrant and alive.

The man-mountain turned to face him.

"Another drink, sir?" Miguel asked, bringing the tray

down to within Grantly's reach. "Compliments of the house."

"Compliments of the house?" queried Grantly, his eyebrows knotting slightly.

"Yes, sir. One for all the board members." It was what all the waiters, whom the man at the bar had asked to deliver drinks to board members, had been told to say. Only Miguel's, however, had the special coaster.

"Thanks," said Grantly, beginning to feel important again. As he took the drink off the tray the paper coaster came with it, condensation sticking it to the bottom of the glass.

The waiter hovered next to Grantly who stared at him distastefully.

"If you're waiting for a tip, forget it. The drink is on the house. Go ask your boss for a quarter." Grantly laughed at his little joke and turned his back on Miguel, who moved away with a look of contempt creasing his face.

Grantly sipped the drink. He hadn't really wanted it, but it was free. He'd finish it and head for home. He took a larger swallow of the drink. As the amber liquid half-revealed the bottom of the glass, he saw there was something written on the coaster. Holding the liquor in the back of his throat and savoring its burning sensation, he removed the coaster and read what had been written on it in a childish backhand scrawl.

You have just swallowed enough poison to kill an elephant. You will begin to feel the effects in around ten seconds and be dead in thirty. YOU HAVE JUST BEEN MURDERED.

Grantly paled and dropped the glass. He spat what liquid he still held in his mouth over the front of his tux. Quickly he stuck two fingers down his throat and was violently sick all over the hall's plush white rug. Twill, watching from the bar, moved quickly to Grantly's side.

"What's the matter, Mr. Grantly? Is there anything I can do?" he asked taking Grantly's arm.

"I've been poisoned," Grantly croaked, not realizing more than thirty seconds had passed since he'd read the coaster.

People around the room were all stopping to stare, thinking that it was just somebody that had gone past his limit —secretly amused it was Grantly making a spectacle of himself.

"It's on the coaster," breathed Grantly. He put his head between his knees, still waiting for the effects of the poison to take hold.

Twill palmed the suspect coaster and replaced it with a blank. "There's nothing on the coaster," he claimed, holding it out for Grantly to see.

Grantly looked bewildered, not comprehending. "But it said I had just been murdered!"

"Come now, sir. Our coasters do not carry any such statements." This came from Miguel who had hovered around to see the results of the practical joke. He was enjoying himself immensely.

"Let me help you clean up and find a cab," said Twill.

"Yes, please," Grantly simpered. He realized what a fool he must appear and wanted to be away from all the prying eyes.

Still bewildered, he allowed himself to be guided by Twill's strong hands. Twill smiled to himself. Now for phase two.

As the cab sped along, Grantly sat quietly, trying to compose himself. He felt rage and humiliation over what happened at the party. He'd made a fool of himself over some kind of a hoax. To top it off, there had been Twill's insufferable superiority. There was also the bit about there being no writing on the coaster, but Grantly was really too upset to give it much thought.

High up on Mulholland Drive, Grantly electronically opened twelve-foot-tall gates to admit the cab to his grounds. The gates were the only break in the brick perimeter wall. Foot-long spikes protruded from the top of the wall.

As the cab crunched on the gravel drive, two low-slung shapes detached themselves from the shadows. Running on silent paws they followed the cab to the entrance steps of the two-story, Tudor structure of Grantly's home. Grantly called softly to the Dobermans, watching as their attitude changed from protective aggression to the subdued joy of having their master home.

Grantly paid off the cabby but did not wait for his change, showing how much the evening's events had shaken him. The cab slid away tripping an electric eye. The front gates opened again for a few moments before returning to their job of keeping the outside world at bay.

As he entered the house, Grantly noticed an unfamiliar, official-looking car parked at the end of the circular drive. He also saw the lights in the sitting room were on. This was strange, as Mary had gone to bed before he left. Fumbling with his keys, he stepped through the oak doors and called out as he walked up the hallway.

"Mary, I'm home."

He heard the scraping of chairs in the sitting room followed by Mary's light footsteps. She rushed into the hall looking pale and drawn. She was a small woman with mousy hair and large dumpy breasts. She was dressed in a pink housecoat that did nothing for her. She wore nothing on her feet save for red toenail polish.

"Phillip! Oh, Phillip," she cried, moving toward him. "They told me you were dead."

Grantly took her in his arms, more surprised at first by her unusual show of affection than by the words she spoke.

A short well-kept man in a nondescript suit walked out of the sitting room followed by a slightly taller, younger version out of the same mold. The two men approached Grantly who still had his arms around his wife.

"Mr. Grantly?" enquired the older man.

"Yes, that's right," answered Grantly. His usual brash attitude was missing under these strange circumstances.

"Mr. Phillip Grantly?"

"Yes, yes. Now, what's this all about?"

"I'm Detective Hadley and this is Detective Ryslip." The older man gestured toward his younger compatriot. "I'm afraid there's a misunderstanding here."

When Grantly only glared without saying anything, Hadley continued. "Do you recognize either of these items?" He took a brown legal envelope from Ryslip and emptied the contents into his hand.

"Yes, I do," exclaimed Grantly. "That's a Masonic ring like the one I'm wearing, and the other item looks like my wallet. I lost it two days ago."

"Did you report your wallet as stolen?" This came from Ryslip in a brash immature voice.

"No, I didn't report it. I thought I'd misplaced it. It's happened to me before." Grantly looked a bit sheepish for a second, but then a cloud passed over his features. As if somebody had flipped a switch, his attitude changed abruptly.

"Now, I asked you before what this is all about. What is the meaning of coming here and upsetting my wife?"

Mary Grantly looked up from her husband's chest, as if becoming aware for the first time of the mess that he was in physically.

Ryslip stammered for a second, and then deferred to his

older partner for guidance.

Hadley took the initiative and began to explain. "The police received an anonymous call tonight regarding a body floating in the wash. When patrol officers investigated, they found a body that looked as if it had been in the water for about six hours. It had this ring on its finger and your wallet in its pocket. When we checked the driver's license, we assumed it contained the correct identification for the body— especially since the physical description was so close." This last part was said in a cautious voice as Hadley ran his eyes over Grantly's immense body.

"We came to notify your wife. She said it couldn't be you as you had only left a few hours previously. We were trying to explain we weren't quite sure how long the body had been in the water when you came home." Hadley defiantly held Grantly's gaze, as if condemning him for still being alive.

When Grantly spoke his voice was menacing, "As you can see, I am still breathing and you're sadly mistaken if you think you're going to be able to sweep this type of mistake under the rug. I will be on the phone to your superiors in the morning to demand a written apology for upsetting my wife!" Hadley tried to interrupt, but Grantly ignored him and continued on. "I suggest you leave now and find out just whose body it was in the wash and what he was doing with my wallet. I pay my taxes. I expect some return on them. If you'll be on your way, maybe I can attend to my wife."

Ryslip had turned red-in-the-face under this barrage, he started to spit out a reply but Hadley grabbed him by his sleeve and started for the door.

Grantly called his dogs and held on to them as the detectives walked out to their car. Ryslip climbed in and started the old Ford, but Hadley hesitated for a second and returned to the door.

"We may as well let you have this back now," he said, handing Grantly his water-soaked wallet. "I'm sorry we've caused you and your wife so much concern."

Grantly grunted and watched as the Ford bounced along the drive and out of the grounds. The electric gates slid closed silently behind the car's passing, and Grantly released the dogs again.

Back inside, Grantly made soothing sounds to his wife and then sent her upstairs to bed before walking down to his darkened library. Turning on an antique lamp he poured himself a drink and opened his returned wallet to make sure everything was there. Inside he found an unfamiliar piece of paper which he unfolded and read. Paling abruptly, Grantly felt his blood chill. The note was written in the same childish backhand as the coaster had been. He read it through.

See how easy it would be? Nothing to it really. You're here one moment and gone the next. The hospital tag would simply read deceased. You're a very vulnerable man Grantly, very vulnerable. YOU HAVE JUST BEEN MURDERED, AGAIN.

Grantly walked over to his desk and picked up his phone. He dialed the operator and asked for the police department. A soft efficient voice came on the line, "Los Angeles Police Department, West Valley Area desk."

"Could you tell me if you have a Detective Hadley or a Detective Ryslip working out of your station?"

"One moment, sir." The voice was gone for a moment, leaving Grantly to stew in his ever-increasing anticipation.

"Sir? Both detectives work in this area, but Hadley is on sick leave, and Ryslip is on vacation. Is there someone else who can help you?"

"Can you tell me if there was a body recovered from the wash earlier this evening?"

"We've had nothing come through the station, and I've seen nothing on the teletype from the other divisions. Is there something we should know about?"

"No, no. It's all right. I'll call back in the morning." Grantly quickly hung up the phone before the desk officer could ask further questions. He stood for a minute with his hand on the receiver and his eyes closed. He could smell something around him which was not just the odor of perspiration. He didn't know it, but it was the smell of fear.

The silent figure standing in the shadows outside of Grantly's grounds watched as the car carrying Hadley and Ryslip drove out of the gates. The figure was dressed in black. A shock of blond hair was visible for a second before the figure slid on a dark, knit ski mask.

The figure reached into a large duffel bag by his side and removed several pieces of black foam rubber. He reached in again and removed an assortment of straps with metal buckles.

Strapping the foam rubber pieces around his calves, thighs, forearms, and upper arms, the figure left spaces at all his joints to allow for freedom of movement. A final piece was secured around his neck giving him the overall effect of a demented hockey player without his skates.

Using the night's shadows for cover, he removed a small collapsible trampoline from the duffel bag and placed it about six feet from the front wall of Grantly's grounds. Satisfied with his handiwork, he stepped back, took a deep breath. Four quick steps and a leap placed him squarely in the middle of the trampoline. He collapsed his knees and then extended them as the springs of the tramp recoiled him smoothly into the air.

With body control developed over long periods of training, the figure sailed over the wall clearing the spikes by a good foot. The figure landed silently on the other side, his knees giving slightly to cushion the shock, his body falling forward into a well-practiced shoulder roll. He was on his feet instantly, all his senses alive to the danger of the Dobermans somewhere on the grounds.

When the dogs did not immediately appear, the figure turned his attention to the house. He could see Grantly's shadow slide across the library window. Moving quickly on crepe-soled shoes, the figure slithered across the lawn to the French doors of the sitting room.

When the dogs did come, it was with such speed they almost caught him unaware. He sensed them rushing towards him and turned to face their attack, his back to a tree of a variety he couldn't discern in the dark. He had to do this right the first time because there would be no second chance.

The first dog leapt straight at him without fear. The figure waited for the exact second the dog left the ground, knowing it would be committed to its course. He started to fall backward, grabbing the dog's outstretched front paws and threw him over his head into the tree behind him. The dog hit the ground with a thud and lay still, not even a whimper from the pain of its broken limbs escaped its throat.

The dark figure rolled over and regained his feet, but not before the second dog materialized from nowhere to sink his bared teeth into his foam-encased arm. Instead of fighting the dog, though, the figure grabbed it by the back of its neck and shoved his arm further back into the dog's jaws. Locked into a death struggle, the two forms fell to the ground—the man pinning the dog with his body and only releasing his hand from the dog's neck for long enough to pull a knife from his belt. He thrust it to the hilt where his hand had been a moment before, killing the dog like a matador would finish a bull. The struggle ended.

Picking himself up, the dark figure started to shake as the adrenaline in his body began to overload. He sat down for a second and breathed slowly before stripping off the foam rubber armor that he no longer needed. Even though the night's air was cool he was sweating from his exertions, and though the dog's teeth had not broken the skin, his arm still hurt badly.

Standing up again, he resumed his approach to the house. At the French doors, which led to the sitting room, he listened to see if there was any interest in the commotion he had caused. When he was satisfied there was no unusual activity, he set back to his task.

Searching quickly around the door he found the alarm wires at the top of the jamb. He removed a length of wire, with an alligator clip at either end, and a pair of wire cutters from one of the two zippered pouches on his belt. Working quickly, he bypassed the systems and cut the main power wire. He stepped back, hesitating for a second before taking another, closer look at the door. This time, he discovered a secondary system—a pressure button hidden cleverly between the crack where the doors met. Using an inch-wide strip of celluloid, he slipped the latch and slid the loid down to hold the button flush as he opened the door. He slid the strip out again once he had entered and closed the door behind him. All remained silent.

Smiling softly, the figure moved across the room and entered the hall. He ran silently to the open library door. Looking in, he saw Grantly was occupied with making another drink.

Moving back to the stairway, the figure light-footed it up to the master bedroom where the regular deep breaths of Mary Grantly were testimony to her slumbering state. Silently, he lifted the covers on the side of the bed furthest from the sleeping woman's form and with one quick movement removed something from his second waist pouch and placed it on the mattress. He lowered the covers again, and moved away.

Like something out of a magic act, the figure made a wraithlike entrance into the library. Grantly turned from his contemplation of the fireplace, expecting to see his wife, and stared at the black-clad figure with a look of fear and puzzlement. Beads of sweat immediately popped out on his forehead.

"W-w-who are yo-you?" he stammered losing all semblance of poise.

"It's time," stated the figure in a deep growling voice.

"Time?" questioned Grantly.

As if the half-question were some kind of cue, the figure lunged from the doorway. He tossed aside the heavy desk blocking his path to Grantly like a child discarding an unwanted toy.

Turning a noticeable shade of green, Grantly started to scream. The noise, however, was cut short as the figure lashed out a long right arm catching Grantly full across the mouth with an open palm. The fat man's triple chins quivered violently, sending blobs of sweat in all directions.

With tremendous aggression, the figure advanced on Grantly. The fat man tripped over an armchair situated to the right of the fireplace and fell to the floor.

Leaning over, the figure landed two sharp jabs flush into Grantly's open face. Defenseless, Grantly rolled onto his stomach and received a vicious kick to his ribs for his trouble.

"Stop. Stop. Anything. I'll do anything," Grantly whimpered.

"Get up," the other man said.

When Grantly didn't move, he received another kick to his

rib area. This one was accompanied by the sounds of cracking bones.

"Now!"

The fat man struggled slowly to his knees, and then found himself propelled into the large stuffed armchair he'd tripped over.

The figure did another magic trick and a gun appeared in his hand. Bringing it up with force, he smashed the barrel into Grantly's forehead and screwed the tip into the skin. Fat curled obscenely around it.

"It was so easy getting to you, Grantly. You might say it was dead easy. But it's all over now."

The sound of the gun's hammer falling on an empty chamber echoed louder in the room than if a bullet had been fired. Grantly, his sweat surprisingly nonexistent, took a half breath.

"You have just been murdered," the figure said in a calm voice. "There is no way I can be caught. All you have to do to live is make the right decisions in life. Make the right decision on Monday." With that statement, the figure turned and glided silently out of the room. One moment the gun barrel was screwing into Grantly's brain and the next second it was gone, leaving only a throbbing bruise as a reminder.

Moving at top speed, the figure ran down the driveway, breaking the electric eye controlling the front gates, and scooted out to the relative freedom beyond the walls.

Pulling off the ski mask and shaking his tousled blond hair, Twill again allowed himself a small, private smile.

Inside the house, Grantly sat in the armchair stunned by the evening's events, unable to catch his breath properly. Suddenly a piercing scream from upstairs propelled him into staggering action. In the master bedroom, his wife was sitting bolt upright in the bed. The covers were thrown down to reveal a small garden snake. It had crawled across her legs while she slept, seeking the heat from between them.

Grantly lifted the harmless snake up gingerly in a meaty hand. Opening a window screen, he flung the snake out to the yard below. He knew there was only one man concerned with Monday's voting who was ruthless enough to do this, to go this far. Only one.

Monday morning broke bright and clear across the Southern California sky. The air was crisp with coolness, and the busy city dwellers scurried along with a minimum of fuss.

Philip Grantly observed all this from the picture window overlooking the front entrance to the KCSB studios. He was alone, waiting for the last candidate to arrive before going down to cast his vote.

With five minutes to go before the board meeting, Grantly observed Adam Twill exit from a taxi on the far side of the street. Grantly watched as Twill paid the taxi driver and started to make his way illegally across the middle of the street. This was a habit Grantly had observed Twill perform every day during the format presentations.

When Twill was halfway across the street, a featureless gray car detached itself from the near curb and with ever-increasing speed pulled towards Twill.

From his aerie, Grantly watched as the car's extra large bumper smashed into Twill, dragging his fallen body under the car's carriage like a hungry python gobbling its prey. A crushed and mutilated mass bounced once as it emerged from behind the car, incapable of caring that the car was racing off into oblivion.

Grantly allowed himself a small private smile and started to waddle down the stairs to cast his vote. *Twill had been right,* he thought. *It was easy. Dead easy.*

Going Postal is a quick little story designed as a one-page mystery for the back of **Woman's Magazine**. It also appeared in an issue of **Detective Story Magazine** in September of 1988. The incident involved was generated by a story told to me by a Postal Inspector regarding his experiences in a small neighborhood where we were both working a case.

GOING POSTAL

The keys of my manual Underwood jammed again and I swore, for the thousandth time, if I ever got far enough ahead on my bills, I was going to leap into the twentieth century and buy a computer. Even an electric typewriter would have been a step up, but they were as antique these days as the ancient model I was typing on.

With a deep sigh, I untangled the jumbled mess and pushed on to the end of the final report on my latest case. It had been a relatively simple matter of employee till tapping in a small department store. The client had been happy just dismissing the quick-fingered employee rather than following through with prosecution. I hoped he would be just as happy to pay his bill.

The rattle of the *gang mail box* in the lobby outside of my office spurred me into frantic action. I quickly typed the last words of my report, tore the page out of the typewriter, signed it, stuffed the completed project in an envelope, and scribbled on an address. I looked out my door to see if the mailman was still around or if he had moved on to face rain, snow, and dark of night at eleven-thirty in the morning on an eighty-five degree LA day.

"Hey, Terry!" I called out, seeing the blue uniform disappearing out the lobby door. "Can you take this for me?" I didn't know the mailman's last name, but since Terry had started to deliver the mail on our route a few months ago, we had become passing friends. He was a good-looking guy in his late twenties with a close-cropped beard surrounding an always-friendly smile.

Terry came back through the lobby door, his charming grin in place. "Sure, Anna. I'll be happy to mail that for you, but it won't get anywhere unless you put a stamp on it."

I looked stupidly at the offending envelope I was waving and felt slightly embarrassed. "Oops! Sorry. I'll just be a second." I dashed back into the office to grab some postage. Before heading back to the lobby, I checked my blond shag cut in the mirror and fluffed it out with my fingertips. After all, Terry was pretty cute, and as far as I knew, unattached.

"Thanks for waiting," I said, handing him the envelope.

"No problem." He gave me that grin again and followed it up with a wink. "You solving any big cases this week?"

"Now you're making fun of me," I said, acting exaggeratingly miffed. "Just because I'm a private eye, people think I don't have feelings. The closest I've ever come to solving a murder is catching a mailman who tried to poison a vicious dog by making him lick the glue off a whole sheet of stamps."

Terry laughed. Making a comment about not letting beautiful PIs keep him from his appointed rounds, he went on his way.

Back in the office, I checked the mirror again. Maybe not

beautiful, the nose reflected in the glass was a little too small, and the thin scar under the chin showed up worse in some lights than in others, but I was definitely passable.

My appointment book confirmed the fact I didn't have any pressing engagements for the afternoon, so I decided I'd drop in at Mama Rosa's for an Italian salad lunch. Mama's is only a four-block walk from my office, but it was enough to whet my appetite. When I arrived, however, I was surprised to find the front door still locked and the lights off. I cupped my hands to the window and peered inside. Lights were on back in the kitchen, but I couldn't see any movement.

All of this worried me a little. By this time, Mama should have been bustling around with the large lunch crowd that provided most of her meager profits. This part of town was not real high-class. The little string of shops where Mama's was located was run by older folks who had been in business for years, but hadn't the cash flow to relocate when the neighborhood started to change around them. Together, they stuck it out. Each helping the other. It wasn't easy and none of them could afford to be closed on a business day.

I walked around to Mama's back entrance and walked in on a scene that made it very clear why the restaurant was still closed. The kitchen looked like something registering a fifteen on the Richter scale had moved through it. Pots and pans were strewn everywhere, cupboards hung open, their contents scattered all over the floor, and food stuffs were smeared across the walls and splattered on the ceiling. Mama herself was standing in the middle of the mess crying her eyes out. Old Moise Kursh, from the cleaners next door, and Helen Snow, from the knitting shop two doors down, were trying to comfort her.

"What happened, Mama?" I asked, knowing the question was stupid. It was obvious what had happened.

"Oh, Anna!" Mama cried. "I'm so glad you are here." She came toward me with her heavy arms outstretched to give me a hug. Her thick, black hair smelled pleasantly of garlic and other spices. She was a heavy-set woman, her smiling face made puffy by the tears. Since her husband passed away five years ago, she had continued to run the restaurant with the help of her son and daughter-in-law, who were away on a short vacation.

"Who did this, Mama? Is there anything missing? Did you call the police?" The questions tumbled out of me.

"Oh, no. Not the police, Anna. I'm too scared. Please, Anna."

"Sure, okay," I tried to reassure her. "But why are you so scared?"

"If I call the police this will just happen again. Only next time it will be worse. The police can't be here to protect me all the time."

"Whoa. Slow down," I said. "You're moving too fast. What's this all about? Let's sit down and you can tell me what's been going on."

We all went through to the dining room and sat down at a small table covered with a red-checked cloth. Mama wiped her eyes with the corner of her apron and tried to pull herself together.

"About a week ago, I had a phone call," Mama started to explain. "It was from a man who said he represented an organization who would protect the restaurant from accidents for fifty dollars a week. I laughed and told him I already had insurance. He became abusive and told me there were a lot of accidents my insurance wouldn't cover. He said I better do as he said and put fifty dollars in an envelope and send it to an address he gave me. Then he hung up." Mama stopped to blow her nose on a crumpled tissue. "I thought it was a prank until I told Moise and Helen about it. They also had the same call. We didn't know what to do, so we did nothing—and then this happened." Mama swept an arm in the direction of the kitchen and sobbed again.

"Did anything happen to your stores?" I asked Helen and Moise.

"Nothing yet," Moise said. "But we both received a copy of this in the mail today." He handed me a small, buff-colored envelope. The plain note card inside read:

Mama's was just a warning! Pay up, or else! The price is now $60.00 a week due to your lack of cooperation. Just send it to the same address!

The note was typed and there was naturally no return address on the envelope. A surge of anger washed over me as I thought about a group of small-time hooligans trying to ring protection money out of these folks. Mama, Moise, Helen, and others like them worked so hard for what little they had. I looked at the envelope again. There was something that struck me as not right, but in my anger I couldn't put my finger on it.

"I think you should go directly to the police with this," I said, holding up a hand to stifle their outbursts, "but since I know you won't, I'll take a quick look into things for you."

Mama gave me another garlic-laced hug. "Thank you, Anna. I knew you would help us."

The first thing I did, after helping Mama clean up and get back in business, was to check out the address she and the others had been given to send their money. The street turned out to be just around the corner, but the actual numbers turned out to be an abandoned house due for demolition. I checked the mailbox and found nothing more sinister than an abandoned sparrow's nest.

Back at my office, I used the phone to contact a friend with the Postal Inspectors. She was able to verify there was no forwarding address for the last occupants of the abandoned house. This was not unusual in a neighborhood where the citizens are usually only a half a step ahead of the repossessor.

I put my feet up on my desk and re-examined the notes sent to Moise and Helen. My nagging thought finally dropped into place. There was something missing. The more I thought about it, the more my hunch grew into a certainty. All I needed to wrap up the case was a little trick I picked up reading Dick Tracy Crime Stopper Tips as a kid.

"I don't understand, Anna," Mama said. "First you tell us to go to the police, and then today you tell us to pay the money."

"Don't worry, Mama," I said. "As long as you did what I told you to do when you mailed the money off, we should be able to get things back to normal in a hurry."

It was the following day, and I was back at Mama's helping her with the early-bird customers. I was also hoping like heck that we were going to have some special guests turn up for lunch.

Terry, the mailman, had come by earlier in the morning to make his delivery, and had taken away the envelope containing the protection money with Mama's outgoing mail. About noon, Terry came back to the restaurant and took a seat at his usual table for lunch. Mama's was the best feeding place on his mail route, and she loved to feed him and worry over him like he was her own son. She wasn't above playing matchmaker either.

"You should go over and sit with Terry," she told me. "Take a break. He's such a nice boy."

"Okay, Mama," I said, surprising her.

I sat in the booth with Terry and turned on the table's small electric lamp. It took my Postal Inspector friend, Pamela Blake, only about ten seconds after I turned the lamp on to reach our booth.

"Terrance Donaldson," she said to Terry. "I'm with the U.S. Postal Inspectors, and you're under arrest for extortion." Pamela flashed her identification.

"But how—" Terry stammered. He was trapped in the booth.

"It was easy," I said. "Moise and Helen's extortion notes were delivered by you with the daily mail. The problem was you were too cheap to put stamps on the envelope."

Terry closed his eyes in disgust.

"When I found out the address where the extortion money was to be sent was an abandoned house also on your mail route, everything became clear," I continued to explain. "I figured you chose that address in case the protection payments were actually put in a mail box instead of with your victims' outgoing mail. That way, they would still be assigned to your route for delivery. It was you who broke into Mama's the other night and vandalized the kitchen to increase the pressure of your threats."

"You've got no real proof," Terry said. His face didn't look half as handsome wearing a sneer.

"Oh, but we do," I said. "Look at your hands."

All of us looked at Terry's hands. Under the radiance of the ultra-violet light bulb I'd installed in the table lamp, Terry's fingers glowed a bright purple.

"I had Mama and the others coat their protection payment with the same dye banks used to taint their bait money—money they want a robber to take because it marks their hands for identification, just like yours. I'm also certain that when we search your wallet, we'll find bills with serial numbers matching those recorded from the protection pay-ments."

"Right, let's go," Pamela Blake said, taking out a pair of handcuffs.

It was really too bad. He'd been so good-looking.